"I don't want to mess my son up any more than I've already done."

Tamara looked at Drew with all the vulnerability she shied away from showing.

Tamara couldn't say exactly when, but sometime during the dancing, they'd let their chests draw close. Her heart rested on his, and she could feel the rhythm, the beat. It had nothing to do with the music.

"You're going to be a great mom because you know how important it is," he reassured her. "You just have to let him see you, see how wonderful you are. And above all, feed him lots of ice cream."

Tamara listened hard. "Right. Boys—ice cream. Dogs—cheese. I hope I don't mix them up."

"It'll work the other way around, too. Trust me. Boys and dogs are simple. Now, women on the other hand?" He gave her one of his very best smiles as he managed to step on her foot again.

Dear Reader,

Welcome back to my favorite town of Hopewell, located in picturesque Bucks County. A northeastern region of Pennsylvania, this rural area is about an hour north of Philadelphia and has a wide variety of attractions: historic towns and villages, beautiful nature and recreational opportunities, unique shopping, and restaurants and cafés to entice the sophisticated foodie or ice cream lover.

For this story, I focus again on the Trombo family, in particular, Drew Trombo, the town's local hero and prodigal son. In the past, Drew was always able to glide through life, even when faced with numerous challenges or natural disasters. But this uncanny ability in no way prepares him for feisty Tamara Giovanessi, a troubled TV news anchor who's looking to make good on the past. Can a mellow adventurer and a determined career woman find common ground and more? The denizens of Hopewell certainly hope so and do their best to speed things along.

Hope you enjoy this return trip to Hopewell.

Tracy Kelleher

PS: I love to hear from my readers. Check out my website, tracykelleher.com, or email directly at tracyk@tracykelleher.com.

LOVE FINDS A FAMILY

TRACY KELLEHER

Harlequin

HEARTWARMING

H Harlequin®
HEARTWARMING™

ISBN-13: 978-1-335-05116-5

Love Finds a Family

Copyright © 2024 by Louise Handelman

Harlequin Enterprises ULC
22 Adelaide St. West, 41st Floor
Toronto, Ontario M5H 4E3, Canada
www.Harlequin.com

Printed in Lithuania

Recycling programs
for this product may
not exist in your area.

MIX
Paper | Supporting
responsible forestry
FSC® C021394

Tracy Kelleher has lived on three continents where she's worked, raised a family and multiple dogs, and had a lot of fun. She's worn many hats: medieval historian, advertising executive, and newspaper reporter and editor. When she's not hard at work on her next book, you can find her gardening, riding horses—and having lots of fun!

Books by Tracy Kelleher

Harlequin Heartwarming

Return to Hopewell

Vet to the Rescue

Visit the Author Profile page
at Harlequin.com.

As always, this book is dedicated to my wonderful family: Peter and Megan; James and Anne; and, of course, Lex. You listen to my moaning, provide editorial insights and allow me to make my deadlines. And you all understand the importance of a good gin and tonic.

Once more, kudos to my editor, Kathryn Lye. We've worked together a long time, and it's always been a pleasure.

Also, I want to give a big thanks to the amazing musician and composer Melody Gardot. Your music makes me smile.

CHAPTER ONE

Hopewell, Pennsylvania

"DREW! DO MY eyes deceive me, or is that really Drew Trombo in the flesh?" The owner of Chubbie's Eatery in Hopewell, PA, let out a cry of surprise.

Andrew "Drew" Trombo held up his hands in mock surrender. "Chubbie Walker, it's good to see you, too. It's been a long time—too long."

"Quick, notify the wire services!"

"No, post it on Facebook!"

"Hey, look. It's already on Instagram!"

"Some photo!"

"Wow! It's Drew, in the flesh!"

Voices cried out. Phones were drawn. And it wasn't even high noon.

Chubbie gave Drew a bear hug. The restauranteur was fit and strong, and in terms of his age, somewhere in the amorphous range of late thirties to fifty. "So, what brings you back?" he asked before crossing his well-muscled arms over his white apron. "Forget I asked. I'm sure it's got something to do with your dad falling off a ladder and breaking his leg. Your sister Jessica's been a real ace, by the way, what with her coming home and taking over his veterinary practice and keeping Norman from doing further damage to himself."

Drew opened his mouth and then closed it, half expecting, half hoping that Chubbie would continue the narrative and that any contribution on his part would be unnecessary. But Chubbie halted, waiting for a response.

Drew shook his head. "Yeah, Jess let me know when our dad fell. Pops is a great guy, but he's never been an ace handyman. What possessed him to go up that ladder and clean out the gutters is beyond me."

"Your dad is known to be stubborn."

"Pigheaded is more like it."

"But we love him just the same."

"Without question—a pillar of the community." Drew placed his hand on his chest. He could have been saluting the flag. And it was warranted. Dr. Norman Trombo had been the town's beloved veterinarian for almost forty years. People even sent him birth announcements when their cats and dogs had litters.

Drew leaned forward as if to share a secret, as if half the town didn't already know. "But the way to maintain a good relationship with Pops is to take periodic breaks. And that's why I'm here this morning. Not only does your food hit the spot, it's also the perfect refuge if I'm going to preserve my sanity. Speaking of which, have you got a spare table for an old friend?"

"For you, Drew, no problem." Chubbie craned his neck and peered around the intimate space. Round tables with bentwood chairs filled the long, narrow room. Potted plants hung in the windows, and flowers spruced up the tables. The place was filled with customers of all ages, including those in baby strollers. And complementing the convivial chatter was the aroma of freshly brewed coffee, homemade baked goods and heavenly concoctions featuring eggs in all forms.

"Hmm, let me just look outside." Chubbie wandered out the side door to a brick patio shaded by a vine-covered pergola.

As Drew rocked on the heels of his well-worn hiking boots, multiple childhood acquaintances acknowledged his presence. He held up a hand and waved, feeling a bit like a celebrity on the red carpet.

Which was when someone slapped him on the back. "So, when'd you get in town?" Robby Bellona had been a classmate of Drew's from kindergarten through high school. They'd been practically joined at the hip, experiencing all of life's milestones together. First illicit puffs on cigarettes. Not-so-stolen kisses at the swimming hole at the old quarry. Speeding tickets? Unfortunately, yes.

"Robby! What a surprise. I got in just a few days ago," Drew answered.

Robby grinned. "In case you didn't know it, a

lot has happened in your absence—especially recently." Robby pushed back his Phillies baseball cap. His black wavy hair had started to recede. "It's too much to explain just now, but maybe later? How long are you planning on staying this time anyway?"

"Not sure. It depends on work."

"Don't I know it. At least your job is more exciting than unclogging drains." He pointed to the logo for Bellona Plumbing on the pocket of his blue polo shirt. "Not that I'm complaining. The more families with young kids who move to Hopewell, the more times I get called for remotes flushed down the toilet."

Drew laughed. Robby always managed to find life amusing.

"Promise me you'll stay long enough for a beer together?"

"You bet," Drew agreed.

Robby grabbed his take-out coffee. "I'll work out the details. I'm booked solid this week with work, and we can't make it too late in the evening either. Nada—that's my wife—"

"You're married?"

Robby displayed his ring finger. "Yeah, I told you that a lot has happened. Anyway, Nada and I always try to have quiet time before bed, seeing as both of us put in the hard miles during the day. I'd complain, but the truth of the matter is, I'm one lucky man."

Robby Bellona was the last person Drew would

have picked to settle down. "I'll be here for a while. I'm sure we'll figure something out."

"I'm looking forward to it. You must have pretty exciting stories—going to all these exotic places."

"There've been moments, no doubt about it."

"Well, I can't wait. Right now, duty calls. Mrs. Horowitz's sump pump is on the fritz. Remember her?"

"How could I forget those Czerny piano drills she put me through." He shivered.

"Then you'll know why I can't be late." Robby saluted and headed out the door.

Chubbie hustled back, moving with the agility of a seasoned short-order cook. "There's one seat available outside. You'll have to share the table, I'm afraid. Someone new to town…"

"Not to worry. You know me. I can talk to a doorknob, and, believe me, I have. And if all else fails—" He pulled a moleskin notebook from a back pocket of his cargo shorts. "Just lead the way."

A couple of people stopped Drew, and he had to hustle to catch up with Chubbie, who had arrived at a small table tucked in the corner of the patio. "If you don't mind sharing a table, I've got a desperate customer here," Chubbie appealed to the woman already seated. He signaled to Drew.

She looked up from her phone and gave Drew a quick once-over—giving away nothing—before acknowledging Chubbie. "Sure. No problem." She went back to scrolling through her phone.

Drew pulled out a metal chair. "This'll work out great. Thanks, Chubbie."

The owner gave Drew a sorry-but-this-is-the-best-I-can-do look. "You need the menu, or will it be your regular?"

"The regular. Why mess with perfection?"

Chubbie gave him a thumbs-up and hustled back to work.

Drew slid into the tiny café chair with the ease of a tall man used to adapting to cramped surroundings. "Thanks for sharing, by the way. Chubbie's fried eggs and bacon are the only things saving me this morning," he apologized.

A beat went by, then two, before his companion looked up. She eked out a strained smile. "No problem. I gotta warn you though. I'm not much of a talker in the morning. In fact, I'm not much of a morning person—period." She went back to her phone.

Drew didn't take it personally. (His life motto, by the way.) Besides, he figured her indifference meant he could study her without inhibition. And he did.

She was petite, with dark, short hair—a cross between an homage to Joan Jett and a high-end coiffure. Punk meets Park Avenue. Although his interest in fashion was basically nil, he recognized an expensive outfit when he saw one: designer jeans, black stiletto heels and a black T-shirt made of some silky material that fit her taut torso like a second skin. Around her neck she wore a slim gold chain with a small pendant—a single gold bean covered in pavé diamonds. Definitely expensive.

Drew had been away a few years, but unless the residents of Hopewell had undergone a radical transformation, it was clear she wasn't a local. And she seemed perfectly content not to fit in.

Whatever. Drew could take a hint. He placed his moleskin notebook on the table and withdrew the pen clipped to the ragged neck of his faded olive green T-shirt. That gesture seemed to get her attention in a way that his friendly overtures hadn't.

She placed her phone on the table and sat up, thrumming her fingers on the metal tabletop. "Planning on taking notes?" She nodded at his pad and pen.

"Something like that."

She crossed her legs tightly. "Are you a reporter?"

"Hardly. I just like to draw." He flipped open the notebook to show her a sketch he'd done earlier that morning of the giant sycamore tree in his father's backyard. Its spreading limbs held his sister's childhood tree house—an architectural wonder that was part medieval castle, part Swiss chalet. The way he'd drawn it emphasized a gnarly fantasy world.

She leaned over to inspect. "Like something out of *Lord of the Rings*." She sat back and uncrossed her legs. She seemed to relax. A bit. That was until Chubbie descended.

"An egg-white omelet for the lady, and two fried eggs over easy on sourdough toast with a side of bacon and home fries for the gentleman." Chubbie placed the orders on the table. "Can I get you anything else? Another latte?" He looked to Drew's companion.

"Why not? Soy milk, please."

Chubbie stared at Drew. "The usual?"

"A must. I managed to grab a cup with my sister before she headed out for work, but it wasn't nearly enough to help me get over the jet lag."

Chubbie nodded. "I can imagine. How long was the trip this time?"

"Eight hours from Pakistan to London and a layover of four hours at Heathrow before almost eight more to Philly. The train to Trenton, then an Uber to Hopewell. You do the math. I'm too tired."

"Depending on the train schedule, I'd say around twenty-four hours," the woman announced.

Chubbie and Drew stared, speechless.

She shrugged. "Simple arithmetic." She picked up her knife and fork and began cutting a neat portion of her omelet. Using a right angle wouldn't have produced squarer corners.

Drew shook his head for a whole host of reasons. "Like she said. In any case, when I arrived home, I fell asleep while Jessica was still filling me in on all the family news. Face-plant straight into a bowl of fruit salad." He mimicked the mishap. "I'm not proud. And I can still taste the strawberries."

"At least they're fresh this time of year," Chubbie said. "How's your sister doing anyway? She always seems on the go, always on a mission. Still, she never forgets to wave and say hello."

"That's Jessica for you. Organized, efficient and always thinking of others, especially if you've got a pet." Drew shook his head. "I used to think her life concentrated solely on furry creatures, but not only has she decided to stay in Hopewell and take over Pops's veterinary practice, she's also found true love. Some fellow named Briggs who moved with his aunt and son to Hopewell a couple of years ago. That kind of blew my mind. You know my sister. She was always all work and no play." He shrugged. "Not that life is completely without challenges. Apparently, this woman suddenly descended on her and the boyfriend. Something about being the guy's son's mother? She'd been out of the picture for fourteen years—that's the age of the boy, but her being here can't help but spell trouble."

Chubbie cleared his throat.

Drew frowned. "Did I say something I shouldn't have?"

The woman held up her empty cup. "My latte?" she asked Chubbie, who seemed all too eager to hustle away.

Then she turned to Drew. "That trouble you mentioned?" She smiled sweetly.

Drew knew to be worried.

"That would be me."

CHAPTER TWO

THE WOMAN HELD out her hand. "I'm Tamara. Tamara Giovanessi. They put me in the far corner for a reason."

Drew cocked an eyebrow. "What's that line from the movie about not putting someone in the corner?" He held out his hand in return.

"Don't believe it. I'm truly persona non grata. Don't say you weren't warned."

He shook her hand anyway. "In my way of thinking, that actually makes you more interesting. I'm Drew, Drew Trombo." He smiled a smile meant to melt the hearts of many a woman—and it had.

Tamara wasn't called the "Ice Queen" for nothing, but even she felt a tingle in her toes.

Drew Trombo was like a sun-kissed god somehow dropped into this backwater town. He towered over her, topping six feet, with a narrow-hipped body and broad shoulders. His drab T-shirt did nothing to hide the sinews in his well-tanned arms. And his atrocious cargo shorts stopped short of his muscled calves.

Yet it was his hair—sun bleached, uncombed and

curling over his neck—that had Tamara thinking. And it was doubtful whether the man had seen the business end of a razor in more than a few weeks. She, who valued a well-groomed appearance, was somehow captivated.

Tamara cut another perfect square of omelet and chewed thoughtfully while Drew dug into his food with gusto. She noticed how he broke the yolks of his fried eggs and swallowed a large mouthful with a piece of bacon. A little barbaric for her taste. But she was willing to give him a gold star for his manners—he'd placed his napkin immediately on his lap, and he chewed discreetly with his mouth closed. Once upon a time someone had instilled the trappings of decorum onto this scruffy mountain man.

She finished chewing and swallowing. "I already know your sister is the Mother Teresa of four-legged creatures. But what's your story? Looks like you're the prodigal son returning to the fold. Don't tell me. Hopewell High School's winningest quarterback ever?"

He shook his head and munched on a crispy-edged potato. Then he forked another. "Nope. Never been much of a team player."

"Then what did you do to warrant all this attention? Save a child who'd fallen down a well?"

"That's Lassie."

"Deliver twins in a blinding storm?"

"Hopewell hasn't had a good snowfall in years."

"Decipher the Rosetta stone?"

"No, that would have been cool, but someone already beat me to it." Drew stared at his half-eaten breakfast. "I can't believe I can't finish this."

Chubbie took that moment to return with Tamara's soy milk latte and a black coffee for Drew. He looked at Drew's plate. "Something wrong? You used to down a double portion."

"I know. This is the best food I've had in more months than I can count."

"I'll have it wrapped up for you to take home."

"That would be great, thanks. And I hate to say it, but could you bring me some herb tea? I'm going to have to work myself back into eating shape."

"You betcha. Anything for our local hero." Chubbie scurried off before Tamara could ask him to wrap up the rest of her breakfast, too. Obviously, she didn't rate the same attention.

She grasped her oversize coffee cup with both hands. "I don't get it. Have you been trapped in the jungle?"

Drew looked up. "Something like that."

TAMARA LEANED IN over her third latte. "Let me get the picture straight. You have no permanent address. You don't go into an office. Instead, you go from pillar to post, until all of a sudden you get a text from this…this group—"

"Usually a call, and it's an international disaster-relief organization based in Geneva," he clarified.

"Right. Anyway, all hell breaks out in Kenya

or Kathmandu—a flood here, a raging forest fire there—and you pack your suitcase and rush in."

Drew sipped his umpteenth glass of water. "I carry a backpack, but you're basically correct. I tend to go from one natural disaster to the next as part of a team of first responders. We're brought in to help provide material and immediate medical aid. By the way, how's the caffeine going? Your hands look a little shaky." He pointed at the jiggling cup.

"Oh, that's nothing. When I'm really into a story I go through buckets of coffee. Still, a little water wouldn't hurt." She grabbed the jug on the table. "And you're a doctor?" She poured herself a glass. She nodded at his. "More?"

He rested his hand atop his glass. "Any more and I'd drown. No, I'm not a doctor, more like a combination fireman/EMT/logistics maven. I coordinate transport and machinery with the local government and aid groups and provide hands-on support as necessary." He neglected to offer more details, like how he recently revived a child who'd nearly suffocated while buried in a mudslide.

Tamara nodded, taking it all in. "But it's dangerous, right? We're talking ginormous natural disasters that can wipe out hundreds of people."

"Hopefully, they wipe out fewer with our help. As to danger? You quickly realize to be careful and learn to anticipate things that could go wrong, not that there aren't surprises." He offered an enigmatic smile.

"If it's dangerous, why do it?"

He wiggled his eyebrows provocatively. The blond hairs had bleached white in the hours of sun. "Because my job sounds glamorous to the people of Hopewell, and as a result I get treated like a king when I return. Just you wait. Odds are my breakfast will be on the house."

Tamara crossed her arms. Sometime during their conversation, Chubbie had reappeared and whisked away the remains of her breakfast and returned with the contents in a cardboard to-go box. Some of Drew's glow must have rubbed off on her. *Not likely*, her inner voice reminded her.

"Okay, you get as many free meals as you want when you come home. But you must have another motivation for doing your job?"

"What's wrong with wanting to help people? Trying to improve the lot of those whose lives are already difficult beyond belief?"

"I certainly applaud your efforts to save the world. But…" She studied his grin. He wasn't so much arrogant as assured, and maybe given his bloodshot eyes, more than a little jet-lagged. "But I also think you may have a selfish motivation."

"You're calling me selfish?" he asked in mock horror.

"Granted, we've only just met. But I've been known to have good instincts about people."

"Do say?"

"Yes, I do." She narrowed her eyes.

"Why do I feel like I've already failed an exam?"

Tamara cleared her throat. "No need to be nervous—not that you are, despite your apparent protests. As to your choice of a job, I think, besides wanting to be a do-gooder, you put yourself in harm's way precisely because you crave the adrenaline rush. You only come alive in anticipation of the next potential disaster. Which leads to the obvious question. Why are you here in sleepy Hopewell? And don't try to claim you've come running home to help care for your injured father because I've witnessed how your sister has that under control. Half the residents of this town will back me up on that one."

Drew forced a smile that didn't reach the crinkly corners of his eyes. "Let's just say I'm between assignments."

Tamara raised her eyebrows. "Don't tell me you got fired?"

"I won't. I believe the correct term is I'm on a leave of absence."

"Self-imposed?"

"By mutual agreement."

"So, you did get fired," she repeated.

"Merely that it was considered best for my welfare if I took a break."

She waited, but he didn't elaborate. "It can happen to the best of us," was her reply. Boy, didn't she know.

He sat up and crossed his arms. A frown marred what had been up until now an I-don't-have-a-care-in-the-world disposition. "Well, it's never happened to me."

"Sounds like you had one nasty surprise that you couldn't have anticipated." Drew's water glass was still on the table, but she raised hers and clinked it against his. "Join the crowd."

He returned her glass bump. "So, what's your story?"

"The usual double-crossing, backbiting corporate wrangling."

"Now I'm intrigued. Nothing like the sordid tale of a wronged woman."

"I wouldn't be so quick as to label me a 'wronged woman.' As far as the good folk of Hopewell are concerned, I'm not that innocent. In fact, as I said earlier, you're likely to tarnish your reputation by hanging around me too long."

"Not to worry, my reputation will survive. I am the local hero after all." He pulled out his phone and glanced at the time. "Unfortunately, I've got to shove off and be the good son. But how about tomorrow? Same time? Same place?" He stood and waited for a reply.

She gave him one. "I was right. You do like to live dangerously."

CHAPTER THREE

Drew headed up the hill to his father's house. It was only a short distance, but it felt like a trek over the Andes. Sooner rather than later he'd have to come clean as to why he'd really come home. That in the middle of a horrific mudslide he'd cracked.

Mr. Local Hero, the man capable of jumping out of burning buildings with a single bound—provided it meant saving four widows and twin toddlers—had failed a mission. He'd been struggling to maneuver in the oozing mud, narrowly avoiding cascading chunks of concrete and tiles from a destroyed home—a home that once held a multigenerational family—when he'd just stopped, overcome by the sudden realization that he felt nothing. Absolutely nothing.

They'd shipped him out on the earliest helicopter, citing fatigue, insisting he take a leave of absence. "You've pushed yourself too hard, buddy," his superior in Geneva had said. "You've been going nonstop for years. Time for some well-earned R&R."

The closest he'd come to admitting his predicament was to provide scant details to, of all people,

Tamara Giovanessi, a virtual stranger. Talk about a fish out of water! Really, who wore designer clothes and high heels in Hopewell? Not that they looked bad on her diminutive frame, which he had noticed was very nicely proportioned. Even more, he admired the way she was forthright—something he couldn't claim to be at the moment.

As he stood on the sidewalk in front of Pops's house, making sure his happy-as-Larry expression was securely in place, a gold-tone Studebaker with white fins honked and pulled over.

"Drew Trombo," the driver called out. "I heard from Mrs. Horowitz that Robby Bellona saw you at the diner this morning."

"Hi, Mr. Mason. You're looking well. Retirement obviously agrees with you." Drew waved at the elderly gentleman with the checked touring cap. Pops had told him that Mr. Mason had sold his garage to a new couple who were planning on turning the place into a brew pub.

"Best decision I ever made. You might let your father know that now that he's cutting back at the office, he's welcome to join our card group. Laura Reggio—you remember Laura?"

"Of course. My sister's best friend. Arty type."

"That's right. She owns a gallery and everything. Anyway, Laura's grandmother plays, too. I'm sure Norman would love it."

Drew recalled something about Laura's beloved *nonna*'s habit of cheating at cards—not that that habit detracted from her admirable qualities, chief among them her renown as a cook. "I'll be sure to pass on the word," Drew responded without betraying his misgivings.

Mr. Mason tipped his hat and pulled away from the curb while Drew headed up the driveway. He didn't bother with the front door and continued to the side of the house. A Queen Anne–style design, the dwelling boasted two turrets and a wrap-around porch. It was painted a colorful combination of mustard yellow, brick red and moss green, the creative handiwork of Drew's late mother, Vivian Trombo.

Everyone thought of Drew as a man's man, but the truth was he was more like his mother. His habit of carrying around a sketch pad? It all began when she gave him one on his tenth birthday.

That memory alone put a smile on his face as he meandered past a row of tumbledown hydrangeas and opened the screen door to the kitchen. "Pops, I'm home." He turned his head and saw his father sitting at the kitchen table. A newspaper was spread atop the checked tablecloth.

Norman Trombo looked up from the sports pages. "You have your regular breakfast at Chubbie's? Two fried eggs on toast, bacon, and a side of home fries?"

"You know me only too well." Drew set the carryout container atop the newspaper and pulled out a chair. "I brought you some leftovers."

Norman undid the flap and sneaked a peek. He sighed before securing it closed. "It looks amazing, but you better hide it in the back of the fridge before

Myrna shows up. Between her and your sister, my diet is mainly limited to rabbit food. Not that it's done me much good." He patted his rounded stomach under his navy polo shirt.

Drew closed one eye. "I have the vague memory of having met her, but who exactly is this Myrna person again?"

"Knock, knock." There was a rapping on the kitchen door before it opened. "Are you decent?"

"Boringly so," Norman replied over his shoulder. He looked at Drew. "You're about to find out."

A sixtyish woman stuck out her capable hand to Drew. "I'm Myrna Longfellow. We were introduced a few evenings ago. You managed to arrive right when my nephew Briggs and your sister, Jessica, made it official—not marriage yet, mind you. But Norman and I are already contemplating venues, am I right?" She nodded at Drew's father.

"In the time we've known each other, I've learned never to argue with Myrna," Norman informed his son. "She's been a wonderful help with my recovery," he went on. "Without her and Jessica I never would have survived. But now that you're here, things will really start hopping."

Myrna slanted a glance at the weary-eyed Drew. "I think the boy will need at least a week's worth of sleep before he can paint the town red. Meanwhile—" she pointed at the table "—what's in the take-out container, Norman?"

"Drew's leftovers from the diner. Chubbie wouldn't let him leave a single home fry behind."

Myrna stashed the container in the fridge, and Norman shared a knowing nod with Drew.

She turned around and rubbed her hands together. "We should get going soon, you know. Your PT appointment is in fifteen minutes."

"I could drive you, Pops, if you want," Drew offered. Frankly, he was amazed to see his father not objecting to being bossed around by this relative stranger.

"Nice of you to offer," his father responded. "But Jessica took the station wagon to work. Which reminds me, maybe Walt Mason has a used car available that you could borrow while you're in Hopewell."

"Funny you should mention Mr. Mason. I just ran into him when I was walking home. He said you should join some card-playing group he's in."

Norman held up a hand. "I'll have to see about that. Jessica's asked me to put in a few hours a week at the clinic. Then on top of PT, Myrna's got me attending a yoga class for seniors."

Drew raised his eyebrows in disbelief. "Yoga? You?"

"You should try it. Keeps the body limber and helps with sleeping," Myrna said, focusing on Drew's bloodshot eyes.

"Thanks, but I'm sure there's plenty of chores to do around the house. I'll have to take a look and see what wood needs replacing and repainting. But good thinking about the car. Once I get one, I'll stop by the lumberyard and get going."

"In which case, a pickup will probably be a better fit." Norman pulled his phone out of the side pocket of his sweatpants. "I'll just text Walt now."

Drew whistled. "Pops! First yoga. Now texting. You're a new man."

His father chuckled. "Who says people can't change their ways, even one who prefers not to alter a thing."

Drew was genuinely surprised by his dad's claim of adaptability. This from a man who once refused to get rid of a sweater even after the elbow patches had developed holes! If this change of heart was Myrna's influence, more power to her. In which case the power she had over him was pretty frightening. He decided Jessica could deal with it—just like he conveniently let her deal with everything else.

And speaking of everything else...

"You wouldn't believe it, but I met the most improbable person at breakfast, improbable for Hopewell, that is," Drew said. "Tamara—Tamara something." He raised his eyebrows and looked around the table.

"That woman." Myrna pulled out a chair and sank down.

"Now, now," Pops placated her. "I know it's difficult, but we need to give her a chance."

Myrna crossed her arms. She looked like a kid ready to pick a fight. "I know you're right, and for Will's sake I'll try. But 'that woman'—" Tamara appeared to be nameless as far as Myrna was concerned "—'that woman' does nothing but rub me the wrong way. What's even more infuriating, she somehow makes me feel guilty. Me? Who's devoted herself to first bringing up Briggs and then Will."

"I gather it wasn't your idea that she visit then?" Drew asked. He gave Myrna his best smile to encourage her tale.

"No, sirree. She and Briggs went to school together in Philadelphia, where we used to live. There's a lot of history there."

Drew looked confused. "History?"

She shook her head. "Look, you're bound to hear talk, that is, if you haven't already heard some of the details. But let me tell you the whole story rather than you having to piece together some hearsay, half of which probably isn't true. You see, when Tamara and Briggs were teenagers, just eighteen, she became pregnant with Will. For a variety of reasons, she made the decision to give him up, and Briggs and I raised him on our own. What's more, we all agreed to keep her identity secret until Will came of age—not exactly how things have turned out, as it happened." Myrna sighed.

Drew sensed some crucial details were missing, but he didn't interrupt the flow.

"Anyway, Briggs hadn't talked with her for all these years until a few months ago when he decided to let her know how well Will was doing, but also to tell her that Will was starting to raise questions about his birth mom," Myrna went on to explain. "Wouldn't you know it, soon afterward this scandal erupted at Tamara's workplace in Phoenix. So out of the goodness of his heart, Briggs invited her to hide out in Hopewell. Not that he has any interest in rekindling some sort of relationship—nor does she, from what I can gather. It was more that he thought her visit could present an opportunity for Will to get to know her and potentially clear up some emotional issues he's been having."

Drew recalled the breakfast conversation. "Okay, I get why Tamara's appeared in Hopewell of all places. And she mentioned something about being put on leave, but she didn't give any specifics. I don't suppose you have the skinny on that as well?" The question wasn't merely rhetorical. Drew figured she knew all.

Myrna nodded. "You're asking the right person. It seems that Tamara's a reporter at this TV station in Phoenix and that she'd done this story that won all these awards and even got her promoted to the anchor spot. It was about some corrupt adoption agency pushing teenage moms to give up their babies. But according to Briggs, a jealous competitor at her station now claims that Tamara falsified the evidence about the adoption agency's predatory practices. As a result, the station's management has put her on leave, pending an investigation. Briggs is convinced Tamara's innocent and will be exonerated. He's good at spotting a phony, so I guess I gotta believe his judgment."

"It sounds like she's in for a fight."

"I don't doubt it. And I suppose I should feel sorry for her, but I'm having real trouble doing so. Between you and me, she was never my favorite person when she was young. But more to the point, there's another complication that has me deeply worried."

"Complication?"

Myrna worked her lower lip. "Some vile person at work also seems to have hacked Tamara's email. She doesn't know who, but my bet's on that same colleague. It appears they've uncovered the correspondence Briggs sent her about Will having questions about his birth mom. And now they've implied that her past personal history is somehow linked to the story. Who knows what could be in store? They could spread lies that Tamara callously abandoned her baby, or that we cruelly cut her off when she was a teenage mom. And if anything like that happens, Will would be the one to lose." She looked distraught.

Drew now understood the underlying awkwardness, not to mention animosity, that had come with Tamara's arrival in Hopewell. The sudden appearance of an outsider was always a cause of gossip in a small town. But Tamara had another strike against her. The Hopewell community, due to actions beyond her control, saw her as a potential threat to Will's future and the rest of the family.

Life and families could be complicated—that was for sure—and Drew preferred to steer clear. He smiled his Drew-smile and offered some feel-good pablum. "It sounds like a difficult time for everyone, especially Will. But I'm sure he'll pull through it."

Myrna wiped the corner of one eye. "I hope so. She's vowed she'll spend her time here building a relationship with him. But I say, promises are easy to make but harder to keep. Frankly, I wish that woman was gone from our lives—for good."

Norman reached across the table and patted Myrna's hand. "Briggs was being kind when he invited Tamara, and now he's trying to do the right thing by everybody. Just give it time. If I can learn to eat yogurt for breakfast and enjoy it—well, maybe that's an exaggeration—if I can learn to eat yogurt for breakfast and accept it, you can learn to think of Tamara as part of the family." Norman leaned over and gave Myrna a quick hug before rising. "We better take off if I'm going to get to PT on time."

Myrna offered a strained smile in return. "You're right. I don't like being late." She rose to her full five-foot-and-a-little-something height. In her warm-up pants and top she looked ready for action. She pulled her keys out of her pocket. "Hold down the fort while we're away, okay?" she said to Drew. "And enjoy checking for rotten wood, though I'm sure you'll be off again before we know it."

Norman ushered her to the kitchen door. "Leave the boy be, Myrna."

"I'm sorry. Thinking about that woman has got my back up!"

"Tamara, Tamara, Tamara. That woman's name is Ta…" His father's voice faded away as they stepped outside and walked farther away from the house.

Tamara, Tamara, Tamara… It sounded like the line from a Shakespeare play. "Tomorrow, and to-morrow, and tomorrow…"

Speaking of tomorrow, after all he'd heard, Drew questioned the wisdom of meeting Tamara for breakfast. Myrna clearly had some serious issues with her, but it seemed to him there was more to Tamara than Myrna's opinions. Besides, when had wisdom ever come into play with his life decisions?

He grinned. He was the man who courted dan-ger. He also couldn't resist Chubbie's.

CHAPTER FOUR

BRIGGS LONGFELLOW WAS waiting at the top of the driveway. He had his hands on his hips in a posture that conveyed a less-than-successful attempt at self-control. "Did you forget that you were supposed to take Will to tennis this morning?"

Tamara shut the door to her rental car—an Explorer SUV—and pressed the button on the fob to lock it. She was staying at Briggs's farmhouse while in Hopewell, a situation that was proving to be not entirely comfortable.

"And like I said before, you really don't need to lock it. The neighborhood's perfectly safe." Briggs ran a hand through his already ruffled hair. Judging from the mud on his jeans and T-shirt and the dirt under his cracked and chipped nails, Tamara figured he'd already spent hours in his precious flower garden and greenhouse. Briggs's full-time job was teaching American history at Hopewell Central High School, but he also had a busy sideline growing flowers and selling them at the weekly farmers' market in Hopewell. Now that it was summer, the sideline tended to take over.

Somehow Tamara couldn't wrap her head around Briggs's obsession. He'd strictly been a city boy when they'd grown up together in South Philadelphia. The closest he'd come to nature was the Cheez Whiz he'd put on his Philly cheesesteak, and she was pretty sure there was nothing remotely organic about that.

She stepped closer. His rapidly dissipating patience was palpable. "Sorry. I thought Myrna was on duty this morning."

Briggs shook his head. "We discussed this at dinner last night. This morning she had to take Norman to rehab, so you agreed to take Will. And then I said I'd pick him up at four this afternoon once he was done. But when I knocked on your door this morning and got no answer, I had to drive him myself. I purposely asked you to do it because I had an appointment with a new heritage-seed provider."

"Like I said, I'm sorry. I'm not used to tailoring my schedule to other people. And I must have zoned out during the dinner conversation. I really have no memory of agreeing to drive him. And if the seed provider's new, I'm sure he's eager for business, and it'll be no problem rescheduling."

Briggs looked away. Tamara could tell he was silently counting to ten. Well, what did he expect? Everybody in Phoenix knew she was self-centered, strictly married to her job and not to a loving (and, naturally, successful) husband. There'd never been a question of 2.5 children with perfect teeth; a Colonial-style four-bedroom house with twin vanities in the master bathroom; and a well-behaved Labradoodle cavorting around the perfect lawn.

And speaking of dogs...

Will's dog, Buddy, chose that moment to wander out of the barn. The medium-sized mutt shook his spotted black-and-tan coat and offered a quizzical gaze before wisely slinking behind Briggs. Buddy was timid on a good day. This was not a good day. He was so petrified of Tamara the brown dots above his eyes kept bobbing up and down as if sending out nonstop SOS signals. Truth be told, she was just as nervous around him.

Briggs bent down and gave the dog a reassuring scratch between the ears. "It's not about the appointment. It's more Will I was thinking of."

Ouch. "Well, we all knew from the get-go that I'd make a lousy mother—which isn't to say, I don't still feel guilty about leaving him with you all those years ago. I told myself then that I was in no shape to be a mother and that you guys were so much better equipped, which seeing as how things have turned out, appears to be true. And my messing up today just goes to show you can't teach an old dog new tricks." She craned her neck to steal a glance at Buddy pretending to be invisible. "Sorry, Buddy. No offense meant."

"Look, I'm not talking about the past. Aunt Myrna and I raised Will, and you had a fellowship for a degree in journalism at University of Arizona. We all made our choices, and we accepted that. But now, now that you decided to get to know Will, you need to do your part."

"I didn't just decide. If memory serves me correctly, you invited me to come."

"You're right. I did invite you, and I believe that you have the best intentions regarding Will. Look, I really don't like to preach—"

"But you will," Tamara joked. Bad timing, she realized when she saw Briggs sigh.

"You need to put those good intentions into practice," he went on. "The last thing we need is an excuse. Will was expecting you to take him to tennis camp. Not being here implied you didn't care. When you're fourteen that hurts."

"It hurts at any age," Tamara responded. She knew what it was like to have family not be there for her. She lifted her chin. "Listen, I get it. I forgot. I screwed up. I promise it won't happen again. I know it's no excuse, but when I woke up this morning, I realized I needed to fill up the car. I checked online and saw there was a station just outside town. One thing led to another. As long as I was in town, I figured I might as well get breakfast. So I googled and found Chubbie's."

"If you wanted to know where to get something to eat, you could have asked us at dinner last night."

"I'm sorry, I'm not used to sharing, and I'm certainly not accustomed to asking for help. Anyway, when I was at breakfast, I met someone who said he knew you."

Briggs raised his eyebrows. "That could be half the town."

"This is a little more immediate—Jessica's brother, Drew. Potentially your future brother-in-law if you play your cards right." Before Briggs could respond, she turned to walk into the house. "I'd talk more but I'm expecting a call from my agent." She paused and struck a more serious tone. "About Will. I promise it won't happen again. If it helps, I'll take him to tennis camp every day this week. Pick him up, too. Heck, I'll let Buddy ride in the back seat. You'd love that, wouldn't you, boy?"

Buddy turned his head away. He wasn't easily charmed.

Briggs forced a smile. "You don't have to go overboard, Tamara. Just be there when needed. That's all kids ask for."

"Far be it for me to set the cruel example of how adults frequently let you down. Like I said, I'm sorry." She tried to sound nonchalant, but inside she was smarting. She'd known she was unlovable from an early age. Not that she cared, or so she'd told herself multiple times during her life.

Briggs squinted. "I'm sorry you feel that way about people letting other people down." Then he gave her a look of reassurance. "In any case, whether you believe it or not, I know that at heart you love Will, and you want him to love you back. And don't quote me on this, but I also think, deep down, you want to win over Buddy. Now that'll be a true test of love and understanding." He paused.

"And liver treats." He walked off, the dog in his wake, leaving Tamara completely confused.

Love and understanding were foreign enough emotions. But liver treats? She shivered in disgust. It was enough to make her a confirmed vegetarian.

CHAPTER FIVE

DREW LOOKED UP from the corner table of the diner's patio. He put away his sketchbook and smiled. "You made it. I was beginning to think you'd moved on to greener pastures."

Tamara plunked her designer handbag on the ground and sank into the other chair. "I forgot to drive Will to tennis camp yesterday morning, so I was trying to make amends." She picked up the laminated menu lying on the table and scanned it before setting it down.

"You've chosen already?" Drew asked. She nodded. He signaled to the waitress.

A teenage girl clumped over in her Doc Martens. Her shaggy hair was purple, and her overalls partially covered a T-shirt advertising a brand of dog food. "What can I get you?" she asked Drew. He indicated with a point of his finger that Tamara would order first. The girl turned to Tamara and frowned. "Yes?"

Tamara asked for her usual soy milk latte but shook things up and ordered a whole wheat English muffin. "One pat of butter on the side. Not margarine. And no jam."

"It's local. The jam. Not some industrial product that's injected into a plastic single-serving-sized container, the kind with a foil top that you can never get off."

Tamara stared at the girl. "In which case, I'll live dangerously. But make sure the jam is on the side." After the waitress left, Tamara leaned toward Drew and whispered, "She's scary."

Drew shrugged. "I like her. She introduced herself when I got my coffee. Her name's Candy, and she'll be a sophomore in high school in the fall. Apparently, she works for my sister at the veterinary clinic part-time and here in the summer."

He drank his black coffee and stared at Tamara. Today she seemed less self-assured, less brittle. Maybe it was the absence of eye makeup. She looked younger, more vulnerable. He put his coffee mug down. "So, let me get the record straight. Will is...?" He rolled his index finger indicating it was her turn to complete the sentence.

Tamara frowned. "I would've thought someone would have told you by now."

"I'd rather you filled me in."

Tamara pondered his question for a minute. "I guess you could say Will's my son. I mean, I'm his mother. That is, I gave birth to him. I really don't know him, a fact due to various circumstances. You could say—life." She scratched her forehead. "It's complicated. I'm here to try to straighten things out. Create a bond, only not the Elmer's Glue kind. An emotional one."

Drew raised his mug. "More power to you is all I can say. I have absolutely no advice to give regarding how to form lasting bonds—glued or emotional— since I don't tend to stick around in one place long enough."

"Well, I've been here less than a week, and so far, I seem to be messing up royally. If that weren't bad enough, I also got this pathetic phone call from my agent."

Just then the waitress reappeared. "Soy milk latte for you." She placed the large cup in front of Tamara before lifting the glass coffeepot in her other hand. "And I figured you could use a top-up?"

"Candy, you're a lifesaver." Drew grinned. He waited for her to retreat before turning back to Tamara. "She's a friend of Will's, by the way."

Tamara groaned. "She probably knows I forgot to take him to tennis camp yesterday."

He shrugged. "Undoubtedly. It's a small town. There are no secrets. In fact, I'm sure that word's already gotten out that you've shown up at Chubbie's with your Lululemon yoga pants inside out."

Tamara shifted her legs from under the table. "Yikes!"

"Yikes?"

Tamara hid her legs back under the table. "I'd been up half the night fretting over the phone call from my agent, and I barely had time to get myself together to take Will this morning. Maybe I should go to the bathroom and fix them."

"That would only make it worse. Besides, this way makes you human."

"Human? I might not be everybody's idea of a good friend—even a mildly okay friend—but I am human."

"Tamara, trust me. I'm pretty sure you scare the dickens out of people." He looked up and smiled in his usual charming way. "Kind of like Candy and her purple hair here."

Candy came to the table with Drew's fried eggs, bacon and home fries as well as Tamara's English muffin. "Strawberry-rhubarb jam on the side." Tamara attempted to say thanks, but Candy had moved on with the blinkered focus that seasoned waitstaff have long perfected.

"Look! Even Candy doesn't like me," she said.

"Forget about Candy. She's a teenager. She's supposed to dislike people. Tell me instead what your agent said and why it's got you so upset." He dug into his food.

Today was going to be a good day, Drew decided. He'd pick up the truck after breakfast, make a list of the jobs he needed to do around the house, and then do carpentry and painting to his heart's content. Maybe even take a short hike, do some drawing. Yes, draw—a lot.

He'd feel revived, in touch with the world. And before he knew it, he'd get a call from his supervisor in Geneva, and he'd be back on the road, going here, going there. Doing what he was meant to do.

But for now, Drew listened to this intriguing woman seated across the table. He found her surprisingly easy to be with. He didn't have to live up to some preconceived—perhaps ill-conceived?—notion about how great he was. He could be satisfactorily mediocre in her presence. He could just listen, not feel obliged to offer praise or any problem-solving strategies. Just be, so to speak.

He bit into a particularly crispy piece of bacon before asking again, "So, your agent. What did he have to say?"

Tamara rolled her eyes. "Not good. It seems he tried to solicit character statements from my work colleagues—his idea of buttressing my case, proof that I've always been aboveboard and treated people with dignity and total honesty." She scoffed. "As if. The problem is no one was willing to defend me because, in their words, 'She's never been nice to me.'"

"And I presume that reaction bothered you?" Drew noticed that Tamara was lathering a generous amount of strawberry jam on one half of her English muffin.

"Not at all." She cut the half muffin into two identical pieces and took a bite. After chewing what appeared to be a requisite number of times, she swallowed. "It was his naivete that bugged me. I mean, he's an agent. What did he expect? That I'd be a regular Miss Congeniality at the office?"

Drew rested his knife and fork on either side of his plate. "I don't get it. You want people to dislike you?"

"Now who's being naive? We're all in competition at work. If I made any attempts at friendship, other people at the station would immediately become suspicious and reject them. They'd want to know what I was secretly up to. Ergo, it makes perfect sense for me to reject them first." She took another bite and swallowed. "This jam is good."

"In your agent's defense, it doesn't sound like a bad tactic to show that as an investigative reporter with an insightful but fair nature, you would never stoop so low as to fabricate a story." He saw her blink with surprise. "That's what you're accused of doing, right? Sorry, but as you already know, word gets around. And full disclosure on my part, Myrna Longfellow was at my father's house to drive him to his physical therapy appointment. She talked."

Tamara gagged. "Not the president of my fan club, that's for sure."

"Forget Myrna."

"If only."

Drew held up his hand. "To get back to the point I was trying to make, what about supportive testimony from a friend outside work? Boyfriend, maybe?" He told himself that he wasn't fishing, but truthfully, he was.

Another guffaw. "Do I look like the type of person who's ever had a supportive relationship, let alone a supportive boyfriend? I don't really buy into the notion of friends—all that 'being there for you through thick and thin.'"

Drew frowned. "That's sad."

"No, that's just reality." She lathered on some more jam.

"Not to be critical, but one might almost think you lack empathy for those around you. I'm just being frank, you understand."

"I understand completely. And no offense taken." She chewed.

"It was simply the observation made by one relative stranger to another."

"If two strangers can't be frank with each other, who can?" Tamara stopped spreading the jam. He noticed she had dispensed with butter altogether. "All right, maybe Sidney—that's my agent—wanted to show that I would never stoop so low. That's one way to go—but not the only way. Consider this instead. Before I go to interview someone, I do my homework and when we meet, I rely on that research—and my gut—to decide whether someone's telling the truth or not. And if he or she is being evasive or lying, there's absolutely nothing wrong with tough questions, especially to people who have power over others. That's the mark of a good reporter. I would never make up things to prove a point or falsify evidence. That would be unethical. A top-notch journalist needs to have an instinct for the truth, and searching for the truth can mean digging in places where people have something to hide or don't want you to go."

"Does that include asking probing questions of vulnerable teenagers who may have been coerced into putting up their babies for adoption? Sorry. Was that too low of a blow?"

She picked up the second half of her muffin. "Not at all. Don't apologize. If I'm willing to ask probing questions, I should be able to answer them." She gathered herself. "I fully appreciated that the young girls in my story were the victims—no doubt about it. But my job is to uncover the truth and expose the bad people—in this case the corrupt adoption agency, the same agency that had exploited them. That being the case, I fully believe that I provided the kind of reporting they deserved."

Drew dug into his home fries and used the silence to think about what she'd just said or, more to the point, what she hadn't. It wasn't a question of her lacking empathy, he realized. She seemed perfectly capable of putting herself in the girls' shoes. Her issue, instead, was the need to champion what was right and, quite possibly, hide her own vulnerability. "So, what are your plans going forward?" he asked.

She cocked her head. "You mean about my life? Well, once I'm cleared of all the charges, I plan to return to Phoenix ASAP and kick butt at the station."

"Have you forgotten about your opportunity to bond with Will? You wouldn't want to just skip out on the kid."

"I'm sure that by the time I leave, we will have

developed some kind of rapport. I'm not sure what kind, but rapport. And I know, I know, it's too important to botch. But it's hard—this people stuff." She sighed. "So, what are your exciting plans for the day?" she asked, conveniently changing the subject.

"My father contacted Mr. Mason about borrowing a pickup truck—Mr. Mason's the former owner of the town's garage, which is apparently being transformed into a brew pub. That information is to bring you up to speed on some of Hopewell's gossip, by the way." He tipped his chin.

"I always appreciate information." She tipped hers in return.

"Anyway, Mr. Mason tracked down a ten-year-old model that belongs to Carl. Carl is Wendy's husband, and Wendy's the office manager at my dad's veterinary clinic, or maybe more accurately now my sister Jessica's."

"Now that's too much information."

"Right. So, Carl—whose name you don't need to remember—is one of those people who seems to have everything that anyone could need. He's a facilities manager at the big pharmaceutical company just outside of town, and he said he's not using this pickup at the moment. His Honda CR-V is more than enough. Wendy would like him to get totally rid of it—not that I'm getting involved with that dispute. But the upshot is, I plan on walking over to the clinic's parking lot where he left it and then go to the lumberyard to pick up some boards to replace some rotten trim at Pops's place." He paused and looked at Tamara. "That really was too much, wasn't it?"

She nodded. "You lost me at Mr. Mason, but since I patiently listened to your story, I am now going to force you to listen to the details of my scintillating day." She turned her cell phone face up. "At four I pick up Will and take him to your sister-slash-father's veterinary practice, where Will is interning for the summer—and, according to you, doing so alongside the hardworking Candy."

"And in between now and then?" Drew folded his hands. "I'm all ears."

"I'm not sure. Perhaps an exploratory outing to the Hopewell Public Library."

Candy rematerialized by the table. "Can I get you anything else?"

"As a matter of fact, your recommendation about the jam was spot-on. If the diner sells it in jars, I'd love to buy one." Tamara offered her brightest smile.

Candy opened her mouth in mock surprise. "I'll see if we have any left." She headed inside to check.

"It's really that good?" Drew asked.

She leaned forward and confided, "It is, but that's not why I asked about it. I want to give a jar to Myrna. As I'm sure you gleaned, she dislikes me with an intensity otherwise reserved for the type of lowlife that'd steal a child's Easter basket. What can I say? She's pegged me for the selfish career girl I am."

"I thought you didn't care what people thought of you."

"I don't. But there's nothing like a little bribe to make my life easier while I'm here."

Drew was about to say something when Candy returned. "Here you go." She deposited the mason jar on the table.

Tamara brushed aside the jute strings tied around the screw top and read aloud the handwritten label. "'Nada's Finest Jam. Made with all-local ingredients and love.' Isn't that a charming sentiment," she commented to Candy.

Candy scratched her head with the eraser end of her pencil. "Anything else?"

"Actually, now that you ask, you wouldn't happen to know if there's a local Pilates Reformer class in town?"

The girl blinked—slowly. Very slowly. "Do I look like I'd know if there's a local Pilates Reformer class in Hopewell?"

Tamara switched to Drew. "I take that as a no."

Candy ripped off the two receipts. "You can pay at the counter." She slipped her pad in the front pocket of her overalls and efficiently cleared the plates and cups off the table, arranging the silverware in an interlocking pattern that kept them from slipping off the top plate. Then she brushed off the table with a dish towel. "Have a nice day," she said in a monotone. "Oh, and don't forget to pick up Will."

She left, and Tamara gave Drew an I-told-you-so look.

"Welcome to small-town life, which just so happens, is also made with local ingredients and love," he responded with a smile. They walked to the counter inside the crowded diner, where a woman stopped him to say hello.

"So, Jessica's big brother returns to the fold. Do you plan on staying longer than it takes the paint to dry on your house repairs?" It was Laura, Jessica's best friend.

Drew grinned and noticed she was drinking what looked to be herbal tea. "What, no double espresso for Laura Reggio, the queen of the caffeinated art crowd in high school?"

She patted her rounded stomach. "No caffeine these days. I've got a baby on the way. And it's Laura Reggio LaValle now. You missed the big to-do. I married Phil LaValle."

"I heard from Jess. A big surprise, I must confess, given that you two didn't exactly hang out together in high school—"

"That's putting it mildly," Laura agreed.

"But Jess said you guys are absolutely the perfect couple now. Congrats." He pointed to Tamara. "This is Tamara Giovanessi. She's new to town."

Laura raised a critical eyebrow. "We've already met. Well, not exactly met. You crashed my wedding reception. Ring any bells?"

Tamara winced. "I'm so sorry about that. My sincerest apologies. I realize it's a feeble excuse, but

I'd just arrived and was pretty distraught. When I asked where to find Briggs, someone mentioned he was at a wedding. Still…"

"Yes, still…" Laura didn't bother with any pleasantries when Tamara apologized again before excusing herself to pay. Instead, she addressed Drew. "Promise me you'll stop by at the gallery—soon. I've got something I need to talk to you about."

"Is it about my mom's artwork that I sent over? I got the email that the opening's next month." It was mid-June now. "I think that sounds great. I can't thank you enough. I've been wanting to set up a scholarship in her name at the school where she taught, and this seemed like the perfect way to do it."

Drew's mother, Vivian Trombo, had been a beloved art teacher at the local Quaker school, and her death two years earlier had left a gaping hole in the family's collective psyche. As far as Drew could tell, his sister, Jessica, was only now coming out of it, thanks to some real soul-searching and the supportive influence of Briggs Longfellow. His father? Pops was a work in progress. Norman claimed to be moving on, but Drew wasn't all that convinced.

As for himself? Drew preferred not to think about himself.

Laura nodded. "I'm more than happy to mount the show. Her work is terrific. I only just got back from a lightning-quick honeymoon—Phil is teaching in a summer school program, and I'm still sifting through the pieces you sent. But there's other stuff I want to talk about, too—and soon."

"No problem. Tomorrow or the next day suits me, but not today. Today I'm on fix-it duty." They said their goodbyes, and by the time Drew got to the cash register, Tamara had already paid and was waiting to leave. "Same time tomorrow?" he asked.

She nodded. "Sounds good. I'm not sure if I'm on chauffeur duty, so I might be later again."

"I could give you my cell number? That way you could let me know for sure." He reached in the pocket of his cargo shorts to grab his phone.

"Not necessary. I think I prefer to leave you guessing."

"Thus, lending you an air of mystery?"

"More like it relieves me of any specific commitment."

With that, he could empathize.

CHAPTER SIX

WILL RUSHED IN the kitchen door. He dumped his tennis racket and backpack on the floor and called out, "Buddy, Buddy, I'm home!" Fourteen-year-old boys weren't much into subtlety. The sound of four paws' worth of nails scurrying along the hardwood floors could be heard coming from the living room.

"Will, what'd Coach Keith say about taking good care of your tennis equipment?" Tamara stood next the abandoned pile. In one hand she clutched her rental car keys, in the other a stack of books. She tried to avoid eye contact with Myrna stirring what smelled like rich spaghetti sauce on the stove.

Will rolled his eyes but doubled back. He picked up the backpack and placed it on a wooden chair, and he was hugging his racket to his chest when Buddy came skidding to a stop next to his super-best friend. Which was when the pooch saw the "evil" racket and cowered, his head scrunched between his shoulders. A stray that Will had rescued only a few months earlier, Buddy was a shy Aussie-shepherd mix whose bravery quotient hovered below the lowest percentile. Some dogs were alpha dogs. Buddy was an omega dog through and through.

Will placed the tennis racket on the floor and clapped for the dog to come for a cuddle. "It's okay, boy. See, the racket's out of the way. It won't hurt you. I promise."

Buddy paused briefly to sniff the strings. Then he launched himself at Will.

"That's my Buddy. Did you miss me?" He rubbed the dog's ruff and gave his back some full-blown scratches. Buddy squirmed and noodled his body in response, all the while lavishing Will with slobbery kisses.

"Did you thank Tamara for picking you up from tennis and taking you to help out at the vet's?" Myrna reminded him.

Will looked up. Buddy was forced to wriggle higher to kiss his chin. "Thank you, Tamara. It was very nice that you drove me all around." There was a singsongy quality to his voice. "Was that good enough, Aunt Myrna?"

Myrna shook her head. "I'd like to think he was born saying please and thank you, but the truth of the matter is it's taken years of practice."

"No big deal." Tamara waved off Myrna's excuses. It was impossible to relax knowing that Myrna only tolerated her presence for Will's sake. "Will was great at tennis. I only got there at the end, but I watched him hit some solid volleys, and he was very helpful with picking up the balls."

"Coach Keith says that's just as important as

learning the shots," Will piped up. He untangled himself from Buddy and staggered to his feet. "And Tamara picked up balls, too. Most of the other moms and dads just stood there."

Myrna raised her eyebrows. "Praise, no less."

"What can I say? I'm a regular whiz with a ball hopper. If nothing else, it gave me something to do," she said, downplaying her actions.

"I'm surprised they let you onto the court in those." Myrna tipped her head to indicate Tamara's high heels.

"Oh, she had on flip-flops. So, there wasn't any problem," Will said, oblivious to the undertones.

Myrna raised an eyebrow. "Flip-flops?"

"This afternoon I got a pedicure at the salon in town. I had to buy the flip-flops there since I didn't want to mess up the nail polish. The owner, Denise, did a great job, don't you think?" She slipped a foot out of her heels and wiggled her toes. "The color's burnt umber. Oh, Denise said to remind you of your hair appointment tomorrow."

Myrna watched as Tamara put her shoe back on. "Nice of Denise to remind you, not that I would've forgotten."

Will rocked from one high-topped sneaker to the other. "So, where's Dad? I wanted to tell him about this surgery Jessica did this morning—reattaching the tendon on the knee joint of a Lhasa apso named Victor. So cool!"

"He's in his room, getting ready for a night out with Jessica," Aunt Myrna answered. She watched

Will start to scramble out of the kitchen. "But knock before you enter. And take your tennis racket, please," she called out to stop him from racing up the stairs.

"Oh, right." Will tripped over his own overgrown feet when he pivoted to retrieve the racket. "C'mon, Buddy. Let's go see Dad." Buddy bounded up the stairs.

Myrna shook her head. "I don't know who's clumsier—Will or that dog. Still, they're both so darn cute."

"At least it looks like the dog is more scared of the racket than of me."

"You wouldn't happen to know where Will's lunch box is?" Myrna suddenly switched gears.

"It's still in his backpack. I forgot to have him take it out of his bag."

Myrna wiped her hands on her striped apron. She walked to the side chair and unzipped the top of Will's backpack. "There's always something with kids. You get used to it with practice—if you stick around long enough." She took out a canvas pouch and brought it to the kitchen counter, where she proceeded to empty the contents—a plastic container with crumbs from his sandwich, the wrapper from a snack pack of Oreos, an empty water bottle and an apple with one bite taken out. She tut-tutted over the last item. "Something for the compost bin, I guess."

Tamara stepped closer. "You don't have to throw

that out. I'll just cut around the teeth marks and eat it later. It's a shame to waste it."

Myrna eyed her. "I didn't figure you for someone who eats leftovers."

"You'd be surprised." There were times during her college days when a half-eaten apple was all Tamara had at the end of the month after paying the rent and utilities. But she wasn't about to share these details with Myrna. "When I picked up Will from the clinic, I saw Jessica, and she also mentioned something about going out with Briggs," she responded instead.

"They're going across the river to Lambertville, first to this funky bar called the Shipyard—it has all this nautical and rowing paraphernalia—and then to dinner at a great pasta place called the Broadhurst."

"Sounds delightful." Her response sounded a bit patronizing when she didn't mean it to be. "If you'd like to have a night on the town with them, too, I'm happy to stay with Will."

"I think Briggs and Jessica would probably prefer to be on their own, don't you?"

"Yes, of course." Was there nothing she could say that was right? "Or maybe you'd like to hang out with Jessica's father?"

"I don't think so. Norman's really looking forward to some quality one-on-one time with his son, Drew. That's important, you see—family."

Tamara picked up the implication that she knew nothing about family, which was, to be fair, an accurate assessment. "You're right, of course, and I am trying to learn how to fit in to family life. And see—" she rifled through her Goyard tote bag "—I even brought you some local jam from Chubbie's that I thought you might like." She held it out.

Myrna took the jar. "Thanks." She looked at the label. "Oh, Nada made it. Then it must be good. I didn't realize she'd branched out into jam. She's famous for her baked goods but not jam. She has a stand at the farmers' market, and everything she sells there is superb. You should come and see for yourself."

Was that actually an invitation? "That'd be nice," Tamara replied. "I've got something else for you, too." She looked through the books she was carrying and passed one to Myrna. "I visited the Hopewell Public Library today and found the latest Louise Penny mystery. I saw you were reading one on your e-reader and thought you might like it."

Myrna looked taken aback. "I didn't realize you'd noticed." She glanced at the cover. "And they let you take this out even though you don't live here."

If the comment was meant as a slight, Tamara ignored it. "It was simple, really. I explained that I was staying with you and Briggs, and Amy— that's the librarian—seemed to know all about me. What amazing curly red hair she has, by the way. She told me that her mother is friends with you. Gloria Pulaski?"

Myrna nodded. "Gloria's like the queen bee of Hopewell—but in a nice way."

"Good to know. Amy also told me that her younger sister, Betsy, who just had a baby and works at the hospital, played field hockey in middle school with Jessica. It was a regular old home week."

"It sounds like you've been busy. First the diner, then the salon—and let's not forget the library. Next, you'll tell me you scouted out the hardware store."

"It's on my list."

Myrna glanced at the book's dust jacket. "I suppose this'll have a short borrowing time, being new and all."

"Not to worry on that score. Amy told me that the borrowing period is doubled in summer." Tamara stretched a smile.

Myrna strained one out in return. "Isn't that handy."

Finally, Tamara couldn't stand it anymore. "I'm not asking you to like me, Myrna. I'm simply hoping we can find a middle ground of tolerance. I haven't come here to take Will away from you—not that he'd even come. Most of the time—and especially at this very moment—I haven't the foggiest idea what I'm doing with my own life, let alone how to take care of a kid." From upstairs she heard the sound of doors opening and closing, murmurs and a toilet flushing.

"Whatever you might think, I'm not threatened," Myrna replied. Her words may have said one thing. Her tone implied another. "I just want what's best for the boy, and, frankly, I'm not convinced your presence is helping matters. I realize now that keeping your identity a secret from Will all these years may have contributed to his lack of self-confidence and shyness, but I don't think your sudden arrival was the way to go about providing reassurance either. In my opinion, a wiser approach would have been to start with a phone call or two and progress from there."

Tamara scratched her cheek. "You're right. Just showing up like that was bad in so many ways."

There came the clump of footsteps and scurrying of paws down the stairs. Buddy landed first, followed by Will, who was chirping away, and finally Briggs, who was half listening while checking that he had his wallet and his phone.

All three of them ground to a disorganized stop. Buddy stationed himself in front of the dog treat jar on the hutch. Will bumped into a kitchen chair as he elaborated on the finer points of taking out sutures, and Briggs tried desperately not to grimace at the gory details.

"Well, how do I look?" Briggs spun around, showing off his lightweight gray slacks and peach-colored linen shirt. When he came to a halt, he glanced down at Buddy. The dog was thumping his tail and waiting patiently next to the ceramic dog biscuit jar. "I take it you approve," Briggs said and tossed him a treat.

Myrna studied Briggs. "The pants are fine. The shirt's a little *Miami Vice* for my taste. Thank goodness you didn't go the slicked-back-hair route."

"If you think it's too much…" Briggs looked unsure.

"Don't listen to your aunt," Tamara declared. "You look very handsome. And just to clarify, I mean that merely as an old acquaintance. More importantly, Jessica will be wowed."

CHAPTER SEVEN

"So, Will, I was at the library today getting books, and I thought next time I'm there I could pick you up something." Tamara rested her fork on the side of her plate. Myrna had prepared penne with Bolognese sauce. It was yummy. Did the woman do everything efficiently and with skill? The other evening, Tamara had spotted her filling out the crossword puzzle in ink. *In ink!*

Will looked up. He'd had his head slanted downward as he not-so-surreptitiously fed Buddy some grated Parmesan cheese. "Huh?"

Myrna cleared her throat. "We use words at this table, not grunts."

"Sorry. What did you say, Tamara?"

Tamara stared at Buddy before looking around the table. "Is that okay for him? I mean the dog?" She pointed at Buddy licking the wooden floor of any remaining gratings.

Will shrugged. "Buddy loves cheese, especially hard cheeses."

"And blue cheeses," Myrna amended. "You remember how he devoured a piece of Roquefort the other day, don't you? But we make sure not to feed Buddy from the table when Briggs is here. It's against his rules. We'll just keep this our little secret, right, Will?" She winked conspiratorially. "And as for the cleanliness of the floor, I just mopped it this morning."

"I wasn't doubting your housekeeping skills, Myrna, it's just that I never knew dogs liked cheese." Tamara smiled brightly. "So, about books. Do you have any favorites?" She was trying to find some commonality with her son. "At your age, I was really into biographies. I already knew I wanted to be a journalist, so I was keen to learn about history and the people who made a big impact on society."

Will speared a large mouthful of pasta on his fork and gobbled it in one gulp. "History isn't really my thing. I mean, I like natural history. Stuff about different species, mostly animals and their habitats. And dogs, of course."

"Of course. Dogs are wonderful." Tamara had yet to work herself up to touching Buddy's favorite liver snacks, let alone trying to pet him. "Any fiction? I guess superheroes are big now, right?"

"I suppose. But I'm so not much into them. Candy tells me that Wonder Woman is sick though. She even lent me a bound copy of some of the comics."

"Candy is Will's friend. She works at the veterinary clinic, too," Myrna provided. She passed the basket of garlic bread. "None for the dog, Will. The last time he ate garlic I had to open all the windows for at least an hour." She waited for Will to take a slice before offering Tamara some.

"No, thanks." She took her cue from the dog. "I actually met Candy this morning at Chubbie's. She's waitressing part-time to earn extra money this summer."

Myrna rested the basket on the table. "My, my, you did meet everyone."

"She even reminded me to pick Will up after tennis," Tamara laughed.

"You did what?" Drew was lazing on the bed in his childhood bedroom, doomscrolling through his phone. On the wall behind him was a Def Leppard "Heaven Is" poster. On the dresser sat a miniature crossbow and a framed photo from his high school yearbook, showing him sporting tinted aviator sunglasses.

"I volunteered you to be the go-between for Tamara and Aunt Myrna so that I can go away for a measly week with Briggs," Jessica repeated. "You see, he proposed the trip over dinner this evening, and I thought it was a great idea. But we need to figure out where Will should go. Briggs is concerned about leaving him alone with Myrna and Tamara."

"Excuse me. Taking a vacation, even a mini one? That doesn't sound like you. Are you sure you're not going to tack on a veterinary convention at the same time?"

"I am capable of separating my work life from my private life."

Drew raised his eyebrows. "I prefer not to imagine the intimate details. But still, can't Tamara and Myrna take care of one fourteen-year-old boy and a dog on their own without my two cents' worth?"

"It's not the boy and dog that are the issue." Jessica sat on the end of his bed. She stared at his feet. "You do realize that both your socks have holes in them, don't you?"

"I've just come from a severe disaster in South Asia, and you're criticizing my socks?" He sighed. "That was a cheap shot at sympathy, sorry. Look, I understand Tamara and Myrna are locked in some kind of personal feud, but surely, they're adult enough to manage."

Jessica lowered her chin and raised her eyes toward her brows. "You gotta understand, Myrna's highly protective when it comes to Will, and she's threatened by the idea of Tamara honing in. And Tamara...well...she's clueless about kids. She claims she wants to get to know Will better, but she hasn't the faintest idea how to go about forming a relationship."

"Did you ever think she might be scared? Insecure, so that even if she tries, he'll reject her?"

"Insecure? The Tamara I've met would eat nails for breakfast."

"As someone who's eaten breakfast with her twice, I can attest to the fact that's not her diet of choice."

Jessica shrugged. "Well, your view of Tamara based on two breakfasts doesn't jive with my exposure. But, hey, I'm just going by way of her interactions with Will."

"And you're such an expert when it comes to raising kids?"

"No, but I think that I have some natural nurturing instincts."

"I can't deny that. I know how well you helped care for Mom and now Pops. Speaking of which, if I take the job of peacekeeper for Briggs's family, who's supposed to look after Pops?"

"We're talking a week and not every waking hour. A bit of quality time. Outings, a few meals. Maybe propose separate activities for the adults? Besides, some of the time, Myrna will be helping out Pops, so it's not as if he'll be totally abandoned. Briggs is explaining the whole situation to Myrna as we speak, by the way."

Drew drummed his fingers on the bedcovers (the original *Star Wars*). He was running out of excuses. But he also wasn't ready to concede. "One last question. Did it ever occur to you to ask if I'm busy?"

"Are you busy?"

He stared at the back of the bedroom door. There was one of those Velcro dart boards. Only two darts had survived the passage of time. He turned back to his sister. "Truthfully?"

She nodded.

"I just about finished all the repair work needed on the exterior of the house. It was in surprisingly good shape. And I fixed your tree house last time I was home. That just leaves a little painting to do."

"Which means you're quickly going to be bored stiff."

"Don't forget all the myriad social invitations I'm going to have to accept. That could tie me down big-time." He folded his arms.

"Oh, please. You'll hear from one or two people at most. People have lives to lead. They just can't go gallivanting around town having brewskies every time you decide to grace us with your presence. And I can't see you listening to stories of diapering babies or the price of a new furnace." Jessica leaned forward and spoke in her most earnest tone of voice. "If you won't do it for me, do it for Buddy. That poor dog is just starting to learn to trust the world. Too much confrontation could send him hurtling backward."

Drew threw his phone on the quilted coverlet. "That was a low blow, Jess. A dog? And accusing me of potentially jeopardizing his emotional well-being?"

Jessica stood and smiled. "I know. But it worked, admit it."

Drew snarled and went back to doomscrolling.

CHAPTER EIGHT

THE NEXT MORNING, Drew dragged his paint-spattered self into Chubbie's. Candy poured a cup of black coffee and handed it to him before he'd even had a chance to sit. "Your usual table?" she asked.

Drew held the mug with both hands. "I'm nothing if not particular." He followed her to the patio, where she pulled out the same café chair. "I like the zebra effect, by the way," he remarked. Today, her purple hair had morphed into purple-and-green stripes.

"She'll be here soon," Candy informed him. No name necessary. "Will texted after she dropped him off at tennis this morning. Seems she talked to Coach Keith about how great she thought the program was. Wanted to know all the details. If he had any publicity for the program. Stuff like that."

"I hope Will wasn't embarrassed. What kid wants his mom schmoozing with the pro?"

"Not me. But Will thought it was pretty cool." She looked over her shoulder at the petite figure rushing toward the table. In sneakers, Drew couldn't help noticing. "Speak of the devil—and I mean that only rhetorically." Candy pulled out the other metal chair. "One soy milk latte coming up, and as far as food, I presume, you'll want to switch to a whole wheat English muffin, while, Drew, that you'll have your usual?"

Tamara settled into the chair and rested her tote on the gravel. She rubbed her hands together. "That would be scrumptious."

Candy silently mouthed the word *scrumptious* behind Tamara's back before heading off to the kitchen.

Tamara turned and called after her. "And don't forget some of that jam by Nada." She frowned before facing Drew. "I get the feeling that girl still doesn't like me."

"I think she doesn't like most people. Or at least pretends not to."

Tamara paused before nodding. "Ahh. The whole teenager rebellion thing. I know I acted that way, too, especially when it came to all my parents' rules. Probably half the reason I took up with Briggs was to thumb my nose at my ultraconservative mom and dad—not that I ever expected the outcome. And I bet you went through the same rebellious stage—convinced your mother and father were holding you back."

"Not at all. Pops may have been überbusy at work, but he fully supported us in everything. And Mom, well, she was our biggest cheerleader, encouraging Jess and me to go off and follow our dreams. And my transgressions were strictly small-time—some underage drinking and a few spontaneous trips to the Jersey Shore. More adolescent bad judgment than rebellion."

"And you never got in any real trouble?"

He shook his head. "Unless you count me losing my license for a couple of months because of speeding tickets. But by then I was in college at Stanford and didn't need a car, and when I came home, I just made Jessica drive me around. So, it's not like I really had to pay any price."

"Of course not. What was I thinking? The halo never slips on Drew Trombo. Or if it did in some teeny, tiny way, it would just endear you more to your fan club." She frowned.

Drew leaned forward on his forearms. "What's got you all riled up this morning? You sound a little ornery."

She shook her head. "It's nothing. I guess I'm a little jealous." She studied her fingernails. "I really need a decent manicure" was all she said as Candy reappeared and set down Tamara's latte.

"Sounds like another trip to Denise's salon." Candy turned away.

Tamara eyed the girl with an open mouth.

Drew took a much-needed sip of black coffee. "Candy sees all and knows all. So, you dropped off Will at tennis again?"

Tamara nodded. She raised her coffee cup and blew on the decorative foam leaf floating on top. "Yes, only this time I stayed to look at the setup. I was surprised how the program attracts kids from all over and at all levels, and that there's a companion tutoring program afterward for those who sign up. It's tied into the program that Laura's husband, Phil LaValle, runs. I was thinking there must be something I could do. I don't know, I have to think about it."

Drew was taken aback (but maybe not) by her determination. "What does Will think?"

"About tennis? He seems to enjoy it. He's not the most outgoing kid, so I can see it's hard for him. But the coaches are super supportive and make sure all the kids are involved."

"I don't just mean the tennis, but your involvement?"

"I don't know."

"Maybe it's something you should ask him about? See if he's okay with you getting involved?"

Candy silently reappeared with the food, and they each sat back. "I brought you extra jam."

"Thanks so much." And before Candy could turn away, Tamara stopped her. "What do you think about me drumming up publicity for the Hopewell tennis camp? Do you think it's a good idea?"

Candy blinked. "Why stop with the tennis camp? Hopewell has other good stuff. It beats a bunch of other places." She moved on to take an order from another table—two young moms with neat ponytails and matching running gear. They were gently rocking their babies in color-coordinated jogging strollers.

"Not exactly the best slogan. 'Hopewell. It beats a bunch of other places.' But I'm beginning to get her drift." Tamara picked up the small glass jar of jam and scooped out a mouthful with a teaspoon. She slurped it straight. "The jam alone is reason enough to come here. This stuff is addictive. Myrna told me that the woman who makes it has a stand at the farmers' market, and I thought that might be a fun thing to do with Will when Jessica and Briggs take their little vacation. And you can join us if you want. You heard about them getting away, right? Of course, you did. You've been enlisted to run interference between me and Myrna." She held up a hand and made clawlike scratching motions. "Grrr."

"I'm sure my help won't be necessary. You do know how to play nice, don't you?"

She dropped her hand. "I suppose I can try. Meanwhile, I have more immediate items to deal with."

"Items?" Drew took his first bite of the combo of eggs, bacon and home fries. The satisfaction of eating food was coming back to him.

"More like plans. For you and me. And in that regard, how are your DIY jobs coming around your father's house? Be honest. As fellow breakfast buddies—"

"Breakfast buddies? That sounds like the title of a kids' show."

"Now that you mention it, I think it's got a certain ring. Speaking of which, I feel it's absolutely essential that this little temporary relationship of ours be based on absolute honesty—kind of a breakfast buddy survival pact. Agreed?"

He shrugged. "Agreed." Why not.

"Good, that's settled." She reached out and snagged a strip of bacon.

"Hey, get your own," he protested.

"I said I would try to play nice. I didn't mean all the time. Anyway, I can tell from the way you're avoiding answering my question that you're not up to your pretty little eyeballs in work."

"You think my eyeballs are pretty?" He looked very self-satisfied.

"Everyone in this place has been admiring those baby blues. Now, answer the question. You just agreed to be frank. You're already bored stiff, aren't you?"

Drew rested the tines of his fork on the edge of his plate. "Correct. The house is in pretty good shape and about all that I have left to do is finish painting some trim. And I hate painting trim."

"Good. Because I found this the other day when I was at the library." She pulled out a black-and-white brochure. "Amy Pulaski, the librarian, says hello, by the way."

Drew narrowed his eyes trying to conjure up distant memories. "Amy Pulaski? I think she was the older sister of a classmate of Jessica's."

"Does red curly hair ring a bell? Midthirties. She's tall, towers over me, actually, and dresses like a futuristic character out of *Blade Runner*."

Drew shook his head. "Not really. All the Pulaskis have red curly hair. Back in my day, their mom ruled the roost in Hopewell. Still does from what I can gather—not that people ever seemed to mind since she has a way of making good things happen."

"So I've been told. I'm beginning to learn that's the Hopewell way of doing things. That, and having a seemingly all-encompassing communication network. But to get back to my plans, or rather, our plans." She spread the brochure on the table. "I think we need to engage ourselves while we're here and while Will's tied up with his own things. Let's participate in something we'd never think of doing."

Drew lifted his chin and glanced at the cover. Hopewell Community Classes was printed in such large, bold letters that a senior citizen with macular degeneration could easily read it. Maybe that was the point. He picked up his fork again. The dripping yellow yolk was calling him. "Like we're going to take a class together? That we would even agree on which class to take? I'm just being perfectly honest, mind you."

"Which you must. It's the foundation of our breakfast buddy-ship. And it's why we're going to take turns. We each get to pick something the other must participate in." She held up a hand. "And before you say no to the idea, let me finish. The reward for the reluctant invitee is that he—"

"Or she."

"—or she, is free to comment in absolutely candid terms, seeing as we need to be strictly honest. Now, doesn't that sound like fun?" She took a very pleased bite of a lot of jam and a little muffin.

"Why do I find your warped plan strangely appealing?"

"Because it comes without consequences—just like your adolescent hijinks."

The weird thing was that the plan did sound intriguing. For one, it solved the conundrum of having nothing to do. For another, if he didn't like what she'd suggested, he could say so without worrying that he might hurt her feelings because…well…because they were just breakfast buddies, right?

He held up another slice of bacon to tempt her. "So, tell me, who gets to go first?"

She reached out and grabbed it. "I do, because it was my idea." She took an uncharacteristically sloppy bite.

"And your course selection is? I presume that's what you're suggesting given that you're flaunting this inspiring-looking pamphlet."

"Don't belittle the graphics. They're simple and direct—the Hopewell way of doing things." She flipped to an already dog-eared page and pointed with the end of the crisp piece of bacon. "This one."

Drew leaned forward. "'Drop-in Ballroom Dancing.'" He sat back. "As opposed to 'Drop-out Ballroom Dancing'?"

"Don't be cute. It simply means you can show up for a class without having to take the whole course. And see, it says, 'All levels welcome. Tuesdays,

1:00–3:00 p.m., town hall meeting room.'" She batted her eyelashes. "And since Will's tennis gets out at four, we have time to go today. It'll save you from having to paint any more of the trim. C'mon. What do you have to lose?"

"My dignity?"

"A small price to pay. Besides, you're the hometown hero. People will think you're just trying to be modest, not show-offy."

"Show-offy? Is that some journalese word?"

She growled.

He held up his hands. "Okay, okay, Twinkle Toes. I'm ready to rumba."

CHAPTER NINE

"DREW TROMBO! As I live and breathe!" An older woman, her gray hair styled in a glossy pageboy with pert bangs (more of Denise's handiwork?), rose from the piano bench and opened her arms. A pin of musical notes twinkled against the argyle print of her twinset. And the rubber bottoms of her Easy Spirits squeaked as she strode across the dull wooden floor.

The floor wasn't the only thing that needed refurbishing in Hopewell's brick town hall. Several years earlier, there'd been a proposal before the planning board to build a new, more efficient building on the southern end of Main Street opposite the bicycle repair shop. But the hue and cry ("How do I know that I'll still get my local tax bill on time?" "How many town halls have cupolas like this one?" Or the real kicker: "Robby Bellona knows how to baby the old boiler perfectly fine.") had been overwhelming. The picturesque old town hall remained intact, a little creaky, its boiler beholden to Robby.

The woman offered a powdered cheek, and Drew bent down to do his duty. "What fates have brought us together again, Mrs. Horowitz?" he asked. "And how is it you never seem to age?"

"Always the charmer. Good to have you home for a change. I know your father's missed you." She eyed him critically. "You need to get a haircut." Before he could protest, she turned to Tamara. "Speaking of fates, I have a feeling you're the cause of this little reunion. I'm Mrs. Ida Horowitz. Call me Mrs. Horowitz. I was Drew's long-suffering piano teacher. And you must be the Tamara Giovanessi I've heard so much about." Mrs. Horowitz patted her kindly on the hand. "Don't worry, dear. I form my own opinions."

Tamara sniffed and tried to regain some composure. "Good to know. And you're right, Drew has agreed to come to today's session of ballroom dancing at my behest."

"More like a dare," Drew qualified.

Tamara turned to address him. "Perhaps a stop-gap measure is a more accurate description?"

"Or how about something to fend off boredom?" he proposed.

They nodded in unison. "Yes, that's it." They turned to Mrs. Horowitz for her concurrence.

Mrs. Horowitz looked first at Drew and then at Tamara. "So you say." She took Tamara by the hand. "Such cold hands. You know what they say about cold hands?" she said with a knowing smile. "Let me introduce you to the others."

Tamara grabbed at Drew with her other hand. "I'm not doing this alone."

"I thought you had it all under control," he whispered. He tucked a stray lock of hair behind one ear—Mrs. Horowitz had a point about needing a haircut—and followed with his best smile.

"This is Mr. Portobello. In addition to owning the wonderful wine and spirits shop in town, Mr. Portobello is our esteemed dancing instructor. He appeared on Broadway," Mrs. Horowitz explained.

Mr. Portobello offered a firm handshake to each. "I was merely in the chorus of the national traveling production of *Cats*. You can imagine the makeup! By the way, Drew, I have a case of that Belgian beer you like. But for you, Tamara, could I recommend a nice Shiraz from South Australia?"

"You can, and you must tell me about the stage makeup when I come to your shop tomorrow," Tamara replied.

"That would be delightful. Ferdinand will enjoy your company. He's my pet rabbit. A devoted patient of Drew's father's—and now sister's—practice."

Ferdinand? Tamara repeated silently to Drew.

"No time for chitchat." Mrs. Horowitz steered the ship onward, making further introductions—Insu Park, Hopewell's mayor. His bull mastiff, Sheba, was sleeping peacefully by the piano, with one paw wrapped around the pedals.

"She particularly likes show tunes," the mayor explained. He was standing next to Gloria Pulaski, she of the family of redheads. Though at this point in her life, Gloria's vibrant-colored hair owed as much to Clairol as it did to heredity.

"I feel as if I've known you forever," she said to Tamara before surveying Drew. "You, I have." She gave him a cuff on the shoulder.

He was still rubbing it theatrically as Mrs. Horowitz moved on to Mr. Mason, the retired gas station owner, and Signora Reggio, Laura's Italian grandmother, or *nonna*, and Mr. Mason's card-playing rival.

"Con piacere," said Tamara.

"What an accent. *Senza dubbio*, we shall have to talk more," Signora Reggio responded with her hands as well as her voice. Then she eyed Drew. "To celebrate your homecoming, I will have Laura deliver my veal scaloppine to the house."

And that concluded the introductions to their fellow classmates, most their senior by about thirty years. ("Age is merely an attitude. And, trust me, I've got attitude," Gloria Pulaski was known to utter on occasion, especially to a passerby who innocently offered to show her how to use the parking meter app. "Excuse me, I was the one who introduced the app's use at the town council meeting!")

Mr. Portobello fingered the curl of his well-manicured goatee and then clapped his hands to bring the class to attention. Mrs. Horowitz glided to the piano stool and eased her way next to Sheba. The participants gravitated to the middle of the empty room. Tamara and Drew followed suit.

"You sure you're up to this?" she teased him.

Drew flexed his fingers. "No problem. Just promise you won't leave me with Gloria Pulaski."

Tamara stood with her chin high. She appeared to be enjoying having Mr. Cool squirm.

"Today's lesson focuses on the waltz," Mr. Portobello briefed the group. "In this first recreational ballroom dance class, we will focus on correct dance postures, dance positions, step patterns, and basic leading and following techniques."

"I'm happy leading," Tamara informed Drew.

He tilted his head in her direction. "Why am I not surprised?"

"The waltz is an elegant, romantic dance done with a partner," Mr. Portobello explained as he sashayed among the students. He gestured with his hands out but kept his elbows in. "We will begin without music and learn the so-called box step, which consists of six movements that form the shape of a box. We'll start by individually performing the lead's steps. Then we'll do the follow's steps. When we've mastered that, we'll partner up and work in pairs. So, to begin with, everyone, please stand side by side, facing the front. Give yourself some room and watch me." He moved forward to demonstrate. "You will love it. Trust me," he said, offering a generous smile.

In between the giggles and stern faces, something that could loosely be called progress ensued as the class mastered the various iterations of leading, following, waltzing with a partner and finally all these elements accompanied by music. Mrs.

Horowitz provided a steady three-four beat that swayed leisurely, encouraging the pupils to enjoy the feeling of dancing rather than agonizing over where their feet were.

"Relax, Mr. Mayor," Mr. Portobello encouraged. "Think of the movements as a celebration of a victorious election rather than a slog through a zoning board meeting." Mayor Park was leading Drew, his current partner, toward the photocopying machine. There was something of a heat-seeking-missile quality to his determination, and his black suit added a particularly menacing aura.

"Maybe it's time for a short break?" Drew suggested when he nearly missed kicking over a metal wastepaper basket. "I know I could use one." The mayor nodded, seemingly relieved, and Drew hustled over to a long table set with refreshments and poured himself a cup of punch.

"Be careful. That's spiked," Mr. Mason warned him.

Drew pointed over his shoulder. "With this crowd? Somehow, I doubt it."

Mr. Mason munched on a chocolate-filled cannoli. "Doubt away, but it's my recipe. I call it my Motor Oil Special, and I can personally vouch for the healing powers of crème de menthe on falling arches." He lifted one of his orthotics-accommodating walking shoes.

Drew peered at the greenish liquid in his cup and cautiously sipped. "You're right. It's not for the faint of heart." He took another mouthful. "There's something else besides the alcohol and fruit juice that I can't quite identify."

"My secret ingredient—Mountain Dew." He gave Drew a playful elbow.

Drew raised his eyebrows and nodded. "That's one way to go." He scanned the offerings and chose a pistachio-filled cannoli. "Signora Reggio made these, I presume?"

"Who else?" Mr. Mason concurred.

At that moment someone clapped with vigorous enthusiasm, (or con brio, as Johann Strauss Jr. had written within those particular musical measures). The sound woke the sleeping Sheba, and she shuffled to a standing position with a grunt and a shake, nearly knocking Mrs. Horowitz off the piano bench. Mrs. Horowitz continued in a rhapsodic rendition of "The Blue Danube."

"Oh, dear. Sorry, Sheba." Tamara held her hands to her chest in apology. Her face was flushed. "I'm the one who made the noise. You see, La Signora and I had just experienced a breakthrough," she exclaimed.

"Who knew that just saying 'sinistra' instead of 'left' and 'destra' rather than 'right' would do the trick?" Signora Reggio fanned herself. "So much more natural to think of dancing in your mother tongue, no?"

"Dancing appeals to a primal sense, which is why thinking in Italian is right for you," Tamara agreed. She passed La Signora off to Mr. Portobello, who twirled her around the room with the ease of a principal dancer, not just a chorus member.

Drew frowned in thought. "You don't happen to know La Signora's first name, do you?" he asked Mr. Mason. "I always thought of her as La Signora or Laura's *nonna*."

Mr. Mason swallowed thoughtfully. "Can't say I do. But somehow La Signora always seemed perfect."

Drew had to agree, and he scanned the group of dancers, appreciating the wide selection of friends and neighbors who were participating. It was good to be with familiar faces again.

"How's the truck, by the way?"

Drew nodded. "Good." They slowly worked their way down the different food offerings on the table.

"It should be, after the number of times I've serviced the engine. I've also banged out a few dents here and there for Carl. You wouldn't think a responsible middle-aged man like Carl would drive like he was racing a hot rod. But you can't ever really tell, can you?" Mr. Mason turned around and watched the dancing. "You gotta admit, she's a character."

Drew needed a moment to realize he wasn't talking about the truck. He tracked Mr. Mason's focus to Tamara, who was presently partnered with Gloria Pulaski. The women were holding their arms aloft and seemed to be struggling regarding the proper positions. "Who do you think is going to end up leading?" Mr. Mason asked.

"Couldn't say. If memory serves me correctly, Gloria Pulaski's used to calling the shots, but I think she's met her match." Drew took a piece of watermelon. If nothing else, it helped soak up the crème de menthe.

Tamara held up her left arm to lead.

"She's met her match, all right," Mr. Mason agreed. He turned to Drew. "So, what's your next move?"

Drew frowned. "My next move? I was thinking of finding a quiet spot in the corner and pulling out my sketch pad."

Mr. Mason shook his head. "That wouldn't have been my choice." He waved off Drew and joined Signora Reggio, who was taking her refreshment break along with some of the classmates.

Gloria and Tamara parted on laughing terms, at which point Tamara went over to join Mrs. Horowitz.

"Enjoying yourself then?" Gloria tracked down Drew sitting in the corner.

Drew looked up. He saw that Gloria held out a cup to him. "No, thanks, any more of Mr. Mason's brew, and I'll be curled up, snoring louder than Sheba."

"This is from my private stash—strictly iced tea with lemon."

"In that case, thank you." He shifted the pad on his lap and took the proffered cup and drank. He was thirsty.

"I wouldn't have thought ballroom dancing would be your cup of tea. Excuse the pun."

"It's not. It was Tamara's idea of how we could pass the time here in Hopewell before we each head off again."

Gloria nodded. "I should have guessed."

Together they watched Mayor Park invite Tamara for another spin around the dance floor, and when he maneuvered them precariously close to the refreshments, Tamara grabbed a dumpling and tossed it Sheba's way. "I want to keep her on my good side," they overheard her explain to the dog's owner. "I've seen the size of her jaws."

Drew smiled. "If she feeds her enough, Sheba will want to cut in."

"Everyone wants to dance with Tamara. Even me," Gloria admitted. She glanced at his work. "A nice picture."

He'd done a quick drawing of Mayor Park propelling Tamara across the room. "The composition of two people together provides a natural dynamic," he explained as he went back to filling out the picture, flipping his pencil every once in a while to erase a line here or there.

"I wasn't talking about the composition." Then she pulled back and narrowed her eyes. "Your hair," she exclaimed, completely changing the subject.

"I know. I should get it cut. I've already been told."

"There's that, but I was noticing the flecks." Gloria poked gently with her index finger. "Paint?"

"Oh, that. I was touching up the trim on Pops's house. You can see it under my nails, too." He flattened out his left hand. The brick color filled some creases and dotted his knuckles.

"Did you ever consider changing the color? Maybe a nice lavender?"

Drew stopped drawing and looked up in mock horror. "What? Make a change to the house? I think Pops would have a fit. The place feels like a shrine to my late mother."

"Knowing Vivian, she would have insisted your father consider a fresh direction. Your mother was an artist, an iconoclast. She'd want to be remembered but not made into some saint." Gloria laughed, and then she saw Drew looking at her. "You seem shocked. You forget that she and I grew up together. A love of life—and sharing that life— was Vivian's hallmark. And in my opinion, nothing says life like lavender." She patted Drew on the knee. "You know, speaking of people's traits, I find myself changing my opinion regarding your Tamara over there."

"She's not my Tamara," Drew protested.

"So you claim," Gloria was fast to reply. "It got me thinking, you see. It can't have been easy. I mean, finding out as a teenager that you're going to be a mom. And from what I can glean—not that she lets much slip—it seems she didn't have any family support either."

"I agree it couldn't have been easy. Still, we have to live with our choices."

"True. But some are easier to live with than others. You know what I think?" It wasn't really a question. "I think Tamara's a little lost. She pretends not to be, but she is."

Drew watched Tamara tactfully volunteer to lead for a change. "Somehow I don't see that."

Gloria stared at Drew. "And you claim to be an artist?" She pointed to his drawing. "Oh, you have talent, all right, but do you really see? The way your mother used to see? Tamara needs us, Drew. She needs Hopewell."

"And you presume to cut in and tell her? She seems pretty much in the lead as we speak."

Gloria tsk-tsked. "It's not the leading that's the hard part. The art is in the following. Trust me. Just ask any woman."

CHAPTER TEN

DREW MANAGED TO extricate himself from Gloria's clutches by feigning a bathroom break. ("Don't think I don't know you're skipping out, Drew Trombo. I'm the mother of five children, grandmother of three. A little thing like a trip to the boys' bathroom never fooled me.")

When he returned, Gloria had luckily moved on. He spotted Tamara by the refreshment table, where she was fanning herself with one hand and holding a glass of punch in the other. Signora Reggio was telling her something that was apparently amusing because Tamara was laughing. She looked relaxed, devoid of the thrumming intensity that seemed to grip her body in their initial meetings. Her skin glowed naturally, and her short haircut lay in easy curls, like it wasn't styled with some lacquered gel. She looked artless. Hopewell-like. He shook his head.

As he did so, Tamara looked up. "Something's bothering you?" she asked when he came and stood next to her.

"On the contrary. Dance?" He held up his arms.

Tamara turned to La Signora. *"Scusami. Potremmo continuare a parlare dopo aver ballato con lui?"*

"Non c'è problema." La Signora shooed her away.

"In which case—" Tamara put her plastic cup on the white paper tablecloth "—never let it be said that I turned down such a delightful offer." She raised her arms, circled into his embrace and drew them across the floor.

Drew let her lead without comment. "What is it about women and dancing? You really seem to like it."

"Who doesn't like to move?" She directed them along with a series of accomplished steps.

Drew pulled her closer. She didn't object. "And you seem to do it so much better."

"Actually, Mr. Mason is pretty light on his feet. Did you see the way his hips move so freely?" She sashayed him around with a flourish, and his boots clipped the toe of one of her white sneakers.

"Oops. Sorry about that. Those are advanced moves," he pronounced.

"Not to worry. You're allowed to step three times on my toes. That's number one." She settled easily into his arms and rested her cheek on his chest. "The material of your T-shirt is very soft, by the way."

"I'm glad, but I was hoping you'd comment on my muscular chest as well."

"All in good time." She turned the other cheek, and they swayed together as Mrs. Horowitz tinkled the ivories.

"You don't mind that I lead, do you?" she asked. And, yes, the contoured muscles of his chest felt reassuring under the baby-softness of his shirt.

He hummed. "Frankly—we are being frank with one another—I find it relaxing to be in such capable hands. It's nice not having to be in charge all the time."

"A man who's secure in his masculinity— amazing." She slipped her hands around his neck.

His large, calloused fingers rested on her shoulder blades. "Admit it. You've done this before— dancing, I mean."

"Just a little. I had to MC a celebrity dance contest for charity, and I didn't want to make some horrible faux pas by mixing up a paso doble with a cha-cha."

"A career killer if ever there was one!"

"Don't joke." She was deadly serious.

"And you speak Italian?"

"Hardly. I had to interview this famous chef from Modena, and I didn't want to make a complete fool of myself. Signora Reggio was being kind to me, humoring me about my language skills. She said my accent was *superbo*!" She glanced over and spotted La Signora dancing with Mr. Mason. Tamara gave her a wink. The Italian grandma made a gesture of approval. Tamara smiled.

"She makes you laugh," Drew commented.

Tamara chuckled. "She doesn't understand how someone with the last name Giovanessi doesn't know how to make lasagna. I explained to her that my mother was Irish, and a meal without potatoes wasn't allowed when I was growing up. She never taught me to cook, and somehow, I've never learned. La Signora promised to give me a cooking lesson if I'm here long enough. I just have to think of an occasion." It was the first time she'd brought up leaving in a while. In the course of the class, she'd completely forgotten the whole reason she was here in Hopewell.

"I'd like to suggest the occasion could have something to do with me." He murmured the comment into the top of her head.

She could feel his breath feathering her short locks. "You're so self-centered," she teased but didn't mention that Laura's grandma had said Drew looked a little adrift during this stopover in Hopewell.

Tamara raised her head from Drew's chest and studied his face. His eyes were slightly closed as he let her set the pace. Lines crinkled the outer edges of his eyes, an indication of fatigue mixed with relaxation. The corners of his mouth turned up in a wistful expression. "So, what do you think of our first adventure outside the box? Did you like my choice?" she asked.

"Full candor?"

She nodded. "Nothing less."

"I've enjoyed it more than I thought. But that may be the effects of Mr. Mason's punch. Never let it be said that crème de menthe wasn't mind-altering." His smile got wider, and he stilled his feet.

She accidentally tripped on one.

"That's one strike against you," he said.

"No fair, you made a sudden stop. But being generous, I'll forgive you. And confess. You enjoy being around people. You're not the lone wolf you claim you are."

"Just because I live out of a backpack doesn't make me a lone wolf."

"No, just..."

"Uncomplicated?"

"On the contrary, I'd say complicated, very complicated."

"Speaking of complicated or more like complications—you cheated," he accused her. "You picked something you already had experience in, and we were supposed to be expanding our horizons."

"For the person going along with the suggestion. Not necessarily the person suggesting," she clarified.

"Aha! A technicality. I can see we have to refine the parameters of our little endeavors."

Tamara set her mouth. "All right. Fair's fair." She stepped forward. "Shall we?" He nodded, and they started to dance again.

Was it Tamara's imagination, or had Mrs. Horowitz slowed the tempo to the pace of a dream sequence in some gauzy French romantic movie? Whatever, it felt nice. She sighed. "This can't last forever, you know."

"I agree. My feet are killing me."

That wasn't what she meant. She could say so,

but she didn't. "I'm not good with dogs," she admitted out of the blue. "I never grew up with them."

"You don't seem to have any problems with Sheba. Even I'm impressed by the size of her jaws. But you figured her out right away. Dumplings. Dogs like food. Actually, mostly cheese."

"Yeah, I found that out about Buddy. But it's easier with Sheba. She's different."

"How?"

"Most obviously, she's not Will's dog." She grimaced. "I don't want to fail, you see. And I don't just mean with Buddy. I mean with Will. I don't want to mess him up any more than I've already done. I want to be a good mom, not like mine." She looked at him with all the vulnerability she shied away from showing. Was this what being candid was all about?

Tamara couldn't say exactly when, but sometime during the dancing they'd let their chests draw close. Her heart rested on his, and she could feel the rhythm, the beat. It had nothing to do with the music. Or did it?

"You're going to be a great mom because you know how important it is," he reassured her. "You just have to let Will see you, see how wonderful you are. Look how great everyone thinks it is that you're here, right? But don't force it. Listen. Do stuff he likes to do when he wants to do it. And above all, feed him lots of ice cream."

Tamara listened hard. "Right. Boys—ice cream. Dogs—cheese. I hope I don't mix them up."

"It'll work the other way around, too. Trust me. Boys and dogs are simple. Now, women on the other hand?" He gave her one of his patented smiles as he managed to step on her foot again.

"That's two," she scolded, but at least she was still smiling. "So, what have you got planned for our next extracurricular activity?"

"I've got an idea. But it may take a day or two to organize. All I can say is, you thought the box step would be a challenge? Wait 'til you see what I have in mind."

Tamara pretended to shiver. "Ooh. I'm nervous."

"You should be. It's going to knock your socks off. I promise." And he attempted to spin her in a circle but managed to completely tangle up their feet.

"That's three times," she announced, laughing.

MRS. HOROWITZ POURED La Signora a glass of prosecco from her thermos. Hopewell women came prepared. "I've had a sudden inspiration." She glanced toward Tamara and Drew enjoying themselves. "Do you see what I see?"

"Our Drew with that lovely Tamara girl."

"She is lovely, isn't she? I don't know who was insinuating otherwise."

Signora Reggio looked at Mrs. Horowitz. "Ida, we all were because we were worried about Will and his family."

"You're right. We can sometimes jump to conclusions about strangers."

They went back to observing Tamara and Drew laughing.

"Do you think we should encourage something that goes beyond dancing a waltz together?" Mrs. Horowitz asked.

"I believe so. But they will need our help."

"I'm already working on it as we speak."

"Anch'io," La Signora agreed.

They clinked glasses. (No paper cups for them.) "To a joint effort."

"To Hopewell."

"To peace and harmony."

"To *amore.*"

CHAPTER ELEVEN

DREW DECIDED TO tag along with Tamara at the end of the dance lesson. She was in a hurry to pick up Will and Candy from tennis camp, after which she'd swing by Briggs's house for Buddy—all a carefully orchestrated campaign to rally the troops for a scheduled appointment at the vet's.

"You're really sure you want to come?" Tamara asked as she walked briskly to the car. "I can't imagine it'll be very exciting."

"Think of it as moral support," he explained.

"For me or Buddy?" She dug her car keys out of her tote bag.

"More like me. These days, all Pops seems to ask me about is whether I think the Phillies will win the pennant this season. And I have absolutely no opinion or any interest in having an opinion, so I keep trying to avoid the topic because if I'm going to be honest—"

"Perhaps selective honesty is the way to go with your father?" Tamara suggested. "Though come to think of it, if that's all he asks about, maybe he's only being selectively honest with you, too."

Just then a voice called out from the art gallery just down the street. "Not so fast!" Laura came bounding down the steps. Her white linen blouse billowed over her baby bump and capped a batik-printed skirt. The green polish on her toenails, visible through her Birkenstocks, matched the streak in her hair.

She eyed Tamara. "Two days in a row. Interesting." She turned to Drew. "You promised to stop by the gallery today, and yet here I see you walking by without so much as a greeting." Her reminder didn't prevent her from giving him a big hug.

Then she liberated Drew from her grip and poked her finger in his chest. "I need your help, and don't say that you're too busy, because I know you're not." Laura glanced at Tamara. "Though, I must say, the ballroom dancing class was a brainstorm. And before you ask, I don't have cameras in the town hall, merely my *nonna*."

The finger ended up in Drew's chest again. "I remembered what a great carpenter you were, and if you could tear yourself away from fixing your dad's woodwork, I could really use your help with the custom framing at the gallery. Even with my obstetrician-approved antinausea medication, the thought of wood glue is enough to make me woozy."

"I have some mints, if you need them." Tamara rifled through her bag.

Laura held up her hand. "I'm okay at the moment, but that's kind of you to offer. And I'm sorry I was not all together friendly the first time we met—given the circumstances."

Tamara nodded. "Completely understandable—given the circumstances."

"Anyway, Drew. Back in high school you were really into art. Why not scratch an old itch? The framing job could be right up your alley."

Tamara pointed to Drew's back pocket. "You know, he carries around a sketch pad. You should see his drawings."

"Whaddaya know? He always used to carry one back then, too. I thought it was so cool. It was your mom's idea, wasn't it?" she asked Drew.

"That's right," he replied. "She always said, 'Never wait for inspiration to come to you.'"

"'You go to it,'" Laura finished the motto. "She was the greatest. So, what I also wanted to let you know is that her show is shaping up nicely." She turned to Tamara to explain. "Drew sent me a whole portfolio of works by his mother that she'd given him. He asked about mounting a show, with the proceeds from the sale going toward a scholarship in her name at the school where she taught."

"Drew, that's so thoughtful," Tamara said.

"I know, not like me at all."

Tamara sent a sideways glance at Laura. "He likes to hide his good nature."

"You think so?" There was a bit of her *nonna* in her eyes. Then Laura focused those eyes on Drew. "The fact is, I could really use some more works to make the show even better—especially later works. It'd be great to get a full sense of how her art evolved." She gave him a steely look. "You know where I'm headed with this one, don't you?"

"You want me to talk to Pops, convince him to donate some of Mom's art still at the house."

Laura nodded.

"Unfortunately, I'm not at all optimistic he'll agree. Mom—and everything about her—is sacred to Pops. Why, the house is like a giant memorial. Nothing can be moved even an inch, let alone leave the premises. It's his way of preserving her memory."

"You could tell him that he wouldn't be parting with the memories. Rather, it'd be like sharing them with the people who loved her and letting new people get to know her as well."

Drew shrugged. "You make it sound so easy."

"Don't you want to help your father move on?" Laura reasoned.

"I'd love to. I just don't know how. I'll tell you what though. Why don't you come to the house and ask him? See how well that goes?"

"I did try."

"How'd that turn out?"

Laura rubbed her swollen belly. "About as well as you'd expect."

"Did you try asking Jessica to talk to him?" Drew grasped at straws.

"Of course. She flat-out refused and suggested I talk to you—said you were always the golden-haired boy. If anyone could convince him, it'd be you."

"Well, no one ever said my sister wasn't sharp." He ran the tip of his tongue along his lower lip. "Look, I get that you want to display the full range of my mom's work. I think it's a terrific idea, Laura. But when it comes to my dad, like I said earlier, I'm not sure what to say to make it happen…"

At which point, Tamara interrupted. "I do."

The others stared at her. "You do?" they asked simultaneously and looked askance.

Tamara sighed. "Look, I really need to leave to pick up Will and Buddy, but do you want my suggestion or not?"

"Yes?"

"What is it?"

"That I deal with it. I'll be the one to talk to Drew's dad. And I'm happy to talk to you about it more, Drew—but while I'm driving. *Andiamo!*" She hustled down the street to her car.

Drew didn't need Laura's *nonna* to translate. "Great! We get to be alone at last, and what do we talk about? My dad." He matched her rapid strides with his longer ones.

"It's for a noble cause," she countered.

"I'll have you know that no one's accused me of being noble before."

She winked. "There's always a first time for everything."

"So where is she?" Candy lay on the grass propped up on her elbows. She had biked to the tennis courts to help Will deal with Buddy getting his shots at the vet's. Tamara was supposed to pick them up after camp, and she was exactly three minutes late.

Will was stepping here and there on the grass in what looked like a drunken pattern. In actuality, he was attempting to balance the butt of his tennis racket on the tips of two fingers. He focused so hard on keeping the racket vertical that he didn't see a divot in the ground. And tripped.

The tennis racket went flying, and Will landed flat on his face. He scrambled to his feet, no harm done except for the grass stains on his white-and-blue tennis shirt. The crest of Hopewell Tennis Camp was monogrammed on the pocket. "Myrna's going to kill me."

Candy got up and retrieved the racket. She held it out. "Maybe you just stick to volleys and serves."

Will rubbed his knee and nodded.

Candy settled on a picnic bench. "Do you want me to text Tamara to make sure she hasn't forgotten? Moms can get busy and forget." Candy's mother, Alice, ran her own printer and copying business besides having sole care of her daughter.

"No, there's no way she'll forget, not after messing up the other day. I've never heard anybody apologize so many times. She blamed it on living by herself, which was a pretty weak excuse, but I've never lived alone, so what do I know?"

"My mom always tells me not to live alone. She says that if nothing else, it's another paycheck," Candy said.

"That doesn't sound right," Will replied.

Candy felt a knot in her stomach. "It's not. My mom should have gotten rid of my dad a lot sooner, believe me. But I think the real reason she talks that way is because she doesn't have enough money to get a new car. She used to love her Audi, said it was pretty spiffy." Candy laid on the irony. "But the last bill for repairing the air-conditioning was anything but spiffy. And we haven't hit August yet."

Will went back to balancing the racket. "Anyway, Tamara will be here soon. She knows we have an appointment for Buddy. She put it on the calendar on her phone and even wrote it on the back of her hand with a Sharpie."

Candy frowned. She couldn't quite picture the woman who wore stilettos and designer jeans writing reminders on the back of her hand. She looked down at her own hand where she had done the same.

JUST AS WILL was making a mess of the balancing act all over again, the sound of tires turning into the gravel parking lot penetrated the air. The pinging of stones off the bottom of the car was enough to silence the starlings in the nearby pin oaks.

Tamara jumped out of the driver's side of the SUV. She left the car running and hurried around to the trunk. "Sorry, I'm late. I had it all planned in terms of timing, but then we ran into Laura Reggio LaValle, Jessica's friend, and it's not easy to… to…to…"

Drew exited the passenger seat. "Get her to stop talking? It's always been that way. I remember during this one school assembly how she got up and started lecturing everybody on the fact that it was Immanuel Kant's birthday and how we should be celebrating such an important philosopher—not that anyone knew anything about philosophy, let alone Kant. It was only a fire drill that stopped her in the end—and I'm not convinced the principal wasn't the one to throw the switch. I'm Drew, by the way," he introduced himself to Will. "I think we may have met at my dad's place my first day back. About a week ago?" He walked over to Candy's bike, which she'd left leaning against a picnic table. "You opened the trunk to take the bike, am I correct, Tamara?"

The two teens appeared dumbstruck, as if they were still trying to digest the tidbit about Laura and, even more to the point, that Tamara had appeared with Drew and that the two kept sneaking glances at one another.

"Don't make fun of Laura," Tamara chastised him. "She's clearly someone who's passionate about things." She paused. "Though I'm not sure Kant was necessarily a good choice. Not that I'm being judgmental."

"Like you're not judgmental?" he teased.

"Well, I am. But I'm trying to be more…more…"

"Open-minded?" he proposed.

"Yes, let's go with that."

Candy and Will shifted their gazes rapidly between Tamara and Drew. Finally, Candy had clearly

had enough and went over and passed her bike to
Drew. "As long as you're here…"

"And I really—really—don't want to be late,"
Will reminded everyone. "Office visits are hard on
Buddy, even though he gets along really well with
Jessica. But it's best to lower his anxiety as much
as possible, and rushing doesn't help."

"Then, Drew, you're on bike duty," Tamara ordered.

He saluted and did as he was told.

She opened the back door of her car. "Hop in,
guys, and we'll be on our way with plenty of time. I
promise." They scrambled in. "You know, I read this
article in *Veterinary Medicine News* about preparing the anxious dog for a trip to the doctor's office,"
she announced as she shut their door. She noticed
Drew staring at her from the other side of car. He
had one arm resting on the hood, and the taut muscles of his forearms stood out against his tanned
skin. "What?" She scooted into the driver's seat.

He got in as well. "You read a vet journal?"

"Just doing my homework. I wanted to prepare
for this little outing. Like I said, I don't know anything about dogs. I wanted to do the right thing by
Buddy—and Will."

Drew shook his head. "And here I was lecturing
you about cheese and ice cream."

Tamara chuckled. She put the car in Reverse and
headed across town to the Longfellow farmhouse
to pick up Buddy. When the traffic light on Main
Street turned red—a given—she glanced in the

rearview mirror. Candy and Will were giggling about something on Candy's phone. Though, given Candy's instinctive smarts, Tamara wouldn't be surprised if they were using it as a cover-up while they were really talking about the adults up front. It was the type of thing she would have done at that age.

"I was thinking," Tamara announced to her back seat passengers. "What about a playdate?" She saw Candy look up.

"I think we're a little old for that," the girl responded.

Tamara waved off the reply. "Not for you two. I was thinking for Buddy."

The light turned green, and she moved forward. "Today at ballroom dancing class, Mayor Park brought his dog, Sheba. Turns out she really likes music. Wild, huh?" Tamara chatted nervously. "Anyway, I got to thinking—Sheba, Buddy. Buddy, Sheba. Why not let them run around together? I noticed that the field next to the tennis courts is fenced in, so it'd be the perfect spot. We could play music—set the mood for Sheba. Something playful—like *Peter and the Wolf*?"

Drew raised his eyebrows.

"You're right. Maybe nothing with wolves," Tamara acknowledged.

Drew patted her arm. "Don't listen to me. I'm sure whatever you choose will be great." His hand lingered for a moment or two longer than strictly necessary.

"Thanks," she said, still mulling over Drew's innocent pat on her arm. It was innocent, wasn't it?

Will ignored the music discussion. "I don't know. Buddy's pretty shy. And Sheba's... Sheba's..."

"Pretty big?" Candy supplied.

Tamara wasn't willing to give up, even in the face of teenage ambivalence. "Granted, I'm not an expert, but I think Sheba's basically a scaredy-cat. That's why she likes music so much. It calms her. Besides, they don't need to play together exactly. Just kind of sniff around." Then she remembered Drew's advice. "And I'll be sure to bring lots of cheese to help break the ice."

"I don't know." Will still sounded dubious.

"C'mon. You don't know if you don't try. Even Drew was telling me earlier that we needed to stretch ourselves."

"Don't rope me in on this." He leaned against the passenger door as far away as possible.

She shook her head. "I'm merely giving you credit for words of wisdom. Look, I've come to realize that I may turn out to be a total fiasco as a mom. And I'll just have to live with that."

"Somehow I don't think you're the type who can live with failure," Drew interrupted.

Candy poked Will.

"What?" He was trying to adjust the damper in the strings of his racket when it slipped out of his fingers. He squirmed around to find it. "Do you see where it went?" he asked Candy.

She leaned forward. "It's on the floor, next to your left foot." She pointed and sat back.

Tamara continued. "Will, you're integral to this plan as Buddy's number one. And, Candy, you're also important to this playdate's success since you're Will's best friend. We'll all work together, kind of a group thing, okay? It'll be fun."

Will fumbled for the damper and looked at Candy. He raised an eyebrow. She turned toward him and raised two. Then she looked at the rearview mirror to address Tamara. "How will it be fun for Will?"

If nothing else, Tamara admired the girl's gumption. "I tell you what. For letting me try this, you both get ice cream from Teddy Sweet." No matter what the weather, the boutique local ice cream shop always seemed to have a long line out the door. "Any flavor, any size, with as many toppings as you want."

"Wouldn't we be, sort of, uh, exploiting the situation then?" he asked.

Tamara felt a proud maternal pang. Her son had a strong moral streak. It had to be Briggs's influence. And Myrna's, she somewhat reluctantly acknowledged.

"Okay," Will finally decided. "Let's do it. Maybe this weekend? It's supposed to be warm and sunny. Perfect weather for ice cream."

Candy nodded thoughtfully. "I'm already thinking about my flavors."

Drew turned and looked at Tamara. "See. Cheese—

dogs. Ice cream—boys. Then at a certain age, it's girls."

Tamara smiled. Small victories. She reached out and turned on the radio. The golden oldies station was playing Jefferson Airplane. Moans erupted from the back seat.

"Hey, if you really want to push the envelope?" Drew angled his head toward her. "Try singing along and see what kind of a reaction you get."

She smiled devilishly. "I like that idea. Let's." She turned the music up louder and belted out the words to "Somebody to Love."

Drew looked at her aghast. "I meant that as a joke."

Tamara grinned. "I know. I just wanted to see the look on your face."

CHAPTER TWELVE

MYRNA LET THE screen door bang behind her as she entered Norman's kitchen.

That was Hint Number One that all was not right in the world.

She pulled out a chair and plopped down with a sigh.

A not-so-subtle Hint Number Two.

Norman tried to decide whether it was wiser to wait for Hint Number Three or go ahead and ask what was bugging her.

He didn't need to decide.

"I got this phone call from Gloria Pulaski, and you wouldn't believe what she told me," Myrna huffed.

Norman ventured a guess. "Knowing Gloria, it could be anything to do with Hopewell, from the latest proposal before the sewer operating committee to Nada Bellona's newest bakery creation. Speaking of which, I'm attending the farmers' market on Saturday morning if you care to join me."

"What's this about the sewer operating committee? I usually get the announcements, and I don't remember any."

"I was just using that as an example. I haven't heard of any issues."

Myrna shrugged. "Good to know. No, the story with Gloria is that Tamara took Drew to a ballroom dance class at the town hall."

Norman looked startled. "That doesn't sound like Drew."

"Exactly. Evidently, they've got some kind of thing going."

"What do you mean by 'thing'?"

"Gloria claims to have sensed some vibes, but I said that's preposterous. What was even stranger was what she said about Tamara. She claimed that Tamara was actually very nice. Danced with everybody. Can you believe it? She even gave Sheba, Mayor Park's dog, a dumpling. She's never so much as tried to give Buddy a dumpling."

"Have you ever had dumplings in the house to give Buddy?"

Myrna threw up her hands. "You're missing the point."

"The point being?" Norman was navigating the conversation as carefully as possible.

"That she acts all standoffish and awkward around her supposed family. But somehow, she has no problem schmoozing with perfect strangers. What does that tell you?"

Norman rubbed his mouth. "I haven't the faintest idea."

"Wait. There's more. I also got this text from

Wendy." She referred to the office manager at the veterinary clinic.

"Wendy? Is everything all right at the office? I told Jessica to let me know if she needed help, but you know that girl. She could organize the Summer and Winter Olympic Games as well as the Girl Scout Jamboree, and still have time to send out holiday cards—with personal messages no less. Though come to think of it, maybe not the Girl Scouts. Vivian didn't believe in children joining organizations that required a uniform. Said there was something suspicious about it."

Myrna rolled her eyes. She didn't seem to have the patience today for one of Norman's stories about his late wife, let alone his daughter. "No, everything's fine. It's just that that woman and your son brought Will and Candy into the office with Buddy. They're still there, according to Wendy."

"Yes, Buddy was due for his regular shots."

"But there's more. Apparently, Candy—Candy who barely tolerates any adult—"

"Candy's just a teenager. She's not supposed to tolerate adults at that age. Besides, she and Will are good friends. That's the most important thing, don't you think?"

"You're not listening to me. I love you dearly, Norman—" she appeared oblivious to the implication of those words "—but you have a tendency to ramble when not held in check."

"I feel like I'm on a short lead here." Norman faked a tug on an imaginary leash.

Myrna seemed self-aware enough to laugh at his joke. "Anyway, Candy volunteered to give them a tour of the office while they were waiting."

"See, you can't complain about her antisocial tendencies."

"But she's never offered to show me around!"

"Well, she probably did it because they were there with Buddy. So the dog didn't have to sit in the waiting room getting nervous."

"I've sat in the waiting area with him getting nervous!"

Norman shook his head. "Then I'm completely confused." The conversation was getting way beyond him, and he decided he needed something with sugar. Myrna, too, for that matter. At the very least, it couldn't hurt.

He went over to a cabinet and took down a cookie tin. He pried off the lid and held it temptingly close to Myrna's nose. "A rugelach? Raspberry or apricot."

Myrna studied the offerings. She raised her eyes to Norman hovering over her. "You wouldn't have a glass of sherry to go with these, would you?"

He smiled. Where there was rugelach there was hope. "I don't think so. But I'm happy to make some tea."

"Aren't you a doll. That'll do." Myrna munched while Norman put up the kettle. By the time he returned to the table—one English Breakfast with milk for her and one with a spoonful of sugar for him (he was trying to be good)—Myrna's stress levels seemed to have abated. She blew on the tea before taking a sip. "Sherry would have been nice, but this hits the spot."

Norman chose the apricot option. "So, what's really got you out of sorts, Myrna? If it's a tour of the clinic you want, I'm happy to give you one."

"It's not the tour."

Norman drank his tea between bites and waited. Sometimes silence was the best response.

"I'm sorry if this sounds selfish, but it just seems like Tamara's taking over everyone and everything that's mine. I've worked hard for what I've got— my whole life I've worked hard. And moving to Hopewell, while I know in my heart that it was the best thing for Will, it wasn't necessarily easy for me."

"I can imagine. Little towns are supposed to be warm and friendly places, but that's mostly how they treat their own. To come in as an outsider can be difficult, like cracking a club."

"Exactly! We've only been in Hopewell two years, but I'm proud of how I've already found my own niche—especially at my age. And now… now after only a week or so, she shows up and fits right in. I mean, if Gloria thinks it's so great to go to some ballroom dance class, why didn't she ask me?"

"Do you like to dance?"

She scowled into her tea. "Not particularly."

"Well, then, there you have it. Otherwise, I'm sure Gloria would have invited you." Norman put down his wildly striped mug. One of Vivian's ex-students had made it as a present for her when she was undergoing chemo. Vivian always loved brilliant colors.

He touched the back of Myrna's hand, and the gentle motion forced her to look his way. "It's not a competition, Myrna. Everyone knows and loves you and what you do for the community. And as far as the whole dance class thing—Tamara's probably just trying to blend in. Either that or she thought it'd be a hoot to see Drew on the dance floor. I'm not sure even his high school prom date got him to dance, to tell you the truth." He chuckled.

Myrna cracked a smile, too. "I suppose you could be right. And I apologize for going on and on like that. I'm really not completely paranoid. It's just sometimes I say things because I'm feeling sorry for myself."

"There're times we all feel sorry for ourselves. The tricky part is getting out of that mood." He was more revealing than he meant to be.

Myrna let it pass without reacting. "At least I know where your loyalties lie, Norman," she said. "Now if we just had that sherry, everything would be perfect."

Norman laughed. And even Myrna made a passable attempt at a chuckle.

DREW WATCHED HIS sister update a client over the phone on the happy outcome of the dental surgery of the cat named Clive. She'd already handled Buddy's exam and injections and asked Candy and

Will to do some chores. Her day might almost be over, but he could tell Jessica was still in business mode because her long brown hair was twisted in some kind of bun and secured with a pencil.

When she finally hung up, Jessica pushed back on the ancient office chair. "So, where were we?" The three of them—Jessica, Tamara and Drew— were crowded in the tiny room that functioned as the vet's private office. Drew seemed to suck up more than his fair share of oxygen.

"I was asking about the dates for your romantic tryst with Briggs," he reminded her.

"I think what Drew meant to ask is the details of your quiet week away, just the two of you," Tamara qualified. She slanted Drew a confirming look. He gave her a silent okay before giving her an I'll-tone-it-down expression.

If Jessica noticed the interplay, she didn't mention it. "To answer your question, we're headed for Chicago, leaving on a Friday evening in about two weeks' time. I'll check in with the partners at my old veterinary practice, and then Briggs and I'll pack up my condo so I can put it on the market."

"That doesn't sound very romantic to me." Drew quickly turned to Tamara as if to check that his question was appropriate. She gave him an iffy hand motion.

This time, Jessica pursed her lips as she studied her brother and Tamara. "To each his own," was all she replied. "Frankly, I like sorting out what I want to save and what to get rid of, especially the getting-rid-of part."

"It's cleansing," said Tamara.

Jessica stood. "Exactly."

"You know, back in Phoenix I interviewed this famous closet organizer," Tamara explained. "And her advice for those people who can't bring themselves to part with possessions—especially ones they no longer used—was to take photos. That way, they could keep the memory but make the physical break. And she had this fabulous list of charities that take all sorts of things."

Drew indicated Tamara. "You heard it from the expert."

"Only the interviewer of the expert," Tamara amended.

"Don't underestimate your role in getting out the information. Your job is important."

She answered with a shrug of her shoulders.

"Hmm," was all Jessica said, and she didn't bother to hide her smile. "I'll absolutely keep that in mind. Meanwhile, I'll talk with Pops after work about the dates, and Briggs can provide the details to Myrna and Will."

Tamara looked around. "Where is Will anyway? Don't tell me I've lost him already."

Jessica shook her head. "Not to worry. He and Candy are walking Buddy and Carnation, a bichon, who's here overnight after a spaying. They're over in the park."

"Thank goodness. I had visions of them running away to the circus."

"No way. Buddy would be afraid of the clowns."

Tamara winced. "That's supposed to be a comfort?"

"That's what I'm here for. And now, if you two don't mind going off on your own—and somehow, I don't think you will—I have a few more calls to make."

DREW AND TAMARA sat on the steps of the front door of the clinic while they waited for Will and Candy to return. Since the clinic was closed to patients for the rest of the day, they were in no danger of being run over by clients and their pets.

Drew picked up a pebble from the ground and tossed it sideways as if skipping a stone over a pond. It hopped off the pavement of the parking lot and smacked into the curb at the far side before coming to rest in the grass. A metal post stood nearby, and a boxlike structure on the top contained compostable bags. A sign gently reminded owners to pick up after their dogs. Needless to say, a garbage can was positioned within handy range. Of all the places to land!

He glanced over at Tamara, expecting her to make some wry comment, but instead of giving him grief, she seemed engrossed in some far-off place. "Wondering why your agent hasn't called?" he asked.

His question roused her out of her reverie, and

she turned to look at him. She was sitting one step up from him so that their heads were actually at the same height. "Sorry, what did you say?" she asked.

Drew picked up another pebble but decided not to try anything special. He jiggled it in his palm, searching for the right words. "I was wondering if you were thinking about your job, Phoenix—you know, the whole thing."

"Not at all, which is weird. For someone who's always been so focused on her work, it didn't cross my mind." She shook her head. "No, I was actually thinking about what Jessica said inside—about going back to Chicago, saying goodbye to her work colleagues, packing up her place. Uprooting her whole life."

"Yeah, it's pretty amazing. She always seemed pretty content with her life there."

Tamara frowned. "That's strange you would use the word *content*. What is contentment anyway? Fulfilling your ambitions? Not having too many ups and downs? A few friends maybe? I mean, can you say that you're content with your life? I'm not sure I can. I got the anchor job, which I may yet still have—who knows—and it's what I've always wanted. But is it what I'll want two months from now, or two years or even ten years down the road? I feel confused." She studied his face. "What do you think?"

Drew tightened his fist around the smooth surface of the stone. "I'm not sure. Frankly, you're sitting next to someone who's never considered whether he was content or not. I've always just done things because they're there to be done and because I was good at doing them."

Tamara gave him a lazy smile. "My man of action." She paused. "Sorry, I didn't mean to tease you. Somehow, you just seem to bring out my mocking side. No offense meant, really."

He bumped her shoulder with his. "None taken. Really."

She bent her chin and stared at the ground. "And the whole way she said that Briggs was going out to help her move. Clearly, she'll still have her career when she comes back to Hopewell, and she's obviously in her element running the clinic, but that's not the only reason she's moving. There's your dad, of course, but more than anything, we both know it's because she loves Briggs. She's moving back for him."

He turned and looked into her downcast eyes. Her eyelashes were thick and dark, but they couldn't hide the questioning nature of her gaze. "I think she's also doing it for herself. He's in love with her, too, don't forget."

She raised her head. "Can you imagine what that must feel like? To love someone so much that you're willing to uproot your whole existence?"

Drew swallowed and wet his lips. "It's something I've never experienced before, that's for sure. But I'd like to think it's possible."

She lifted her head and studied him in a way that

made him nervous. "For true? You really think it's possible?"

And for the first time, he recognized that he was starting to think just that. This unexpected realization imbued him with an overwhelming sense of exhilaration, akin to jumping off a high waterfall—something he'd actually done. But, at the same time, it frightened him beyond all belief—and fear was an emotion he was used to suppressing.

He suddenly felt the need to turn his gaze away. He wasn't ready to admit either of these thoughts out loud. Instead, he shifted his gaze back to Tamara and offered a large wink. "Anything is possible. In fact—" He raised his hand and shot the pebble across the parking lot. It dinged right off the garbage can. "Bull's-eye," he shouted.

She looked at the target. "Really? I thought we were baring our souls about the meaning of true love, and all you're excited about is hitting a can of poo?"

"Hey, what did you expect from a breakfast buddy?" He leaned over and gave Tamara a playful kiss on the tip of her nose. Then he stood up, thrusting his hands in his pockets, and ambled off a few paces. "Where are those kids anyway?"

WHILE TAMARA AND Drew were waiting outside the front door, Will and Candy returned from their walk by the back. Being careful not to bang Carnation's big plastic collar on the metal sides, Will placed the bichon, who was recovering from surgery, in her crate and then joined Candy and Buddy in the staff room. He knelt down to give Buddy a cuddle around the ears before retrieving his leash from Candy. "You know, I wanted to ask you. While we were walking the dogs, how come you kept talking about money? It's kind of boring, you know."

"Not if you don't have it. I'm saving up for a car, and I gotta admit, Tamara's generous tips are helping out a lot. Who'd have thought? I guess she's not completely hopeless."

"Don't forget she's promised us ice cream," Will added. And she was getting better about all the driving, he thought. She even seemed interested during the car ride this morning when he explained why it was important to brush your dog's teeth.

"How could I forget about the ice cream? Anyway, it'll be a few years before I can drive, but it might take that long to get enough money to buy a car. And once I do, I'm out of here."

"Don't you like Hopewell?"

Candy scoffed. "It's not bad compared to the last place we lived. But I want to go away to college. Then travel. See the world."

"I thought you wanted to study gorillas."

"I do, but there aren't exactly any gorillas in Bucks County." She pushed open the swinging door to the front waiting room, and they all went through.

"Duh, that's not what I meant," Will said. He waved at Wendy, the office manager, who was on the phone. She acknowledged him with a smile while she pulled up the appointment calendar on her computer. Seeing her do that made Will realize that he should find out if she'd gotten the hang of the new software update yet and whether or not she liked his surprise—he'd uploaded all the photos she'd taken of the pet patients and put them into a continuous loop on the clinic's home page.

He turned back to Candy. "I've got to talk to Wendy a second when she's free. But after that, I guess I'll find Tamara and Drew so we can take off." He went to the desk, but Candy held him back.

"I've got a question for you," she whispered. "Do you want to have two moms and one great-aunt?"

Will shook his head in confusion. "What are you talking about?"

"I mean, your dad and Jessica are the real deal. It's just a matter of time before they tie the knot."

"Really?" Will was happy that his dad was happy, but he hadn't given much thought to any changes to their family life.

"For sure. And that's a good thing—at least where they're concerned. But the situation is fraught with possibilities."

"Possibilities?"

"I'll tell you what. We'll hatch a plan."

"A plan? What kind of plan?"

"I'm still working on that part. In the end you'll have two moms and Aunt Myrna. And I'll keep my tipping spree intact—trust me."

Will wasn't so sure about the trust part.

CHAPTER THIRTEEN

"Hi, Pops, I'm home!" Drew announced as he came through the kitchen door.

Jessica dumped her keys in the key basket on the side table and discarded her shoes on the mat. "Me, too. I decided to call it a day."

Will and Buddy followed, the former heading directly for the cupboard where he knew the cookies were usually kept. Buddy was hot on his heels.

Aunt Myrna shook the cookie tin on the table in front of her. "I think I've got what you're looking for."

"Oh, sorry. I didn't see you." Will came over and placed a quick peck on his great-aunt's proffered cheek. "We worked hard at the clinic today, Aunt Myrna. Really hard." Buddy thumped his tail in agreement.

Hidden behind them all was Tamara, who'd been watching the scene unfold.

She raised one hand. "Hi, everyone. I was just dropping off Drew on our way home, and he insisted we all come in."

"Of course you should come in. I need you to verify that I had a very productive day," he joked.

"I can't comment on how your paint work went, but you did master the box step." She grinned.

"We've already gotten word of your dancing class exploits," Norman chimed in. He nodded to Myrna, who seemed to pick up on his cue.

"That's right, Gloria mentioned you two lighting up the place." She glanced back at Norman as if to say, *See, I'm trying*.

"Really?" Tamara was surprised. "I didn't think we made that much news."

"That's Hopewell for you. And don't underestimate your being here," Drew added.

If she didn't know better, Tamara would say she was blushing. She rubbed the tip of her nose, attempting to cover her rosy glow. The action instantly reminded her of Drew's quick kiss on the same spot, and she blushed more.

"I think it's more your being here with my gadabout brother," Jessica said as she padded over to the fridge and took out a beaker of cold water. She held it up as an offering to the others, but nobody bit. She poured herself a glass.

"I think it's time to give your brother a break, Jessica, especially when we're so lucky to have him home after so long," Norman reminded her.

"And, please, enough about Drew—and me," Tamara interjected, not quite sure she wanted to be the topic of conversation—alone or in connection with Drew. "Instead, I'm sure Dr. Trombo wants to hear about what went on at the clinic today. Will?

You started to tell us in the car, but why don't you fill in Dr. Trombo."

"I can't think of anything I'd rather hear more about. Why don't you have one of these to give you some extra energy. I'm sure you have lots to say." Norman held up the tin of cookies. "And you," he addressed Buddy. "I bet you were a brave dog getting your shots today."

Will wasn't shy about taking Norman up on his offer. He munched as he related his contributions at the clinic. "First, I helped Candy clean the cages and change the water and feed the pets staying overnight. Then Wendy let me put in the orders for new supplies of dog and cat food and hypoallergenic treats. The new software package arrived at the office, too, and I was showing her how to use it."

"We would have been lost today without Will." Jessica came over to the table and drank her water. "You wouldn't believe the other clever thing he did." She described how the practice's home page now featured the pet photos. "Wendy was really chuffed to see her work displayed like that."

"That's my clever boy. I'm glad you could be helpful," Myrna said with pride.

"Wendy says there're good reasons to have teenage boys around," Will echoed her words with complete sincerity.

Norman chuckled. "They're even useful past their teenage years. I'm sure Tamara would agree."

But before she could respond he rattled the box at Drew. "Rugelach?"

"Well, I can't say no," Drew accepted. He made a sharing gesture to Tamara and Jessica, but they shook their heads no.

Will reached over to take another.

"I know you worked hard, Will, but maybe you should ask your aunt if you should have a second? I'm sure she spent a lot of time preparing dinner," Tamara said, deferring to Myrna. It was a simple gesture, but she was still trying to learn this whole family-dynamics thing.

Myrna looked surprised but pleased. "It's just a light meal tonight—chicken tarragon and asparagus. So, I don't think another cookie is out of the question. But thanks for asking, Tamara." That last comment seemed to show she, too, was also trying to adapt.

Will took the baked good and continued his narration. "Then I walked Buddy while Candy walked Carnation. Carnation had just had surgery, and I thought it'd be good preparation for Buddy for his playdate on Saturday afternoon."

"A playdate for Buddy this Saturday? It looks like something else to add to the calendar along with Jessica and Briggs going away in another week," Myrna commented.

"And don't forget I've got my PT appointment at ten tomorrow," Norman piped up.

"Oh, that's right." Myrna covered her mouth.

"That might be a problem because I've got a dentist appointment at ten thirty."

"I'm happy to take Norman. There'll be plenty of time after I drop off Will at tennis," Tamara suggested. "I haven't worn out my welcome driving you around, have I, Will?"

The boy swallowed. "Nope. You even laugh at my corny jokes. I like that. I'd even like to go to the library with you after I finish up at the clinic. You can show me some books instead of just bringing them home."

Tamara grinned. Then she put her fingertips to her forehead and looked at Drew. "You weren't planning your surprise outing for tomorrow morning, were you?"

Drew gave her a cocky grin. "You can't wait to see me again, admit it."

"Well... I'm... I'm just trying to work out the schedule here."

Jessica stepped between them and reached for the tin. "From the tone of this conversation, I think I'll have a rugelach after all." She waggled her eyebrows at Drew.

He made a show of ignoring her. "Let me check the weather." He pulled out his phone. "It looks like clear skies on Thursday. We'll just wait until then. I'll confirm at breakfast tomorrow—we have time for that, right?"

"I should. Which reminds me, don't forget you promised to help Laura with some framing jobs at the gallery."

"That's right. Thanks. See, already you've become my indispensable social secretary."

"Indispensable in more ways than one, perhaps," Norman observed.

Myrna cleared her throat. "Perhaps."

Drew and Tamara both reached for the cookie tin at the same time, an act of desperation. Their hands touched briefly before they drew them back as if avoiding a burning flame. (Well, Tamara did feel the heat on her skin.)

Norman bit back a smile. "Well, if it's all right with you, Tamara, I'd love it if you could swing by and pick me up. It sounds like you'll be free after dropping off Will and getting breakfast at Chubbie's with Drew." He turned to his son. "See, I've got your interests at heart." This time he didn't bother to cover up his smile.

Drew groaned. "How about everyone leaving my interests to myself?"

"But that wouldn't be the Hopewell way, would it?" Tamara quipped and then quickly turned to Norman. "I'm looking forward to seeing you tomorrow. And there's no problem with me sticking around until you're finished. We can even have a little outing afterward. To tell you the truth, I'm curious to find out what Drew was like as a boy."

Drew groaned again, louder this time.

Jessica laughed. "So, it's all settled then. And just to be clear, this doggy playdate on Saturday doesn't involve me, right?"

"That would be my doing," Tamara explained. "And I still need to contact Insu Park to see if Sheba's free."

"In which case, I'll make sure to prepare extra liver treats," Myrna announced. At the sound of that, Buddy rested his head on Myrna's lap. She fondled his ears. "Not to worry. You'll get dinner as soon as we get home."

Tamara could tell Myrna was trying to make an effort—for both Buddy and her. "Thank you. That's very thoughtful. As you know, I claim absolutely no expertise when it comes to things in the kitchen. I figured my contribution would be to download some music to my phone for the occasion—for Sheba, that is."

"Good thinking," Jessica agreed. "But I've got a boom box and some CDs kicking around my old bedroom. That might be easier." She waited to see if anyone else had something to contribute. They didn't. "So, as long as that's settled—"

"Is anything ever truly settled in this family, let alone Hopewell?" Drew asked.

"The fact that Buddy always gets his dinner at six o'clock?" Will suggested.

The adults all laughed. Poor Buddy immediately worried he had done something wrong and hid behind Will.

"You know, son, you might come to appreciate how things work around here in—I don't know— a few weeks' time or maybe a month from now." Norman eyed the room.

Tamara rubbed her nose and thought about the kiss, while the rest of them all laughed again. Drew—a little less freely.

CHAPTER FOURTEEN

THE NEXT DAY, Tamara met Drew at Chubbie's, where he was standing by "their" table.

"Don't tell anyone, but I woke up this morning, suddenly unsure whether we were meeting for breakfast today," he confessed. "I forgot to enter it on my phone."

"Frankly, I'm surprised your father didn't send around a follow-up memo. Boy, when he decides to take charge, he takes charge." Tamara sat in her chair.

"And how. I took my chances and went ahead and ordered you your coffee and breakfast. I got it to go just in case."

"That's very thoughtful, but what if I hadn't shown?"

"I would have dropped it off at the house for Pops to give you."

"Smart."

"I know. I was very pleased with myself, too."

Tamara threw a paper napkin at him.

He picked up her unguided missile and slipped it in a front pocket of his cargo shorts. "I've got mine to go, too, because I'm heading out early for the gallery. Apparently, in addition to my mom's art, Laura had another big framing order come through."

"Are you excited about that? The show, I mean? I think it's a wonderful idea."

Drew beamed. "It's kind of cool."

Candy approached with two white paper bags with handles. She passed one package to Tamara, who rose to take it. "One English muffin, extra jam. And a soy milk latte. I made it extra hot so it wouldn't be stone-cold by the time you got to drink it."

"That's so thoughtful." Tamara scrounged around in her tote bag for her wallet.

"And the other one's for you." Candy held out the second bag.

Drew smiled sweetly. "No extra-hot joe-to-go for me?"

"Nah, I figured you wouldn't know the difference."

He scrunched up his mouth. "The sad truth is you're probably right." He noticed Tamara open her wallet. "I already got it. My treat."

"He can be sweet sometimes, don't you think?" she remarked to Candy. "Still, I'm sure he doesn't tip as well as I do." As Tamara handed over some bills, her phone rang. It could only be one person given the "Eye of the Tiger" ringtone. Her agent, Sidney. He would have to wait until later.

Candy pocketed the money in her overalls. "You're right—" she narrowed her eyes at Drew

"—on both counts. Tamara's generosity is why she gets extra hot."

"I will remember that next time." He bent over and dropped a quick kiss on Tamara's cheek. "Gotta run. I'll text you the time about when I'll pick you up tomorrow." With his hand raised in a wave, he worked his way back through the diner and out the door.

Tamara touched her face and frowned. "Did he just kiss me?"

"One of those half kisses. I don't even know if he knows he did it," Candy answered.

Tamara looked up. "Ya think?"

"You're asking me? I'm the kid here. Why don't you ask him yourself?"

Tamara frowned. "A wise suggestion." She sprinted to the sidewalk. Drew was just about to round the corner to Main Street. He had a look on his face of determination—or maybe something else. Distraction? Confusion? "Drew," she called out. "Wait a sec."

He turned at the sound of her voice, and a broad smile replaced whatever had been marring his cheerful countenance.

She pulled up next to him, panting after racing down the street.

"You couldn't get enough of me, could you?"

"It wasn't that. Well, maybe a little." She was still catching her breath. "Actually, I wanted to ask you a question."

He waited.

"It's…it's…ah…"

"Cat got your tongue?" he teased. "That's a change. I guess there's a first time for everything."

"It's not that. I just want to get my words right. It's about the kiss back there." She pointed over her shoulder toward the diner.

"The kiss?"

"Yeah, the one you planted on my cheek. And don't pretend you don't remember."

"Who said I didn't remember?"

Tamara rolled her eyes. "For once, no little games."

He nodded.

"That's the second time you kissed me. The first was the other day, outside the veterinary office. You planted one on my nose." She touched the tip.

"So I did, didn't I?" he agreed.

"I want to know what you meant by them. Were they just kisses between friends? Like some off-hand way of saying goodbye?"

"Hello, goodbye. One of those." He ran his hand through his hair. It was particularly unkempt today, and the untamed locks gave the impression that he'd just rolled out of bed. "I just kind of thought they were the right things to do at the moment. Something spontaneous. Not as formal as shaking hands or as empty as just walking away."

"That was all? Are you sure?"

He shrugged. "Why? Do you want more?"

She set her lips in a line. "I don't know. Do you?"

He frowned. "Let's leave it with spontaneity for now, okay?" He brushed a quick kiss on the top of her head before hustling off around the corner. The white to-go bag bounced against his thigh.

Tamara shook her head. "Okay? You call that okay?"

"WHEN YOU SAID to come first thing in the morning, I took you at your word." Drew was lounging on the front steps of the gallery, blocking the entrance, when Laura showed up.

Laura placed one sandaled foot on the bottom step and took a few moments to study him. "Is that pair of shorts and gray T-shirt the only clothing you own? And I say that with your best interests at heart, of course."

"Of course," he replied good-naturedly. "No, I have two more pairs of the same shorts and black and olive green versions of this gray one. Anything wrong with that?" He handed over a take-out cup. "Lemon tea with honey and—" he located a white bakery bag from the paper carrier on the top step "—one raisin scone, courtesy of Nada Bellona. I have it on good authority—"

"Chubbie's or Candy's?"

"Chubbie's. He was working the counter, though Candy did the handover. Anyway, he says it's the best."

Laura took the tea. "It's a close tie with the cranberry, but I'm not complaining. You can come by early every day if you show up bearing goodies like this." She fished in her woven shoulder bag for the keys. The colorful stripes and checks somehow

blended with the bold batik print of her skirt and
deep purple blouse. "Hold on to that for a sec, will
you, while I unlock the place."

Drew stood to the side. "I thought you lived over
the gallery?"

"I do—with Phil, but there's no direct entrance
between the two floors. The building was originally
set up for two separate apartments, and truthfully,
I like it that way. Keeps work at work and home
at home."

Drew followed Laura inside as she switched off
the security system and turned on some lights. He
put the bag on the large framing table in the back
room. A partition separated the workspace from the
display area in front. Samples of various wooden
and metal frames were attached with Velcro to the
padded wall. He waited for Laura to sit on one of
the metal bar stools before pulling out another for
himself. "Makes sense about the work/life balance,
I suppose. Not that I would know. Usually for me,
it's either all on for work or all off. And when I'm
off, the location can be anywhere."

"Don't tell me you're still doing that silly Airbnb
thing, living in any old place in whatever part of
the world that's convenient?"

"Don't forget cheap. Any old place that's cheap."

Laura flapped an eager hand. "Pass over the
scone. I'm starving. Eating for two and all that."
She took the small bag from Drew but hesitated.
"I hope you don't expect me to share."

He shook his head. "Not to worry. I already ate my usual."

"Two eggs over easy and a side of bacon and home fries?"

He nodded.

"Geez, you might have the most unstable living situation, but you're completely predictable when it comes to breakfast. I guess some things never change."

"Give me the rolling-stone life, as long as I have Chubbie's Eatery to come home to," he mused.

"You have other things to come home to as well."

"You're right. Jess and Pops. And it's great to see all the townspeople and my old school buddies, including you, whenever I can. But I'm sorry. Nothing and no one can compare with Chubbie's."

"What about Tamara?"

"Tamara? You mean, what's her opinion of Chubbie's? Well, her go-to order is an English muffin with Nada Bellona's jam."

"I'm not talking menu choices, Drew. Tell me. Do you know how long she's here for?"

"Not really."

"But just look at the two of you. Shouldn't you want to know?"

He shrugged. "Maybe. Right now we refer to each other as breakfast buddies."

"Breakfast buddies? Is that what they call eating together daily? Going to dance classes together? Accompanying each other to the vet clinic? Gathering at your dad's house?"

"My, you are informed." And a little too relentless for Drew's taste. He wasn't so sure how long he could remain nonchalant.

"I'm just trying to find out what's really going on. I'm also looking out for my best friend. Jessica? Your sister? Now that she's with Briggs, don't you think having Tamara around might be awkward for her, especially with Will in the mix?"

"It's not as if Tamara has any romantic interest in Briggs. Besides, I'd think a reconciliation between Tamara and Will would only make Jessica's life easier, not harder. Tamara's the one taking him to tennis camp, listening to his experiences working at the vet's, arranging outings."

"That sounds pretty involved to me. And what's your part in all this family bonding?"

Drew looked upward, but the recessed lighting in the ceiling didn't do much in the way of enlightenment. Stuff was going on between him and Tamara. He sensed that. But the feelings were all too new, too unfamiliar for him to try to identify them, let alone share with his little sister's best friend. He straightened his shoulders. "Hey, enough with the questions! I won't help you out at the gallery if you don't treat me with respect." Pretending to take offense, he clutched his coffee cup in a protective motion against his chest—and managed to dribble some of it on his shirt.

"I'll get a towel." Laura started to rise.

"No need." He fished out the crumpled napkin from his pocket and tamped the cotton material.

"I've had far worse. Believe me." He lifted away the damp napkin and stared at it. Without even thinking, he wet his lips and smiled.

Laura raised an inquisitive brow. "Something special about that paper napkin."

Drew shook his head a little too emphatically. "Nah, it's just from Chubbie's. Where else? Tamara left it."

"Oh, did she now?" Laura arched her eyebrow higher—no mean feat. Then she balled up the pastry bag and tossed it at his chest.

He startled. "Hey, what's that all about?"

"Consider it a reality check."

Reality or not, he kept smiling.

NORMAN HELD OPEN the front door. "Why, don't you look nice."

"Sorry I'm early," Tamara apologized. "I stopped by the library to let Amy Pulaski, the librarian, know I'd be coming in with Will later this week to help him look for books. Somehow, from our meeting the other day she sensed that might be the case, and she'd already pulled some new fantasy works. How she had time to do that, I don't know. She was in the middle of filming a reading-aloud session for kids that she's posting on the library website later. In any case, I glanced over them, and they're completely after my time. Will and I will have to read them together and compare notes."

"What a wonderful way to get to know each other! Please, do come in."

Tamara crossed the threshold into the spacious entryway. The first time she'd been in the house, Tamara had followed Drew in by the side door and had only ventured into the kitchen, which was painted in a bombardment of hues, a true coat of many colors. The front entrance gave an entirely different perspective. Large pocket doors stood open to a sitting room on the left and a formal dining room on the right. Ahead, a majestic stairway led to the second-floor landing and the bedrooms. And to the side of the stairway, the hallway continued, giving access to a smaller sitting room or den and the kitchen. She remembered that there was also a back stairway and a ground-floor guest room, both accessed directly from the kitchen.

The stately public spaces in the front of the house were the real points of interest though. Large, color-saturated paintings depicting the rolling hills and valleys of the rich Bucks County countryside hung on the dark paneled walls. Tamara could only assume they were works by Drew's mother.

"Thanks for complimenting me on my new outfit," she responded to his initial remark. She had on a new denim skirt and a striped sailor's shirt. "I bought it at a boutique in New Hope." New Hope was a colonial town along the Delaware River not far from Hopewell and a well-known tourist destination. "I figured my skirt suits from work weren't quite the ticket for schlepping Will around. I also bought a few pairs of Levi's at the army and navy store. I figured it was time I started dressing like a local. And speaking of locals, did your wife paint the landscapes? They're amazing."

"Yup, they're Vivian's. Remarkable, aren't they? She was smitten by nature and loved being out-doors. But she also did abstracts, and even portraits of people and animals."

"She sounds incredible. And she certainly pro-duced two outstanding children—with your help, of course."

"I can only claim a little bit of an influence. It was Vivian who really encouraged both kids to go out in the world and follow their passions."

"I'm sure you had more influence than you're giving yourself credit for."

"Not really. But speaking of influence—I was hoping to use my avuncular charm and persuade you to stop at the Hopewell Historical Society after my physical therapy session. It's pretty modest by big-city standards, but it has a nice exhibit of the history of the area, and it's widely known for some remarkable baskets and well-preserved tools from the Lenape Indians, who were the original settlers in the area."

"You absolutely found the right person to invite, and it'll be my first trip there. I have to warn you though that I'm a real information hound. I can spend hours looking at art and artifacts. And I've always been interested in the history of this part of Pennsylvania since I grew up nearby in Philadel-phia."

"Then I'm surprised you've never visited the museum before, seeing as you lived so close."

"My parents weren't into vacations, even day trips. In all fairness, my dad worked pretty much all the time. He was a tailor."

"A craftsman. How interesting."

"I don't think he had any choice. His grandfather had been a tailor. His father, too. So, he became a tailor. If only he'd passed his skill on to me! I can barely thread a needle."

"And your mom?"

"She was a homemaker. I'm not sure she had a choice about that either. Anyhow, my dad and she didn't talk much. Didn't talk to me much either. Not a lot of hugging happening."

"That's a shame. No brothers or sisters then?"

Tamara shook her head. "I'm an only child—classic personality of one, too, I suppose. Introverted. Independent. I like to do things my own way—sometimes to my detriment."

"But I'm sure your parents are proud of you. Becoming a famous TV news anchor and all. How could they not be?"

"I wouldn't know. We haven't spoken in years."

"Really? I can't believe that."

"What can I say? After I found out I was pregnant, things went downhill. The silences were almost unbearable. And in the end, it just seemed simpler for everyone if we went our separate ways. I guess it sounds more tragic than it was, but sometimes families aren't meant to be together. And I had Myrna and Briggs to help me in the beginning before I went off to college. So things could have been a lot worse."

The conversation was not going at all the way Tamara had wanted. This was supposed to be an opportunity to talk to Norman about donating Vivian's art. Instead, she was divulging information she preferred not to share with anyone. Gloria Pulaski had somehow wheedled some vague information out of her at the dancing class, and now she was opening up further. There was something about Norman though. As he had said, he had a certain avuncular charm. He made her feel like he cared. That he took a genuine interest in her well-being.

"Tell me more about Vivian," she said, changing the subject to one she was more comfortable with.

"What can I say? She taught art full-time, but somehow, she managed to make it all happen at home and in the classroom." He stumbled over the words and cleared his throat to recover. "It was pretty chaotic, but that's the way she liked it. Always something going on, something to challenge the kids. I remember the time she had them up on the roof to help her clean out the gutters. I was hopeless at home repairs and chores—still am, as is evident from my recent spill." He pointed to his leg. "But Vivian—no worries."

"No wonder Drew travels the world practically looking for danger."

"Which is why I worry about him—not that I'd

ever tell him that. No, Vivian's lack of fear was different. She didn't seek danger. She was just curious. And that curiosity was contagious—for Drew and Jess and for her students. I still get some of them stopping by the house years after she taught them to say thank you and tell me stories about her. It's remarkable."

"Maybe all the movement and color in her landscapes reflects her vibrant personality then?"

"Exactly. Come to the den. You'll see it in action when it comes to portraying the family." He motioned over his shoulder, and even though he wasn't wearing the boot on his leg this morning, his gait was still a little awkward.

Tamara followed him past the stairway. The first thing that struck her about the room was the abundance of color: the walls painted peach, the curtains made of paisley-printed silk, and a crocheted, patchwork afghan that screamed sixties psychedelics thrown over a worn leather recliner. The comfy chair was clearly Norman's domain from the way it was angled toward the TV screen.

The wall behind the recliner was another world altogether. Tamara stepped closer to get a better look at the framed portraits. "You're surrounded by your family!" she exclaimed.

"Every year she insisted that we all gather in a different spot in the house or the yard so that she could record what she liked to call 'our progress.' But when the kids were little, they didn't have the patience to sit for long—not that they got much better as they got older."

Tamara studied each group portrait. Some were watercolors, others quick sketches, one or two were in oil. But all of them captured the liveliness and utter joy that expressed the moment. In one, Drew held a hose and was dousing Jessica and Norman. In another, they squeezed together on a picnic table bench, proudly holding ice cream cones. A large German shepherd waited patiently for drips. In a third, Drew and Jessica sat on Norman's lap while he read to them from a large children's book.

Norman peered along with her. "Those were good times. Unpredictable but good." He pointed to the dog. "That's Zebra. She was Jessica's. A wonderful companion. And there's Drew, playing games and not getting into trouble for it."

"And the ice creams must be from Teddy Sweet." She turned her head to Norman. "I'm taking Will and Candy there."

"You're keeping up a long Hopewell tradition then. Bringing yourself into the fold, so to speak."

Tamara studied some more of the paintings. "But there're none of Vivian. Didn't she ever do any self-portraits?"

Norman shook his head. "She claimed she was her worst subject. But this one here—" He moved over to close the door and revealed a delicate pencil drawing that had been hidden behind it. "This is the only one of Vivian. Drew did it right before she lost all her hair to chemo, the first time she was treated for breast cancer."

Tamara stared at the drawing, the profile of a handsome woman with a tentative smile. Her hair was pulled back in a long braid, while a few wisps escaped at her temples, giving her an angelic quality. But there was nothing cherubic about her eyes. They conveyed a singular purpose, a pride in being. "She was so young."

"Just forty-two. It was right before her birthday. She never complained when she lost her hair. In fact, she was proudly bald for those months."

"To me the drawing captures that strength, her determination. But it also shows her sensitivity. Quite a testament to her and Drew's artistic ability." Tamara looked at Norman again. "You should move the drawing to a place of honor, not bury it behind the door. She's too special to be hidden. And the drawing is too beautiful."

Norman nodded slowly. "You're right. One of these days." Then he looked at his watch. "We should get going if we don't want to be late to my session. And I think that you're family enough to leave by the kitchen door, wouldn't you say?"

"I'd be honored."

CHAPTER FIFTEEN

TAMARA AND NORMAN sat on a wooden bench in front of the historical society and rested their feet after their leisurely perusal of the museum's collection. "I'm still marveling over the elaborate beadwork of that bandolier bag on display," Tamara exclaimed. She referred to the linen shoulder bag traditionally carried by Lenape men. "No wonder the Metropolitan Museum in New York City has borrowed some of the society's other items for a special exhibit—I mean, given the high qualities of the things we saw. You know, we should make a trip to New York and see that show when we get a chance."

"I'd like that very much. But right now, I'm glad we're taking the time to rest. Between the PT session this morning and then walking around the exhibition, my leg's a little sore," Norman admitted.

"Oh, no. I hope we didn't overdo it. Since you're out of a cast and weren't wearing that boot today, I actually forgot you broke your leg. And the way the physical therapist really pushed you. Wow, a real drill sergeant! Maybe I should drive you home immediately, let you get some rest?"

He patted her knee. "Not to worry. It's more restful—and more fun—just sitting here and watching the world go by on Main Street." He gave her a genuine smile.

Tamara was marginally relieved. But speaking of driving… "I didn't mean to be eavesdropping at your rehab session, but I couldn't help overhearing the therapist say you could start driving short distances. Why not going home today?"

"I'm not sure I'm quite ready," Norman begged off. "And in your rental car? I'd feel more comfortable in my old Subaru wagon—the one Jess is borrowing."

"I understand." Tamara presumed his reluctance went beyond the fact of driving. It provided an easy excuse for not getting out in the world again, but she decided not to press him. Instead, the two of them sat contentedly and watched the passing cars.

Mr. Mason happened to amble by and stopped to greet them. "Good to see you. I'm on my way to play cards with the gang. You want to join us? This week we're meeting at Signora Reggio's house. You know the refreshments will be top class."

"I'm not much of a card player, but thanks for thinking of me," Norman answered.

"Maybe I wasn't inviting you, Norman. I was thinking that Tamara might like to get out and about. She's already met most of us at the ballroom dancing class, and she seemed to fit right in."

Tamara grinned. "That's very generous, Walt."

"See, we're already on a first-name basis," Mr. Mason informed Norman.

"Maybe some other time," Tamara deferred. "Norman has my attention today, but please keep me in mind. I haven't the faintest idea how to play bridge, but I can hold my own at Go Fish."

Mr. Mason laughed. "We're strictly a gin rummy crowd."

"In which case, if the invitation stands for next week—and I'm still here—I'll be sure to study a YouTube video ahead of time. I don't want to totally embarrass myself."

"You'd never do that," Mr. Mason assured her. "'Til next week then." He tipped the brim of his tartan touring cap and sauntered down the sidewalk.

A few minutes later, a thin woman with platinum-blond hair trudged by pushing a dolly loaded with two large bankers boxes.

"Alice, you look like you could use a rest," Norman called out. He motioned to Tamara. "Alice, this is Tamara. She's staying with the Longfellows. Alice is Candy's mom, and she runs the printing and copying store in town. She also owns two dachshunds—Peanut Butter and Jelly. Sometimes I can't remember the names of the pet owners, but I always remember the names of their pets."

Alice tucked her glossy hair behind one ear, and Tamara noticed she had multiple piercings running up the side. Kohl rimmed her green eyes, and moist red lipstick emphasized her mouth. Her pencil skirt and fitted white blouse showed off her curvy figure. It was hard to link Alice to Candy, seeing as the teen's purple hair and baggy outfits were stylistically at the opposite end of the spectrum.

"Hi, Dr. Trombo. Nice to meet you, Tamara. Candy's mentioned you to me." Alice blew upward, causing her bangs to flutter. "I'd love to stop and chat, but I'm on a job. Busy, busy, busy. You know how it is."

Tamara used to know how it was, but her time in Hopewell had slowed her pace down substantially, not that she was complaining.

"I just want something to go right for once," Alice continued. "I've got this printing delivery for Laura—it's to do with the upcoming art exhibit. You must know all about that, Dr. Trombo, seeing as it's your wife's work."

Norman eked out a tense smile but didn't respond beyond that.

"And wouldn't you know it, today of all days, my car decides to die on me. It's been giving me trouble for the past few months, but I was hoping it'd last a while longer. Anyway, Laura needs these announcements right away so that she can mail them out, and I really don't want to let her down." She patted a handle on the heavy moving cart.

"I'm sure we can help you out, Alice," Tamara offered. "My car's just around the back, in the historical society lot. I can bring it around and we can load the boxes in the trunk. That way, it'll be an easy drive to the gallery and save you the job of pushing them. I'll even volunteer to unload them myself once we get there since I'm missing out on my usual Pilates classes. I could really use the workout."

"Oh, that would be *so* helpful. I've already sweated bullets pushing this trolley three blocks, and—you see—I kind of have this date tonight," she confided. "I'm certain I already look a sight."

"I think you look just great. I doubt he'll notice," Tamara said. It was the truth.

"Aw, that's so nice." Alice looked at Norman. "She's so nice, isn't she?"

"Hopefully, not at all like Candy described me." Tamara laughed.

"No, she said you were cool, weird but cool. That's high praise from my daughter, trust me. She also mentioned something about you and Dr. Trombo's son—him being back in town and all. Have I got that right?"

Tamara offered a cheerful if disingenuous smile. "You know teenagers. Always imagining this or that." Tamara silently cringed. "I tell you what, why don't I bring my car around now? That way we won't keep Laura waiting."

By the time she returned Tamara could see Norman had retreated into his smiling, semi-taciturn mode while Alice kept chatting away. Tamara rushed to open the trunk. "I hope I didn't keep you waiting."

Alice stood and smoothed the material of her skirt. "Not at all. Dr. Trombo was just giving me tips on how to keep PB and J in check when new people come to the door." She pushed the cart toward the back of the car and began lifting one of the bankers boxes with the assuredness of a stevedore.

"You want me to help?" Norman offered.

"No, I think Alice and I have got it covered. You've had enough exercise for one day," Tamara said. While the two women finished loading, Norman settled into the front passenger seat.

Job accomplished, Alice leaned next to the driver's side. "Are you sure I can't come along and help you unload?"

"Not at all. I'm sure you have enough to do. And it was nice meeting you, Alice."

Norman slanted a look at Tamara as she pulled away from the curb. "Don't think I didn't notice what you did back there. The fact that you didn't respond when she mentioned you and Drew."

"Did she mention Drew? I barely remember." She applied the brakes when the light turned red.

"Don't play dumb with me," Norman teased. "One thing you're not is dumb. And then there's the whole thing with the boxes. Laura already came and talked to me about the art show, you know. You didn't have to fabricate some elaborate plan to get me to come to the gallery."

"Okay, I admit that I promised Drew and Laura that I would talk to you about the show. But whatever you may think, I didn't time our outing so that Alice would just happen to come by and need help taking all the invitations to the gallery. If nothing else, I'd like to think I'm subtler than that."

"All right, I'll buy that. But something else you just said really intrigues me. Why did my kids ask you to talk to me about the exhibit? Vivian was their mother after all."

"Well, not to be too blunt…"

"Be blunt. I can take it."

"Then let me just say that it's probably easier for me to bring up the matter because you aren't my father."

"Now you've lost me."

"Look, when it comes to you and me, there's no emotional baggage. I can say something that you might disagree with, but it doesn't threaten you in some intrinsic way. We agree to disagree. If Drew or Jessica say something you don't want to hear, you're more likely to take offense. Why? I'm not sure, and I'm certainly no expert on families or friends. But from my observations, disagreements between loved ones have a tendency to somehow become personal. Someone says the other person's wrong, and their immediate reaction is to get upset. Then everybody digs in their heels, the disagreement escalates and feelings get hurt."

Norman listened, nodding thoughtfully as she spoke. "I admit I can be difficult to deal with."

"I wasn't necessarily singling you out, Norman. We all have moments where we feel offended and get our hackles up." She smiled, trying to soften the blow. Their time together had been brief, but Tamara realized that she'd already grown to care about Norman and care about his family. But this conversation wasn't about her or her feelings about the Trombos as a family—or maybe one family member in particular. (Or so she told herself.)

He pointed out the window. "I think the light has changed."

"So it has," Tamara acknowledged. "And just to set the record straight, I volunteered to talk to you. Nobody twisted my arm."

"Out with it then. What exactly are you planning to say that I won't want to hear?"

"That maybe you'd consider donating some of Vivian's pictures to the exhibit. The works that Drew has given apparently date from an early period of her output. Your contribution, especially of her later works, would allow for an appreciation of the full scope of your wife's talent. And if donating is a step too far, perhaps you'd consider loaning the art on a temporary basis, getting it back when the show's over? Think about it, Norman. You could share Vivian's vision with others. Let the entire breadth of her work touch as many people as possible."

Norman shook his head. "You've already seen how I'm not ready to move Drew's drawing of Vivian to a different location. You think I'm about to let some of her pictures actually leave the house?"

"Maybe you don't touch the ones you've already got hanging? I'm sure you must have lots of her art stored away, right?"

Norman wet his lips. It was obvious he couldn't deny her question. "Let me think about it. No promises."

"What is it that Vivian liked to say? I heard Laura mention it the other day: 'Never wait for inspiration to come to you.'"

"That's a low blow."

"I know."

They drove on in silence—Tamara with her eyes focused on the road, Norman looking out the side window. Finally, he turned to face her. "What about you?"

"What about me?" She wasn't sure what he was getting at.

"When are you going to stop waiting for inspiration and visit your parents? Reestablish a link? I think you might find it's beneficial going forward. Besides, you don't have any excuse about them being too far away."

"Talk about low blows. Like I said, it was never a warm and fuzzy relationship. And as for trying to establish one? Who knows? The point is, I'm just not ready to take that plunge."

Norman frowned and then chuckled. "It looks like we're both set in our ways. Two peas in a pod. But you know what?"

"What?"

He lifted his chin. "After we drop off the boxes at Laura's gallery, if—and I mean if—she doesn't hound me about Vivian's art, I'll agree to drive home part of the way."

"Fantastic, Norman. It's a deal." Tamara put on her indicator and pulled into an empty parking space in front of the gallery. "One thing you have to promise though." She turned off the ignition and shifted to look at him head-on. "No telling Myrna about me letting you drive, agreed? She scares me."

Norman laughed.

"I'm serious. Don't laugh," Tamara warned him.

"Sorry. It's just that she's scared of you, too."

CHAPTER SIXTEEN

TAMARA WAS WAITING outside the farmhouse when Drew picked her up Thursday morning. She opened the passenger door to the pickup truck and climbed in. "See, as ordered—comfortable clothes, no jewelry and tennis shoes, with laces, mind you." She held up one foot as she spoke.

Drew did a close inspection. "Good to see you took my advice, especially about wearing a fleece jacket."

"I hope this doesn't mean I'm expected to climb Mount Everest."

"No, we're not going quite that high. Seat belt." He nodded toward the shoulder harness.

Tamara grabbed the strap and clipped her seat belt while Drew turned around on the gravel drive. "Should I be worried?"

"You'll be in good hands, I promise. Meanwhile, see the bag at your feet? There's two muffins and two bottles of orange juice. This way we can still have our Chubbie's fix."

Tamara reached for the bag. "Oh, yummy. Blueberry. If the rest of the day is as good as this, it'll rank as an all-time high."

Drew glanced her way before turning onto the road. "It'll be high all right."

A LITTLE TOO high for Tamara's comfort.

"When you said you were going to stretch my limits, I didn't think you actually meant it," Tamara said over her shoulder to Drew. "Truthfully, sky-diving's not something I'd ever expected doing."

"I'm a certified skydiving instructor," he assured her.

"If that news is supposed to quell my fears, it's not working." She was so nervous she could hardly breathe, let alone regulate her other essential physiological functions.

She and Drew sat on molded chairs in the terminal of a small, private airport while they watched a video about skydiving. Afterward Drew gave her instructions about the equipment and the jump itself.

"You're sure we're not headed to the State Penitentiary?" Tamara asked as they rigged up in orange jumpsuits. Humor was her way of covering up her fear.

Drew gave her a crinkly smile. Clearly, he wasn't buying her flippancy. "You don't have to do this if you don't want, and I'm not trying to force you. I just thought because you talked about pushing our comfort zones that you'd be game. And it's something I've always found amazing—a freeing experience." He held her helmet and waited.

Tamara breathed in deeply and finally nodded.

"Okay, you're right, but I gotta admit that this is challenging me. But as long as you're near..."

"I won't leave you, trust me. You do trust, don't you?"

Tamara took in his pleading expression. "You know, as unbelievable as this seems even to me, I do trust you—explicitly. Or is it implicitly? I'm all mixed up."

Drew chuckled. "If you, the wordsmith, are mixed up, then I know you're nervous. That's okay. It's perfectly normal to be nervous. If you weren't in the least, then I'd be worried." He passed her the helmet and helped her adjust it.

Then came the visors and harnesses. Tamara's pressed into her pelvis and rib cage, and she squirmed to get comfortable. Drew also had cables hanging from his. And when they were finally ready to go, she and Drew headed outside to a Cessna 182, the workhorse of the skydiving business, and boarded.

"It'll take about twenty minutes to get to the drop zone." Drew sat next to her on a narrow bench, while up in the cockpit, the pilot completed his checklist and started down the runway.

Drew slipped an arm around her shoulders and squeezed. "Just remember, you'll be clipped to me the whole time, and I'll do all the work. I've probably logged more hours skydiving than anyone around here, so you're in good hands."

Tamara nodded. "All part of your job, right? At least this time we won't be landing into the aftermath of a hurricane or something." She had to shout over the noise of the plane's engine. Then she braved a glance out the side windows. The journey was taking them over rolling hills, dense woods and a patchwork of farmland—green squares juxtaposed against plowed fields.

She turned back and saw Drew talking to the pilot, and she waited anxiously.

"Okay, he's just about to give the go signal," Drew shouted to her before bending to slide open the door. A cold rush of air blasted the plane. Next, he leaned his head close to hers. "We're just going to scoot over. You'll cross your arms and lean your head back. And don't forget to keep your knees bent. Then I'll tap you on the shoulder, and that'll be the signal to jump. After we jump, you'll open your arms, and we'll have about fifty seconds of free fall before I deploy the chute." He rubbed her upper arm. "You ready?"

She felt the warmth of his touch through the layers of clothes. "Ready and more or less willing."

"That's my Tamara! Not many people would have your gumption."

She smiled at his reassurance. "So do I get a prize for agreeing to do this crazy stunt?"

Drew brought his visor close to hers. "I promise a special celebration with me. Because no matter what, I'm there for you. I'm your wingman."

But before she could respond, he tapped her on the shoulder. They moved in tandem to the open door. And together they took the leap.

Tamara felt like an engine was blowing full force on her when they hit the open air. She managed to pry open her eyes, which turned out to be less scary than keeping them tightly shut. More than anything though, she was aware of the closeness of Drew's body and could sense his smallest adjustments. For the first time in her life, she realized, she was willingly letting someone else take charge of her fate. But she trusted Drew. And that awareness was amazing!

Here she was, spiraling through the air, and she actually felt safe knowing that he was with her. She stretched out her arms and let the sun run through her fingers.

Then came a sharp jolt, and Tamara felt her harness snap against her thigh. Drew had opened the parachute, she realized. They were no longer in free fall.

Immediately, an enormous feeling of calm penetrated every muscle, every pore, and Tamara let her body relax into Drew's. She felt the rise and fall of his chest and synchronized her breathing with his. And as they floated downward, Drew pointed out the sights. She looked around and tried to take it all in.

And after what seemed an eternity but, according to the video she'd watched earlier, had merely been about five minutes, Drew let her know they were close to the ground. "Remember," he shouted. "Lift your feet and prepare for landing. And don't wait until we hit to start running."

Tamara gave him the thumbs-up and began to windmill her legs. To her surprise, the impact was no big deal, like jumping from maybe three feet off the ground. Drew grabbed her as soon as they landed, then unclipped the harness.

With her knees still shaking, she pushed up her visor and sought out Drew. "Oh, my gosh. That was fantastic! Not at all what I expected. And without your prodding, I never would have done it."

He started the long chore of stowing their gear. "And you weren't afraid after all, were you?" He had pushed aside his visor, as well.

"The truth?"

"Nothing but." He offered a wide grin.

On top of everything, that almost tipped her over. Tamara inhaled deeply and tried to organize her thoughts. They were running amok, something that would normally freak her out, but this time didn't at all. "At first, I gotta admit, I was pretty scared. My heart rate was racing, but...but sometime, some-where, in the middle of it all, I experienced this... this sense of total freedom—of letting go. Which, frankly, goes against the grain of all my desired behavioral patterns—me, Ms. Control Freak."

After feeling steadier on her feet, she moved closer. "So explain to me, since you're the expert on skydiving—how can that be? How can some-thing be so liberating on one hand and so...so... beyond my power on the other? I mean, it was prob-ably the most...the most exhilarating, most mind-blowing experience I've ever had." Even now, she sensed the implications of her words.

He stopped fussing with the chute and stared. "Sounds to me like you had one heck of an adrenaline rush. The fact that you were stressed out going into the jump but overcame those fears just compounded the high. And it's everything I'd hoped you'd achieve."

"And more." She went to give him a thank-you kiss but stopped short when she saw him take a step back. Why, when he was the one who seemed to offer kisses at the drop of a hat? "But what about you? How do you feel?" She wasn't merely questioning him about the jump. She was searching for an admission of his feelings for her.

Drew narrowed his eyes. Then dropped his head and went back to focusing on the equipment. "I'm happy." (That didn't sound genuine.) "Happy that you're happy." (Only marginally better.) "How does the line from the old song go?" he asked. "'Who could ask for anything more?'"

She could. His response wasn't at all what Tamara had expected, or, indeed, wanted. She angled her head and tried to get a good look at his face. At those baby blues that had the ability to sparkle in a way that made her feel that she was the center of the universe. Within a heartbeat—her heartbeat—those amazing eyes had turned gray. Not stormy, nothing so obviously trite. But dull. Profoundly dull. This was a different Drew, a listless Drew, one she didn't recognize. "Did I say something wrong? Something that bothered you?" She was worried—for him and for her.

Drew shook his head and forced a smile. "Not at all. I think the jet lag just kind of hit me all of a sudden. Sorry about that. I meant this to be a joyous experience, and I think I'm somehow dragging it down." He hoisted the packed gear to his shoulder. "But enough about me. I say we should go for beers to toast the occasion anyway. Like they say—the first time is always the best." He forced a wry smile.

Not good enough. Tamara could spot a phony gesture when she saw one. "You know what, I think I'm going to have to take a rain check on the celebration. That adrenaline rush you mentioned before? I think I'm definitely having a downswing after my over-the-top high. I promised I'd meet Will after his tennis and go to the library together, and the way I'm dragging now, I'm going to have to work just to get through that." Then she pointed gamely at Drew. "But don't think I'm not going to hold you to it."

"It'll be my pleasure," he responded. "I can't think of anything I'd rather do than celebrate with my breakfast buddy."

Tamara could tell his heart wasn't in it. Maybe it was the tiredness of his recent travels combined with the stress of his job all catching up with him. Whatever the cause, it didn't leave her feeling comfortable. And the way he referred to her as his breakfast buddy? It wasn't what she wanted to hear, even if she'd been the one to initially come up with the term. She shook her head.

It seemed that it was one thing to successfully dive into the heavens. But quite another to come back to Earth.

CHAPTER SEVENTEEN

WILL AND TAMARA stood at the front desk in the library and waited while Amy Pulaski checked out their books.

"All on the same card?" Amy asked. Today she was wearing a black suit and white dress shirt buttoned to her chin. She looked ready to attend Hogwarts School.

"You can put it all on mine," Tamara answered. She was delighted to be sharing the outing with Will, especially after the confusing end to her skydiving excursion.

"I've… I've got my own card, you know," Will said softly.

Tamara smiled at him. She had to look up, she realized. "I'm sure you do, what with having a teacher for a father and the good influence of Aunt Myrna. But I'd like to do it for you. My way of participating."

Will shrugged. "Sure, I guess." The ins and outs of blossoming parental pride seemed to pass him by.

"Well, I can think of no better way of sharing than exchanging books," the librarian said. She scanned Tamara's card and the barcode inside the front covers of the books. "You must tell me how you like them." She moved the pile to the side, then reached down and pulled another book from the shelf below. "I'm also going to add this volume that I came across the other day. I understand from Tamara that you are a dog aficionado, and I thought you'd find it interesting."

Will peered at the title embossed on the thick hardcover. "Wow, *The Illustrated Atlas of the Anatomy of a Dog*. That's amazing." He began thumbing through the pages and studying the colored drawings.

"It might be too much detail," Amy warned.

Tamara waved her off. "I don't think there can ever be too much detail about dogs as far as Will is concerned."

Will agreed and passed over the book so that Amy could check it out. "I'll let you know. And thanks." He gathered up all the books and accompanied Tamara with ungainly strides as they exited the building. The heavy wooden door closed behind them, and they stepped into bright sunshine.

Tamara turned her face upward and let the warmth soak in. The sky was the same cloudless stretch of azure that had surrounded her on the skydive earlier in the day. But how different it was—for many reasons—to have two feet back on the ground.

"I've had a really good time together," Will declared.

Tamara looked over and saw he was walking with his nose pressed close to the open pages of the anatomy book. She felt a sense of delight. "I'm glad you enjoyed it. I did, too. And I can't wait to start on those fantasy books and compare notes with you. It'll be the first time for me, too." (What had Drew said about the first time being the best?)

The toe of Will's sneaker stubbed against a bump in the sidewalk, and he had to catch himself from tripping. "Oops. I guess I should pay better attention. That's what Aunt Myrna is always telling me." He closed the book and held the stack close to his chest.

"If Aunt Myrna says so, it must be true. She seems to know everything."

Will nodded. "I know what you mean. Sometimes it's a little scary."

"For me, too," Tamara said. She saw the way he had to fight from opening the anatomy book again and smiled. Then she wet her lips and decided to be brave. She had acted bravely once already today. Why not do it again? "You know. Sometimes I'm scared around you, too. Not so much because you're frightening, but because I'm scared that I'm going to say or do something that you might not like or think is pretty weird."

Will stopped as if to mull over her confession. "I thought I was the only one who worried about being out of place."

Tamara shook her head. "Not at all. I mean, on my job, I know what I'm doing. But otherwise? I'm constantly convinced that I'm behaving the wrong way with people. And then to make up for it, I tell myself I don't care what they think. That I don't need any friends."

Will shifted the pile of books in his arms. "That's not good."

"Here, let me take some of those," Tamara offered, and together, with the load redistributed, they went on walking to the car.

"You know, when I first got Buddy, he was so scared he wouldn't come to anyone—not even my dad," Will related. "He had to build up trust and learn to let people in. And now, he's so much happier. Not perfect, but happier. I like to tell people that he's a work in progress."

Tamara nodded. It was the first time Will had shown enough confidence to open up to her about something near and dear to his heart. "Do you think I can learn like Buddy?"

"Why not?" he said with the surety of a young teenager. "With Buddy, I discovered that praise works best, and I developed all sorts of cues to teach him how to act around people and how to behave in a way that made them and him happy to be around each other. And you know what the amazing thing was?"

She shook her head.

"I found out that by teaching Buddy, I learned how to be more comfortable around other people myself. That it's wonderful to have friends—like Candy."

"You're so lucky." He was. "So maybe I just need praise and cues to act better with you—and other people?"

"If you want, I can tell you when you're doing good things. Like me letting you know that taking me to the library was a really good idea."

"I think I'd like that." She paused. "But we'll also need some kind of cue so you can remind me to do the right thing."

"A cue? Let me think." Will pursed his lips. "Well, with Buddy, before I give him a treat, or when I want him to calm down if he's getting a little out of control, I make him sit."

Tamara smiled. "I'm not sure sitting will work for me."

"You're right." He was very serious. "But the hand signal for 'Sit' goes like this." He shifted the books to one arm and bent his free arm at the elbow, bringing his fist to his chest. "We could use that."

Tamara studied his gesture. "That's a great suggestion. It's like you're bringing your hand to your heart." She mimicked the movement.

"That's it. It can be our secret signal. And you can use it with me if you want, too."

"That'll work, and it'd be our secret." When they reached the car, Tamara scrounged around in her bag for her keys. "Should we go home, or do you want to stop first at the supermarket and get some cookies for a treat?" she asked. The outing together had turned out much better than she'd anticipated.

Unlike this morning, she felt the timing was right for a celebration.

"Cookies are a great idea, but I think Aunt Myrna's probably made some already."

Tamara couldn't help squeezing the keys in her fist at the mention of Myrna's name.

Will immediately performed their secret signal.

"What?" Tamara was taken aback.

"Don't get all nervous when I mention Aunt Myrna. She might bark, but she doesn't bite, you know."

Tamara laughed. "It sounds like I'm learning so much from Buddy—and you. Thank you."

"Anytime." Will smiled. "See? Praise works with everyone."

"TAMARA, I FINALLY have some news." Tamara's agent, Sidney, caught up with her in the evening. They'd been playing telephone tag since he'd left a message the day before.

Tamara was lying on the guest room bed in Briggs's house. The time with Will at the library had been productive in more ways than one, and that was deeply satisfying. The skydiving itself? A blast. The aftermath, not so much. And now, she was just plain tired. Any deep evaluation of the events would have to wait.

"Tamara, are you there?" Sidney wondered.

"Sorry, it's been a long day. But before you begin—is your news good or is it bad? Just tell it to me straight what's going on."

"Okay. Just the facts, ma'am." His voice was gruff.

She frowned. "If you're making some Hollywood-type reference, it's totally escaping me."

Sidney laughed. "Joe Friday? From the old TV cop show *Dragnet*?"

"Sorry."

"Never mind. I realize I'm dating myself. But anyway, it's like this," he went on. "First off, even the bozos at the station realized that the fact that you had given up a baby had absolutely no bearing on the case and was strictly out of bounds. A total invasion of your privacy, and they've made it known. So, no one's going to use that against you."

"Thank goodness. I couldn't bear the thought of Will's happiness being jeopardized by lies and innuendos. I'll let everyone here know so they can breathe a sigh of relief. It's been weighing on them—understandably. But what about the accusations that I'd fabricated the evidence against the adoption agency? Is the network still buying that?"

"That's where it gets interesting. The private detective I've hired found that an unusually large sum of money had been deposited into your colleague's checking account right before she publicly broke the story alleging your corrupt practices."

"Wait a minute. How did the detective get access to her bank account? I can't imagine that it was legal."

"Let me just say that he's someone I've used before. He gets results. I don't ask how."

"But bottom line, the implication is that someone bribed this person at the station to lie about me?"

"That would appear to be the gist of it. And get this. The payment came from a law firm, but apparently one of the firm's clients is the adoption agency you exposed in your story."

"Of course! The agency! They gaslight me to divert attention from their own crimes." She paused. "Wait a minute. Whatever you do, I don't want any of the poor teenage moms getting caught in the cross fire. If the agency was willing to bribe a reporter, I can imagine them trying to twist the girls' arms in some way, threaten to spread lies about them, too. They've gone through enough already."

"Whoa! What's happened to the take-no-prisoners attitude that I've come to expect from you? Never mind. I kind of like this softer side. In any case, just listen. We'll definitely try to keep the kids out of the picture. We can't control everything, but we'll do our best." Having defended his plan of action, Sidney got to the crux of the matter. "Tell me one thing. Do you want your job back or not?"

"Of course I want it back!"

"Are you sure?"

Was she? She hadn't worked so hard all these years simply to wave bye-bye on account of a few old people making nice at a dance class and Norman taking her to the historical society. (Though that had been special.) And Will. Did she really want to give up on that connection? It was just starting to click and was more rewarding than she could have ever imagined. But they could still see each other during school vacations, maybe a holiday or two, right? And they had their special signal. They'd never lose that.

And then there was Drew. Oh, dear. She had no idea where that relationship was heading, but was she ready to give up on it completely?

"Just see what you can find out," she decided, bowing to Sidney and her own ambition. "But remember. If it looks like the agency is starting to put pressure on the young moms, pull the plug on the investigation. I want the truth, but I want it without harming the kids any more than they've already had to go through."

"You're the client, you call the shots. I'll wait until I have more solid information before tackling management."

"Just keep me updated," she said.

"Will do. Meanwhile, I've got a call from another client I need to take."

"I thought I was your favorite client." It was a running gag between the two of them, which was true to the extent that Tamara had always felt she'd deserved to come first.

Sidney laughed. No explanations were necessary. He had his part to play, too.

BY THE TIME Drew rolled into the Hopewell Inn, Robby Bellona was already standing at the bar. The celebration with Tamara might have been put on hold—thank goodness, was all Drew could think at the time—but Drew didn't stand a chance of turning down Robby. His old school pal had called him in the afternoon with a firm and enthusiastic invitation—so enthusiastic that Robby started ordering two Rolling Rocks on tap as soon as he spotted Drew at the door.

As far as Drew could tell, the place hadn't changed from the times they used to sneak in as seniors in high school. The hardwood floor was dark with umpteen layers of wax and ground-in dust. The taps still strictly served American beer and ale, and the television sets were tuned to Philadelphia teams—mostly losing ones. The place was such a time warp, there were still bowls of peanuts on the bar counter. No nut allergies as far as the Hopewell Inn was concerned.

"We can sit at the bar or in a booth, whichever you prefer," Robby offered. "We'll run a tab," he said to the barkeep.

Drew liberated a tall, frosted glass from Robby. "How about a booth? I went skydiving with Tamara in the morning. The jump may have been smooth enough, but I can tell I'm getting older. My hip bones are a little sore."

Robby laughed. "The town hero feeling aches and pains? Tell me it isn't so? I'd like to believe one of us is invincible to the passing of time."

Drew slid into the booth. "Sorry, but the aches and pains are definitely real." He clinked glasses with Robby.

Robby took a long swig and smacked his lips.

"So, you took Tamara skydiving, did you? That's really cool. I remember when we went years ago."

"How could I possibly forget? It was Halloween, and you came dressed as a clown." Drew laughed.

"If only I could get Nada to try. I'm the luckiest guy in the world to have her as my wife—what she sees in me is beyond comprehension. But I'd like for her, just once, to experience that sense of… of…?"

"Freedom, of letting go," Drew echoed Tamara's words. He'd been overjoyed by her reaction. Why couldn't he have just accepted her wonderful news instead of mulling over his own surprising and troubling response? He was sure he'd ruined her happiness, not to mention his own.

"That's it. Freedom." Robby closed his eyes and seemed to savor the feeling. He raised the glass in a mock toast. Then he leveled his gaze at Drew. "You know, when I first saw Tamara in Chubbie's the other day, she didn't look like she'd fit into Hopewell at all. Too big-city, too driven. But since then, you'd be surprised. All I hear around town is Tamara this and Tamara that. It's like she's bewitched the whole lot of them."

"Don't get too excited. She's only here until she gets her TV anchor job reinstated. Once she's gone, I promise you she won't be looking back, except from time to time to see her kid, Will Longfellow." Who was he kidding? He wanted her to look back for more than just Will. But could he promise he'd still be around?

Robby frowned. "Won't look back? What brought on all this cynicism? You used to be so upbeat, always putting a positive spin on things. Just having you around made people want to go out and have fun."

Drew leaned his head against the padded back of the booth. "Come off it, Robby. Back then, what did we know? And what did we have to worry about?"

"You want to talk about worries? How about your mom getting cancer when we were in high school? Or my dad dying of a heart attack driving home after seeing the Flyers play? They'd lost the game, for pete's sake. He didn't even get the chance to go out happy."

"You're right. Stuff happened to us, but at least in Hopewell there were people around to help out, make tuna casseroles, shovel the driveway if it snowed. But when stuff—bad stuff—happens far away, most people don't care. Or if you do, it can feel like you're just spitting in the wind."

"I'm sorry to hear you say that. Really. Listening to your dad talk about what you've been doing always made me feel I should do more. But what's opening up your wallet compared to being in the trenches like you are? I always admired you for that, but I can see how it might get to you."

Drew shook his head. "You're right, and sorry for the negative vibes. Between you and me, my relief organization and I had decided it was time for a short break, and clearly my attitude reflects a bit of burnout." He pulled out his phone and scrolled through his email. "But look here," he said and pointed. "A message from one of the organizers. He claims he's merely checking in. Says he knows I have tons of vacation days racked up, but he just wants to be certain of how many people he has in place if and when the next call comes out." Drew closed his phone. "How do you think I should respond?"

"I'm no expert, but it sounds like you need more than a short break."

"You're saying I should take a longer sabbatical?"

"No, I'm asking if you ever considered doing something else."

"You mean like sticking around Hopewell? And do what? Listen to Pops complain that Jessica makes him drink low-fat milk? I love the guy, but he drives me crazy. That's one of the reasons I started hanging out with Tamara—just to get out of the house."

"Then keep doing that—for as long as she's here. There're worse things than passing the time with a smart, great-looking woman who you know from the get-go isn't looking for a long-term relationship."

Drew shook his head. "And this is the counsel I get from a married man? Maybe I should tell Nada about your thinking?" he teased.

"Ha. Nada knows how much I love being married to her. And even you, Mr. Rolling-Stone-Who-Gathers-No-Moss, I have a feeling that if you stayed in Hopewell long enough, you'd start singing another tune—maybe even with Tamara. I'm not so convinced she'll fly the coop so quickly as you claim."

Drew shook his head. "I wouldn't count on anything between me and Tamara. After skydiving today, I really blew it. I knew she was excited, really happy, and wanted to share that happiness with me. I could sense she wanted to kiss me even. But I backed off. Gave her the cold shoulder. A really dumb thing to do. I guess I was scared to admit my feelings for her."

Robby finished off his beer with a flourish. "There comes a time for all of us to admit our feelings. It's scary, don't I know it. But it's worth it. For you—and for her. Trust me, asking Nada to marry me was the best thing to ever happen."

Drew watched his old friend slowly stand and stretch to one side and then the other. When he reached for his wallet, Drew held up his hand. "Let me get it. I might have another drink anyway."

Robby nodded. "Thanks. It was great getting together—certainly beat installing a new dryer for Mrs. Horowitz. I let one of the new workers do it for me instead. She's a great lady, but her dog Schubert scares me. He's one of those little furry things, and his breath? Phew. You don't want to know."

Robby started to head for the door but stopped and turned back. "You know, Nada's this amazing cook. And her baking? To die for. But like all great cooks, she likes to try new things—which is good. It stretches her imagination. But sometimes it doesn't work out. And you know what she does?"

"Feeds you the mistakes?"

Robby laughed. "I wish. No, she's a perfectionist. She'd never allow that. Instead, she just starts all over again. And you know what happens then?"

"I think you'll tell me."

"You're darn straight. She keeps working at it until she gets it right." Robby slapped his hand on the well-worn table. "Let that be a lesson to you. So, you screwed up today? There's always tomorrow. You just have to keep trying to make it better." He gave a final wave and headed for the exit.

"Later." Drew watched Robby head out the door. To think Robby Bellona of all people could give him lessons in baking and in life. And Drew knew he'd be a fool not to take note.

CHAPTER EIGHTEEN

ROBBY WAS DEFINITELY RIGHT. Schubert's breath was nothing short of lethal. Especially when the dog decided to make Drew the chosen one and curl up on his lap.

It was Friday afternoon. Drew had first met Tamara for breakfast as usual. He'd still been feeling a bit down, but Chubbie's could not be denied. And if he was being honest, he'd been eager to see Tamara. He was going to try to take Robby's wisdom to heart and give it another try—maybe open up about why he'd held back.

But before he could get a word in edgewise, she immediately began talking, excitedly brimming with an idea for what to do next. And as Drew listened to her eager conversation, he decided now was not the time to inject too serious a note. After all, it was her turn to choose.

"You'll never guess who I ran into when I was parking the car by the old train station." She took a bite of English muffin. And waited. The muffin had morphed into a modest carrier for the jam.

"You're going to tell me anyway, so why keep me in suspense?"

Tamara nodded. "Mrs. Horowitz! She was on her way to Robby Bellona's plumbing store to tell him what a nice job his new assistant—Mr. Mason's niece, of all people—had done putting in her new dryer. Apparently, Georgie—I think she said that was her name—anyway, Georgie showed her how to clean out the filter. Wasn't that thoughtful?"

"I would have expected nothing less from a niece of Mr. Mason's." Drew didn't even know that Mr. Mason had a family, let alone a niece who knew how to repair and install appliances. He'd always pictured Mr. Mason popping out of a carburetor fully formed.

"Anyway, Mrs. Horowitz was so nice to me, saying that she was delighted to meet me at the dance class and that I had natural rhythm."

"Please tell me that you didn't sign us up for a tango lesson." He sipped his coffee with trepidation.

"Gosh, no, the tango's not for a couple of weeks. In between is the foxtrot and samba, but only on Tuesdays. No, she had a much better idea, for this afternoon, for both of us."

"I hope she didn't volunteer us to install a washing machine to go with the dryer."

"No washing machines. It's piano lessons." Tamara leaned back in her café chair and enjoyed the strawberry-rhubarb jam—Candy's recommendation. She seemed quite pleased with herself.

"Piano lessons? You do realize that my mother made me take piano during my middle school years? She thought it would 'focus me'—her words, not mine." Drew found himself making air quotes to go along with his words. How low had he sunk in so short a time? He shook his head. "After a few years, Mrs. Horowitz told my mother that while she enjoyed our weekly lessons, she didn't want to waste my mom's money. I was not cut out for practicing. And now you want us to take piano lessons?"

"Look at the upside. She didn't say you had no musical talent—only that you lacked perseverance. How many kids have musical perseverance when they're eleven or twelve years old anyway?"

"I don't know. Lang Lang? Daniel Barenboim? Name another famous pianist."

"They're concert pianists. We'd be amateurs, amateurs looking to broaden our horizons during this unique and fortunate sojourn in Hopewell." She smiled brightly and batted her eyelashes. They were long and thick, he noticed.

Drew almost succumbed to her enthusiasm. Almost. "So, now you've rebranded this enforced period of idleness as 'unique and fortunate'?"

She made a hand motion as if to say *Pshaw*. It was almost as bad as air quotes. "I'm sorry you feel that way. My advice is to keep busy—and think of my needs."

"Are you being serious or attempting humor?" A smile managed to wrangle its way onto his face.

"Both." She shrugged. "But really, look at it this way. I like Mrs. Horowitz. I always wanted a grandmother, and she fits the bill. Besides, I took piano lessons as a kid. They were part of a free afterschool program. And I wouldn't mind seeing what it's like to pick up playing again as an adult. Kind of an intellectual exercise."

"Good, then you take the lesson this afternoon and tell me all about it. We can hang out—just the two of us—doing something less taxing." See, he was following the Nada Bellona theory of baking—try and try again until you get it right.

"That's not our deal. We're supposed to expand our horizons. Do something we'd never dream of doing on our own. Anyway, I'm just carrying out Mrs. Horowitz's orders. She says adult pupils learn much more rapidly when they work together as a team. Apparently, working together provides an incentive." She finished the half of the English muffin with a flourish.

"So, you're telling me it's decided? That you've already agreed to us taking piano lessons together?"

Tamara nodded. "This afternoon. Two o'clock sharp. She said that she was thinking of having us learn a duet. That's true togetherness. Just you and me."

It wasn't exactly what he had in mind. Drew groaned and rose. "It sounds like torture. In which case, I better get going to Laura's gallery. There's a boatload of framing to be done, and I promised

I'd cover for her over lunch while she's at a prenatal appointment."

"Oh, could you please let Laura know I'm making progress with your father about donating some paintings."

"You're a brave woman—in more ways than one."

"Keep that thought in mind for our lesson. And I was planning on meeting you there, if that's okay? You know where to go, I presume."

"Unfortunately, yes. And just for organizing our little afternoon adventure, I'll let you pick up the bill." He bent over and snatched the other half of her English muffin.

"Hey, that's mine!"

"I need all the nourishment I can get before our lesson. I don't know about you, but I'm afraid."

"Not to worry. I'll protect you. I'll even take the harder part in the duet."

TAMARA'S SUV WAS already parked in the driveway of Mrs. Horowitz's split-level when Drew arrived that afternoon. Built in the late fifties, Mrs. Horowitz's modest house was half brick, half cedar shingles. Located on a flat stretch of land behind the bank, the property had originally been a dairy farm before evolving—or devolving, in some people's eyes—into a sod farm, only to be sold to a developer in the post–Korean War population boom. Mrs. Horowitz (Drew had never met a Mr. Horowitz) must have bought the house when it was brand-new because nothing much had changed except for the evergreen bushes planted around the foundation. They had grown so much that they threatened to take over the living room picture window.

Drew pressed the doorbell and listened as the chimes played the opening bars from Beethoven's Fifth. High-pitched barking followed this serenade. Drew sucked in the air. He would need all his strength.

The front door opened, and Tamara greeted him. "I'm glad you came. Mrs. Horowitz was just showing me her new dryer. It's beautiful. Even has a freshen-up cycle."

"I might need it after the lesson."

"Don't be such a scaredy-cat. If I can jump out of a plane, you can share a piano lesson." For a moment, her gaze became unfocused and her breathing a little deeper.

He couldn't help noticing. "You wouldn't consider letting me…"

She blinked rapidly. "Letting you what?"

"What I mean is…"

"I'm in the living room, you two," Mrs. Horowitz could be heard saying. "I've located something for you both to play."

And that's how Schubert ended up on Drew's lap while Tamara sat on the piano bench next to Mrs. Horowitz. "Ladies first," Mrs. Horowitz announced. She was dressed for work: navy twinset, gray pull-on pants and her broach of musical notes.

"After I'm done with you, Drew——" the words sounded ominous to Drew's ears "——I'll get you both going on this one duet."

MIRACULOUSLY, TAMARA STILL remembered how to read music and locate the notes on the keyboard—well, the ones in the central octaves. She stumbled with the fingering on the scales in the beginning, but once Mrs. Horowitz marked which finger to use on the sheet music she got better and could do one or two scales with sharps. Flats would be reserved for the next lesson. Next came a few exercises for each hand individually before Mrs. Horowitz judged that Tamara was ready to attempt a simple minuet that Mozart wrote when he was a mere five years old. But she insisted again that Tamara work on each hand separately, and she marked the fingering where necessary.

"Let's keep it to one hand at a time for the first lesson. That will be enough to practice in addition to your scales and exercises, not to mention the chords I've introduced," Mrs. Horowitz instructed as she wrote out a lesson plan on a small assignment pad with musical lines. She'd given it to Tamara along with a folder to hold the sheet music. Tamara had picked the one with Moana on the cover. "I'm sorry, my students tend to be children. Hence the limited selection," Mrs. Horowitz had apologized.

"That's okay. I'm not much of an Ariel person, but Moana is just my type."

Mrs. Horowitz smiled. "I know what you mean. I think she's terrific, too. And I must say, you're doing remarkably well for someone who hasn't played in, what, twenty years?"

"But you're sure I can't try two hands together yet?" Tamara asked.

"It's not a competition," Drew piped up from the couch. He'd been silent until now. Perhaps he was concentrating on breathing in as little as possible to avoid the effects of Schubert's halitosis.

Tamara looked over her shoulder. "You better believe it's a competition," she answered. She couldn't help noticing that Drew had made an effort to tame his hair with some ruthless combing, and she found his boyish attempts endearing.

The thing was, after her phone call with Sidney, Tamara had decided that the best move forward was not to dwell on what had happened after the skydiving. Instead, she would go about making the best of her time in Hopewell. If that meant forming a deeper relation with Drew (and his many endearing qualities), so be it. If it didn't? Well, they'd had a good time together, shared a few laughs. And truthfully, candor being a hallmark of their breakfast buddy pact, he'd become the closest thing to a friend she'd ever had. And maybe more…

And meanwhile, this closest thing to a friend shifted Schubert to the side and leaned forward. The Pekingese snored contentedly. "Did you cheat and look online before we came?" he asked.

"Of course I looked online. That's not cheating. That's being prepared."

"Some of us actually work and don't have time to cheat."

Mrs. Horowitz clapped her hands. "Children, order, please. Tamara, you'll have to be patient with your studies. Trust me. I've had years of experience. And now, Drew, it's your turn, and this lesson is the one instance where you're allowed to sight-read. But hereafter I expect you to practice before each lesson. Hussle up. Let's see what you can recall."

With some helpful prompting, Drew unearthed his long-hidden knowledge of reading music and translating the written notes to the piano keys. He stumbled through the scales and exercises but persevered despite sweating under the pressure. Then he tackled a minuet where…yes, timing was an issue.

Mrs. Horowitz reached for the assignment pad and wrote out a guide to the various notes and rests as well as simple exercises that combined whole, half and quarter notes in different measures. "I want you to work on these exercises especially. I can loan you a metronome, but I'm sure you'll grasp the timing again quickly. I remember how you used to pick up things easily—facts and figures, drawing, all sorts of things with your hands." She paused. "Speaking of which, I just have to ask—not to be impertinent, mind you, but merely inquisitive. Given all your natural talents, why didn't you graduate first in your high school class?"

"I did manage to place second," Drew admitted reluctantly. "It was because I got an A minus in physics. The teacher had it in for me."

"His mistake, I'm sure. So, don't be discouraged with today's lesson." She patted him on his knee.

Drew dropped his head. "I'm not discouraged." He sounded like he was discouraged.

"It's not a competition," Tamara reminded him.

He turned and growled. She raised her eyebrows and grinned back, letting the smile linger. He caught his breath. And growled again. Only this time it had a different tone. Tamara responded with a low-pitched hum.

Mrs. Horowitz quickly looked at her watch. "Unfortunately, I think we better leave the introduction to your duet until the next lesson. We've already used up the hour, and I don't want to push it any more."

Tamara sighed with regret. Drew sighed with exhaustion.

"Now, given your short time in Hopewell—I'm right that you're only here temporarily?" She looked at them both for confirmation. They nodded at each other and at her. "Given that, I insist that we meet twice a week."

Drew opened his mouth to speak. "I'm at the gallery—"

"Yes, I understand. But mixing two artistic endeavors can only inspire you that much more. Luckily, since it's summertime, I'm flexible with my schedule. As I see it, we shouldn't have any problems."

Drew closed his mouth. Mrs. Horowitz had decreed.

"That'll be terrific if you have the time to spare," Tamara gushed. She stood, unencumbered by Schubert, who'd abandoned the couch and made a beeline for the window, where he'd taken up a post, monitoring the street.

Drew gathered up his assignment book and folder. "Thank you for supplying everything, Mrs. Horowitz. And I happen to love *Star Wars*, by the way. Which reminds me, we never settled on a price."

"That's right," Tamara said.

Mrs. Horowitz walked them to the front door. "We'll work that out later. I don't want anything to get in the way of all our fun! Now, as to practicing. You still have the piano in your family house?" she asked Drew. He nodded. "Then that settles it, Tamara can practice on the upright as well."

Tamara waved off her suggestion. "That's not necessary. I'll order a keyboard online, and it'll be delivered in a day."

"No student of mine plays on a keyboard! It simply isn't the same touch, the same feel as the genuine instrument. Tamara, I insist you go to the Trombo household and practice there every day. And you, too, Drew. You're an adult now—I presume. My adult students are serious about their music studies."

Who had the power to deny Mrs. Horowitz her wishes? Certainly not Drew.

"Let's settle on Tuesday for our second lesson then," she declared. "I'll text you the details. I love texting, don't you?"

The next thing Drew and Tamara knew, they were walking down the brick path to the driveway.

"Did we just get played?" Drew asked. He fingered the truck's keys in his pocket.

Tamara buried her head in her tote before she withdrew her own keys. "I'm pretty sure we did. Only, what's her game?" She stopped at the side of the SUV. "Before I forget, one question. Who was number one?"

"Number one?"

"In your high school graduating class. Who was the valedictorian?"

"Remember when I said I didn't remember her?"

"Who?"

"Amy Pulaski. The librarian. She was valedictorian."

"Figures."

Now that the lesson was over, Mrs. Horowitz and Schubert headed for the kitchen. The Pekingese curled contentedly at her feet when she settled herself at the table and dialed Gloria Pulaski from the wall phone. (Mrs. Horowitz still had a taupe-colored wall phone. "It works perfectly fine. Why should I get rid of it?" she'd say when asked. People learned not to ask.)

The cord hung by her elbow, and she flicked it away from her tumbler of dry vermouth on the rocks. "It's all in motion," she said conspiratorially when Gloria picked up. "I was a little concerned we'd let too many days pass since the dancing lesson when we all first talked about getting Drew and Tamara together, but I've finally gotten the ball rolling on my end. In fact, it was easier than I thought it would be. I even insisted Tamara practice at the Trombo house. I used some excuse about not letting her get a keyboard. That the feel wasn't the same."

"And she bought that? The savvy professional woman from the big city?"

"Yes, I know. I've still got it." Mrs. Horowitz chuckled and took a sip of her go-to celebratory drink.

"What about Drew? Any suspicions?"

Mrs. Horowitz considered Gloria's question while she rubbed Schubert's fur. She stretched her feet, after having gladly removed her navy pumps as soon as the couple was out the door. For the first lesson, she had felt it important to dress appropriately, to establish a certain professional air.

"None that were obvious. I think he was traumatized just sitting on the piano bench. He kept insisting it wasn't a competition, but you could tell he wanted to do a good job."

"And did he?"

"Not bad for someone who's never practiced

a day in his life. He has natural talent. It makes learning easy—perhaps too easy. Whereas she's a worker. A real terrier. Talent, yes, but determination in spades."

"What did I say—a perfect mix!" Gloria exclaimed.

"To tell you the truth, I wasn't sure in the beginning. The way they teased each other—it was so sweet, but I wasn't sure it was going anywhere."

"But did you see sparks?" The noise of a truck applying its brakes could be heard in the background.

"Are you on the road? I thought I heard a car," Mrs. Horowitz commented.

"Yes, I'm off to meet my daughter Amy. She wants to film Mr. Portobello's upcoming lecture at the library on organic wines—another edition of her series Library Happenings. It should be entertaining if it's half as good as his presentation on boutique gins. She wanted to get my input from an audience member's point of view. You know how her videos are so much more than just one camera angle pointed at the speaker. But enough about Amy, tell me about the sparks. They were there, am I right?"

Mrs. Horowitz nuzzled the phone receiver under her chin and bent to pick up Schubert. She settled him on her lap and replied, "Sparks?" She thought a moment. "Definitely. Only they don't seem to know what to do about them. And I'm still worried about the possibility that they'll leave Hopewell without ever really giving themselves a chance."

"That's why we need a concerted effort on everyone's part—kick this into high gear. You've done your bit. Now Signora Reggio and I have to get going, too. We've been a little lax, I agree. But the time to act is now. Pronto."

Mrs. Horowitz agreed and rang off. All this matchmaking brought up fond memories of the evening Mr. Horowitz proposed to her on the verandah of his parents' house in Queens. She and Samuel were sitting on the sofa opposite Morris and Gretel. Morris had a small button business in the Garment District. Gretel was a housewife. They'd both been smiling.

She sighed and kissed Schubert again. Then she pulled back. Schubert looked up and gave her a crinkly dog smile. "You know, the last time we saw Dr. Jessica at the clinic, she was correct," Mrs. Horowitz admonished. "I absolutely need to make an appointment to get your teeth cleaned."

CHAPTER NINETEEN

NORMAN AND DREW were seated around the picnic table at the end of the day, nursing some beers. Norman faced the rear of the house so he could enjoy the rosebushes in full bloom. The pink and red blossoms and an occasional white accent danced against the freshly painted clapboard.

"You did a nice job with the woodwork and the painting," Norman complimented. He grabbed a handful of popcorn from the ceramic bowl on the table.

Drew took a slow sip from his bottle. It tasted good, really good. "Thanks, Pops. It wasn't a big job, really. The place is in pretty good shape."

"Thanks to you. I couldn't possibly do it on my own."

"On that we can agree." They clinked bottles. "And I wanna thank you for the brilliant suggestion to get the beer."

"Long day at the gallery?" Norman cocked his head.

"Yes, but a real pleasure. I love the whole picture-framing thing—I get to use my hands and be a bit creative at the same time. It's a real puzzle how to show off the art as best as possible. Surprisingly, I also enjoy working with the customers. Laura will be pleased to hear that I sold two etchings by this new artist she's just started representing. He used to be in an orchestra in Mexico, and his work depicts musicians."

"Makes sense."

"Well, the couple who bought them happen to be in a rock band. They just played the Stone Pony on the Jersey Shore. You know, the place where Springsteen got his start?"

Norman grinned. "Even I know Bruce Springsteen. And I'm not surprised you made a sale. You've always had a way with people."

Drew munched on the popcorn. "Actually, someone got the better of me today—Tamara. It was her turn to choose a mind-expanding experience, and you'll never guess where we ended up. At Mrs. Horowitz's for a piano lesson."

"Ooh, that was a low blow. Just you then?"

"Both of us. We're even going to learn a duet. A duet!"

Norman chuckled. "That'll be something to hear, seeing as you haven't had a lesson in twenty years or so. I presume Tamara's in the same boat?"

Drew nodded and took an exasperated sip. "Correct. Get this. Not only does Mrs. Horowitz expect us to play at her annual recital, but she's having us come in for two lessons a week. And we've got little assignment pads to record our practice schedule. To top it off, she insisted that Tamara practice on our old upright in the living room. She said an electronic keyboard won't cut it."

Norman cocked his head. "Did she, now? Interesting. I always said that Ida was a sly one."

Drew frowned. "Ida? I never knew Mrs. Horowitz had a first name."

"There're many things you don't know about Mrs. Horowitz."

Drew waited, but all he got was the sound of his father munching on popcorn.

Norman sniffed. "Speaking of Tamara, you know how the other day she drove me to my physical therapy appointment?"

Drew nodded.

"Afterward we hung out, and she brought up the upcoming art show of your mother's work."

Drew's last gulp went down the wrong way, and he sputtered a cough. Then he cleared his throat. "I knew that she'd volunteered to talk to you. I wasn't sure how well you'd take it."

"Mostly I was surprised that you or your sister didn't come talk to me about it first. But we got over that hurdle."

Drew appreciated that.

"Anyhow, Tamara suggested I consider donating more of your mother's paintings, especially her later works. Apparently, the stuff she gave you was from an earlier period—not that I would know since you didn't consult me about having an exhibit to raise money for a scholarship in her name."

"I didn't think you'd go along with the idea. You always felt the need to guard Mom's work close—that somehow by holding tight, you'd keep her memory fresh in your mind. I get that. I miss her too. I don't want to let go of how important she was and still is to me." He used his thumbnail to pick at the label on his beer bottle. "And I'm sorry I didn't talk to you earlier about the show. It's just that I was worried you'd lecture me on why I shouldn't give away her art, even if it was for a scholarship fund. Call me a coward, but I figured you'd say I was trying to forget Mom, even if that wasn't true. And, to top it off, in some irrational leap of my imagination, I pictured you telling me I should have come home more—that life was too short to put things off, as Mom's early death proved all too well. So, I felt guilty for selfishly following my quest around the world without bothering to check in as often as I should have."

Norman was quiet for a while. "There's no need for you to feel guilty. You're right. I probably would have lectured you. I might still. But that's no reason to feel guilty about not being home. Your mom and I were always so proud of your work, your courage at dealing with all that adversity. We knew it was your calling. We never wanted to tie you down."

Drew kept chipping away at the label. This heart-to-heart stuff was all new to him. He'd always preferred not to examine his relationships with others, let alone himself. Was it any wonder he was all at sea about where things were going—or not—with Tamara?

Norman munched thoughtfully. "Help me remember here. Your mom gave you her artwork near the end, when she knew there were no other treatment options. Am I right?"

Drew stopped his nervous fiddling and concentrated. "Exactly. She died just a few days later." He stared toward the far end of the yard at the Japanese garden his mother had designed and planted. He noticed how neglected it was. The evergreen shrubs needed shaping, and no one had raked the small pebbles back into swirling lines. He should do it. His mom would have appreciated it.

All Drew remembered of those final days was rushing home and seeing the pain his mother suffered despite the drugs. In the end, he had held one of her hands while Jessica held the other. His father had stood at the foot of the four-poster bed. He hadn't uttered a word or shed a tear. Yet, somehow, when the ordeal was over, Pops had shrunk by more than an inch.

Drew shook his head.

"I've got a question for you," Norman declared. "Do you know why your mother gave you those works?"

Drew refocused on his father. "It was a mystery. Not that I don't value them. I mean, she was an amazing artist, and they're precious to me. In fact, when I decided to donate them as a way to keep her memory alive, there was one work I couldn't part with. It's a portrait that, for her, is surprisingly sedate, even modest, one might say." He waited a beat. "It's of you, Pops. You're sitting in your recliner, reading the sports section of the newspaper. Zebra is curled up at your feet, a large pile of dog fur. You're not wearing any shoes, just socks. Mom even painted a big hole in one sock." Drew laughed quietly. "It's so perfect. Just the way you always looked on a Sunday afternoon, wrapped up in the baseball box scores, close to a beloved pet and oblivious to the fact that your socks were a mess. It's amusing but not critical—a quiet depiction of love." He studied his father's face but didn't see any visible signs of nostalgia or sadness. Pops's way of grieving was an enigma.

"So why did she give them to you? You say it was a mystery, but you can do better than that. Think," his father pressed.

Drew shrugged. "Maybe because I was the one person in the family who also drew and was into art. But it still doesn't make sense. Back then, I didn't have a permanent place to live. I mean, really? Where would I have displayed them?"

Norman pushed aside the bowl of popcorn that sat between them. "Maybe that was her point? Maybe she thought that it would make you find a place, a place to call your own. But knowing your mother, I think it goes deeper than that." He placed his elbows on the table and knitted his fingers together. "She and I accepted—even applauded— the idea that you were a wandering soul. Maybe you still are, though I'm not so sure anymore. But she also understood that you were a naturally social person, always ready to give of yourself and help others. And I think the combination of the two factors was why she gave the art to you. She could have left them with me, but she knew I would have just kept them on a shelf in some random closet. I think she wanted you to share them with others, the way you've always felt compelled to share yourself. And your decision to donate them was precisely what she'd hoped would happen. It's what she loved so much about you."

Drew felt a lump in his throat. "I'm not sure at that stage she was thinking that many steps ahead."

"I'm pretty sure you're wrong because I don't believe it was a last-minute decision by any stretch of the imagination. She may have seemed a loosey-goosey arty type, but deep down, your mom had this strategic brain. I just loved that about her." Norman smiled with a great deal of satisfaction. "Which is why I can't help thinking that somehow by keeping all her remaining art, all her things— her very presence in so many ways—I've missed what she had planned for me." He stared down Drew. "And don't you start trying to figure it out."

Drew pulled back. "You get to analyze her gift to me, but I'm supposed to remain silent as to yours? That's a bit one-sided, don't you think?"

"I suppose so, but I won't give you the pleasure of showing up the old man. Vivian was a wonderful mother, wife, artist, gardener—a lousy cook, unfortunately." They both chuckled. "But above all she was a teacher. I look at the art she left me as a gesture of love, but also as a lesson—a series of questions, if you will—for me to ponder and to solve."

"Well, you know what Mom always said—about art and life?"

"'Never wait for inspiration to come to you'? I know. And I won't. And I promise you and Laura that I'll make up my mind about the exhibit—soon."

THAT NIGHT DREW couldn't sleep. The conversation he'd had with Pops wasn't the only factor.

After having tossed and turned till after midnight, he grabbed his sketchbook and switched on the bedside lamp, the one with the *Star Wars* shade. He hadn't been lying to Mrs. Horowitz when he told her he'd loved *Star Wars*.

The drawing came quickly. When he had finished, he sat back against the pillows piled up at the head of the bed and studied his work. Tamara playing the piano. Her posture was ramrod straight, and she'd narrowed her eyes in concentration. The set of her jaw showed determination, but the tufts of her dark hair, even though short, seemed to curl and sway along with some silent melody. And the slight upturn of the corner of her mouth betrayed her utter happiness. She was enraptured by the music.

He looked—and discovered—what his fingers and his talent were telling him—that he was enraptured with her.

Drew placed the pad on the floor and rested the

soft pencil on the table. "Breakfast buddies," he reminded himself. Maybe that's all they were meant to be. "Breakfast buddies." Could he be content with that?

CHAPTER TWENTY

THE NEXT MORNING, Briggs had such an overflow of flowers for the Saturday farmers' market, that he and Tamara needed both cars to transport the buckets, flowers, tables, folding tent and all the sales paraphernalia—in addition to squeezing in Will and Buddy. Oh, and an enormous bag of treats for the doggy playdate in the afternoon.

Myrna had planned to join them, but the beginning of a migraine had come on quickly when she and Tamara were loading the dishwasher after breakfast.

"Do you think it's all right to leave her?" Tamara asked as she wedged a portion of the flowers into the trunk of her SUV. She stuffed the dog bowls and treats and the stand's fold-up tent around the flower containers to keep them from falling over. When she lifted the sandbags used to weigh down the tent, she was surprised to find how heavy they were. She put her hands on her hips and took a breather.

Briggs was maneuvering more flowers into the trunk of his station wagon. The back seat was already packed with milk cartons containing packing paper, a stapler and tape dispenser, a money box and credit card reader, and a bunch of other stuff that Tamara didn't know how to name. Atop were two watering cans and stacks of metal buckets to hold bouquets that were currently nestled on cardboard box tops. "I think she'll be fine. I told her to call if it gets worse. Myrna gets the occasional migraine, unfortunately, but she prefers to handle it on her own rather than have someone hovering over her. Pride, I guess." He kept bending and lifting up as he spoke.

"You don't know what brought it on, do you?" Tamara asked. She was ready to give Myrna kudos for trying to tough it out, and she knew Will would be proud of her reaction. She was trying to show patience and give praise. She put her hand to her heart—mimicking their private signal.

"It probably came on from overdoing it— You know how much she has on her plate right now."

"And don't forget she stayed up late, cooking homemade liver treats for Buddy's playdate—the one I arranged," Tamara added.

"Just remember it was her choice. No need to feel guilty. She wouldn't have done it if she didn't want to."

Kind words from Briggs! Will's advice was bearing fruit. She'd have to tell him. Smiling, she examined the front passenger seat to see if she could pack in more bouquets. Will and Buddy would be sitting in the back, so she didn't want to risk the back seat.

But once they got to the market, she was too busy

to take the time to confide to her son, who was hard at work, erecting the tent. Buddy knew his role, as well, because as soon as Tamara set up one of the large white folding tables, he scurried underneath and hid from all the action.

"Is it usually this much work?" she asked Briggs as they lugged the flowers out of the cars.

He studied the colorful array that flooded the stall. "It's always kind of hectic, but this week is particularly wild. Since I'm not here next week—going away with Jessica and all—I brought almost twice as much as usual. Problem is, with all the extra merchandise, I'm not really sure where to put it." He rubbed his chin.

Tamara looked at the layout. Three tables, covered with white cloths, lined the sides and back of the tent. They'd already put the tall metal buckets with the bouquets on the left table and the cut bunches on the middle one. The right table was free for wrapping flowers and ringing up customers. But with so many flowers, the overflow had taken over the ground and blocked customers from being able to get a closer look.

"I've got an idea," she said. "You know the milk crates under the checkout table? We can turn them upside down, place them at the outer corners of the stall and put buckets on top of them and around them in tiers."

Briggs nodded. "Good idea, and we can take some of the leftover mason jars still in my car, put the shorter flowers in them and then nestle them among the tall metal containers. What do you think?"

"I like it. Meanwhile, we can keep any extra buckets of flowers behind the tables on the ground and pull them out as we sell the stuff already on display."

Briggs returned to the car to get the jars while Tamara emptied the milk crates and put them in place. Then she took a moment to admire their handiwork. For once, they weren't tiptoeing around each other (at best) or acting like hostile house-mates (at worst). *Progress*, thought Tamara.

Will had just finished writing on the chalkboard that the flower stand would be closed next week when Briggs motioned to him to come over.

"Hey, a new setup," Will remarked when he saw the different arrangement.

"It was Tamara's idea—a way to fit everything in."

"Sweet. It looks great." He bent his arm and shared their secret signal. She smiled and returned the favor.

If Briggs saw the subtle exchange, he didn't comment. Instead, he pulled his wallet from his jeans. "Can you do me a favor, Will, and go to the Bean World Coffee truck? You can get Tamara and me two coffees and a lemonade or something for yourself. Take Buddy, why don't you, while we move stuff around. That way he won't get upset." Briggs held out a twenty.

"Sure thing, Dad. You know, Buddy likes those

gourmet dog cookies from the lady across the way. Do you think…?"

"No problem." He pulled out another bill. "And get some stuff at Nada's stall for us humans, too."

"Any preferences?" Will asked.

"Surprise me," his dad said. Then he looked at Tamara. "What about you? Do you want anything in particular?"

"Anything with Nada's jam on it would be amazing," she replied. "What about for Jessica? She's coming, right? And Norman and Drew." She held up her hand. "Hold on a minute." She pulled out her phone. "Drew's just texted to say that he had to take Norman on an errand. The two of them will be running late."

"And Jessica's working first thing this morning, but we might as well pick up snacks for them all."

"Got it, Dad. C'mon, Bud." Will skipped along the pavement, intermittently stopping to let Buddy explore the many mysterious smells.

Briggs and Tamara got back to work. She recognized the roses, scented geraniums and red peonies, but she had to ask about the other varieties. Briggs identified daisylike feverfew and buttery-yellow yarrow, white and pink phlox, purple baptisia and cheerful blue forget-me-nots. She just hoped the names would stick so she could answer potential questions. Then she barely had time to take a photo of the full display when the first customer arrived.

It was the last time they had the luxury of dealing with one person at a time. Tamara fielded inquiries about the flowers where she could. As for creating bouquets, she let the maestro do his thing, while she proved adept at wrapping and handling the payments. "Years of waitressing prepared me for this," she explained to customers, surprised at how many she knew.

As the morning progressed, the crowds swarmed the market. The stalls offered all sorts of temptations: veggies and fruit, meat and poultry products, baked goods and handcrafts. But Briggs's flowers were by far the biggest draw. It wasn't just that the flowers were beautiful, Tamara realized, but that everyone bought into his passion. He eagerly shared his knowledge, and the customers found his enthusiasm infectious. Purchasing bouquets—he referred to them as bundles of beauty—was as essential as buying a dozen eggs. She felt proud that she could help.

The double cappuccino that Will got her, along with the amazing Linzer cookie from Nada (apricot jam this time), helped keep her adrenaline up.

"Tamara, *buona mattina*," came a familiar voice. Signora Reggio wished Tamara good morning with a kiss on each cheek. She carried a string bag stuffed with eggplants, zucchini and tomatoes. *"Ho qualcosa da dirti,"* she explained in Italian that she had something to tell her before switching to English. "I had an appointment with the—how do you say?—*il fisioterapista*."

"The physical therapist?" Tamara guessed. She handed a wrapped bouquet to a young mother with a stroller full of twins. "You're okay, Signora? Nothing wrong, I hope?"

"I am fine. Just my wrist. Sometimes I knit too much, and the tendon…it gets sore. But that's not what I want to tell you."

"No?" She turned to the next customers, a middle-aged couple with coordinating Patagonia fleece jackets. "Will that be cash or charge?"

"No," Signora Reggio continued. "I happened to see Myrna Longfellow there recently—she was driving *il dottore*, Signor Norman, for an appointment. We got to talking, and I discovered that her birthday is a week from today, *il prossimo sabato*."

"Oh, no, and she's looking after Will with me then. Not much of a celebration." The tension between Myrna and her had eased, especially after Tamara told her and Briggs the news from her agent, Sidney, that Will was no longer in jeopardy. Even still, Tamara was never quite sure how to act around Will's aunt. Clearly, the strain caused by her unexpected pregnancy all those years ago had affected them both deeply, and Tamara was unsure exactly how to rationalize the past and move on. Neither of them seemed prepared at this point to have some deep, soul-searching discussion. Patience and praise, she tried to tell herself, echoing Will's advice. To say it was a work in progress was an understatement.

Signora Reggio tapped her chin. "Myrna does deserve something special. And you know, I have an idea. A surprise."

"You think a surprise is really a good way to go when it comes to Myrna?" Tamara asked. Then she smiled at the Patagonia couple and made change after they handed her a fresh fifty-dollar bill.

"She will like this surprise—trust me. Because for a change you will cook for her instead of the other way around! And I know just what it will be. My lasagna—just like we talked about at the dancing class. I tell you what, why don't you suggest to Dottore Norman that he take Myrna out to dinner on Friday? That way she'll think it is the celebration of her birthday. But in reality, on Friday, you will come over to my place, and I will teach you how to make the meal. We'll start in the morning and finish the preparation when they are out for dinner. Then you will be all set to surprise her on Saturday." She obviously saw the dubious expression on Tamara's face. "Don't worry. It's much better reheated anyway."

"But I'm hopeless in the kitchen. You don't understand. I've never even turned on my oven in Phoenix. I keep my shoes in it."

"You keep your shoes in the oven? *Oddio.*" Signora Reggio seemed to ponder the challenge facing her. Then she raised an index finger. "I have an idea. You get that Drew to come on Friday, too. He is very handy, no? He should be able to help in the kitchen with no problem."

"I don't know if he'll want to give up his Friday to cook lasagna for someone else's birthday."

"Nonsense. When he finds out it is for the friend

of his father, he will be happy to do it. You will tell him that he and *il dottore* will also be invited to the dinner. He will come. You will see. He is a good son. He does not want to see his father hiding in his house and…and…" She searched for the right vocabulary. "And sulking. Yes, that is the correct word, I am sure. And the meal will be the perfect celebration for Myrna. She won't have to cook for a change, and she will have the company she adores—*il dottore*, the lovely boy Will, also that girl who is Will's friend…"

"Candy."

"Yes, Candy, that's her name. And of course you and Drew. *Che uomo!*" La Signora gestured with both hands in tandem. No translation was necessary.

"I guess you're right." Tamara still wasn't entirely sold, especially if the festivities relied on her culinary skills. "Why don't you give me a list of ingredients, and I'll go to the supermarket on Thursday."

"Supermarket! Absolutely not. Italian cooking is all about fresh ingredients. I'll speak to the butcher now about the meat. The farm stand also has a proper selection of vegetables. I will convince the farmer to make a special delivery. But we will use my Parmigiano-Reggiano. Nothing else will do."

Tamara nodded. The whole thing was going straight over her head. But she had to trust La Signora. "Please, you'll let me know how much I owe you."

Signora Reggio waved her off. "We will finalize the bill on Friday. Meanwhile, I will talk to Nada Bellona about making a cake. Normally, I would make one, but the truth of the matter is, Nada is a better baker than I am. I recommend her plum cake. It is superb."

"If you think so, I'm sure it's wonderful."

"I will arrange for you to pick it up on Saturday morning." She clapped. "You are in good hands. Do not doubt. I will see you Friday around nine in the morning. Laura will give you my address, using that email thing. I have decided not to understand computers." She went up on her toes and gave Tamara a kiss on each cheek before scurrying off.

Tamara touched her face and tried to figure out what just happened. Which was when she realized that a young man holding a bunch of poppies was waiting to pay. "Oh, I'm so sorry. I didn't see you standing there." She looked at the prices listed on the jar and took his credit card.

"Don't worry. I was fascinated by the whole conversation," he said. "Do you think she can teach me how to cook lasagna, too? My girlfriend's parents are coming over, and they'd be so impressed."

SIGNORA REGGIO DID indeed talk to Nada Bellona at her baked goods stand. She put in the order for a plum cake and picked up two walnut crescent cookies to have with coffee later in the day. (An indulgence, but it was worth it!)

She was adjusting the various purchases in her

carry bag when she spotted Gloria Pulaski paying for a very nice-looking apple strudel. Gloria was a wise woman in many ways. It was also time to check in.

"Thank you so much, Nada. Just one more thing." Gloria reached back in her purse and pulled out several bills. "I know my grandchildren will be stopping by with my daughter Betsy—you know, the one who's the receptionist at the hospital. Could you make sure the children get some cookies on me—whatever they choose."

Nada smiled. "Your daughters are wonderful, Gloria. You did such a good job raising them. I am coming to you when we have the baby."

Gloria leaned forward. "Are you saying…?"

"I just found out, but I haven't told Robby yet," Nada whispered. "Keep it between you and me, will you?"

Gloria nodded and took her carefully wrapped strudel. She turned and waved to Signora Reggio. Then she ambled over. "Did you hear what I just heard?" she asked, her voice low.

Signora Reggio nodded and guided Gloria by the elbow to an open space near the stall for artisanal soaps. La Signora only trusted olive oil soaps to cleanse her face, and since at eighty-one she was nearly wrinkle free, she considered her choice the correct one. She might get some for her *nipote* Laura. Pregnancy was difficult on the skin. Perhaps she would get some for Nada as well, but not yet. She would wait.

"Did Tamara buy it? Our little plan?" Gloria asked. The question had nothing to do with baked goods or soap.

La Signora was almost offended. "Did she buy it? Is there anyone in Hopewell that can bluff better than I can?" She rolled her eyes. "People think they are so smart when they say the way to a man's heart is through his stomach. This is true. But even more important, the way to a happy relationship with a man is through his mother, or in this case, Aunt Myrna. You wait and see. Together we have designed the perfect strategy, and I am putting it into place with just the right touch."

Gloria sighed in relief. "I'd already mentioned to Ida Horowitz that I was worried we might have left it too late. But now with you two working your magic, I am convinced there is no reason to be nervous. Why, La Signora, you're practically Machiavellian, which I suppose is a testament to your worthy heritage. One thing else though," she said in all seriousness.

"What is that?"

"Remind me never to play cards with you."

CHAPTER TWENTY-ONE

WILL WAS COMING back with the coffee and baked goods when he saw Jessica headed to his dad's flower stand.

"Sorry I'm late," she apologized. "I had to do an emergency endoscopy on a rottweiler who'd swallowed a flash drive."

Will, with Buddy in tow, immediately rushed to her side. "Is the dog all right? Did you manage to get it out with tweezers?"

"Precisely, tweezers attached to the end of the scope. Good news all around except for the owner's pocketbook. And I'm not completely sure about the flash drive."

During her description, Will sipped on his lemonade with a serious expression, but as soon as the story concluded with a happy ending, he held up the paper bag. "There's a brownie for you in here, too." He stopped to let Jessica dig through the bag.

"Ooh, this looks wonderful," she cooed when she'd retrieved the brownie. "Nada's, I presume?" They continued walking toward the flower stand.

Will nodded before looking down at Buddy,

who was anxiously eyeing Jessica. "None for you, Bud. You've already had two of those gourmet dog treats."

Jessica winked. "Only the best for Buddy."

"Oh, speaking of the best for Buddy, I want to thank you—for calling Tamara." He took another sip. "Candy thought you'd be able to reassure her about the doggy date we've got later today—give her good advice and stuff. And what you said must have relaxed her because she didn't seem to freak out when I told her on the way to the market this morning that the two of us—Candy and me— would have to leave her alone for a little while during the whole thing. I know it sounds weird, but we just realized that this afternoon was the only time to get Aunt Myrna a birthday present."

"Actually, when Candy asked me to speak to her, I thought it was a good idea—for her, the dogs and you guys. Even more, I realized it was a way for me to reach out to Tamara. I can see how she's really been trying to get along these days."

"Yeah, she is." Will involuntarily brought his hand to his chest in his and Tamara's secret signal.

Jessica was about to take a bite when she stopped. "Hold on a sec. You know, I can't help wondering."

"What…what's that?" Will looked away, uneasy at how the conversation seemed to be shifting.

"You mentioned suddenly needing to get your aunt a birthday present? You and Candy aren't trying to cook up some scheme to get Tamara and my brother alone together today, are you, all while making sure Buddy and Sheba were okay in the process? I know your priorities, after all." Jessica looked at him suspiciously. She took a thoughtful bite and waited.

"Me? Plot something like that? I mean, it's great that Tamara and Drew are friends, but do you really think I'm the kind of person to be that devious?"

Jessica smiled. "No, but I can think of someone else who might be." Will held his breath at her remark and she hurriedly added, "Don't worry. Mum's the word. Anyway, it looks like we're here." She strode over to Briggs and planted a kiss on his outstretched cheek. His arms were otherwise occupied with four bunches of Asiatic lilies.

"Ah, always a welcome face," he said with a wide grin, and he smiled even wider when Will set down his coffee. "Just in time. I was starting to lag."

Will passed around the treats, and Jessica joined him in moving new bunches of flowers from buckets in the back to refill the emptying display in the front. All the commotion was too much for Buddy, and he wisely wriggled under a table.

A few minutes later, Candy showed up, and was put to work. Meanwhile, Briggs finished helping a mother of a bride-to-be pick out flowers for the bridal shower, as Tamara efficiently kept ringing up sales with the speed and accuracy of a snack vendor at a baseball game.

Which was when not only Drew, but Mayor Park arrived to join the organized chaos. The crowd went *ooh* and *aah*, and some moved timidly back with

Mayor Park's bull mastiff, Sheba, appearing on the scene.

Jessica knelt and pulled a dog treat from a pocket of her khaki pants. "'Some enchanted evening,'" she warbled, and Sheba, ever a sucker for a good love song, lay down and panted. Any fears that some shoppers had shown around such a large animal quickly dissipated.

Will peered under the table on the left of the stall. "Why don't you come out now, Buddy? I bet Jessica has something for you, too," he cooed. Sure enough, Buddy, ever guided by his nose, crawled out on his belly and gobbled another snack from Jessica.

Briggs chuckled. "Looks like you're performing your usual canine magic, Jess. But do you think you'll be able to handle the onslaught of shoppers with just me now that we're about to lose the rest of the team?"

"I'll try my best." She called out to Tamara, who was ringing up a sale. "How about I liberate you of that apron?"

Tamara thanked the customer and untied the butcher's apron. "It's all yours." She handed it over.

Jessica fished out the few remaining treats from her pocket. "You might as well take these for the car ride. And if I were you, I'd let Drew take Sheba in his truck while you bring Buddy separately. Just easier that way. He can serenade Sheba and keep her calm. I know he knows the songs from *The Music Man* because he played the con man Harold

Hill in the Hopewell Central High School production his senior year."

Tamara laughed. "Figures." She watched Jessica efficiently tie the apron strands. "I know I won't be able to deal with the dogs as well as you do, but I really appreciate what you said over the phone about handling the playdate."

"My pleasure. I don't know about a lot of things, but with dogs I'm aces."

"Well, it was still very kind of you to reach out. I don't mean to make your life complicated, you know. And I apologize if my presence makes things a bit awkward."

"We all have to learn to deal with things," Jessica conceded. "And I can tell you're trying. On top of which, you seem to be the only person who's able to keep my brother in line. You're good to have around—for all our sakes."

Tamara sniffed. "If you say so." She didn't say anything more but clapped her hands and turned to the others. "Troops, I think it's time to gather for our little doggy get-together. What do you say?"

Will had been silently listening to the conversation and had a smile on his face. "Aye, aye, Captain." He saluted and untied Buddy's long leash. Candy dumped out the water in the dog's bowl and stood at the ready.

Drew tore himself away from several female customers of varying generations and joined the group. "So, are we ready to roll?" he asked.

"Just about. And in case you were wondering,

I've got sandwiches and lemonade on the floor of the front passenger seat of my car. Courtesy of Myrna, naturally."

"Sounds about right." He then spoke to the mayor. "Insu, I know you have the planning committee meeting, but you're sure we can't tempt you with a free lunch and an hour in the sunshine?"

"'Fraid not. I just wanted to say that it's so nice of you to think of inviting Sheba. Lots of people are afraid because she's so big and looks ferocious, but at heart, she's just a pile of mush."

"I know that already from the dance class," Tamara agreed. "But to make sure we handle this with as little drama as possible, Jessica suggested Drew drive Sheba in his truck. Will, Candy and Buddy—you're in my car. And for our time at the field, I've already got Jessica's boom box and a CD of *Oklahoma!* It's the Broadway production with Hugh Jackman, apparently Sheba's favorite."

"Count on my sister to know all the tricks," Drew said.

Jessica bowed humbly. "I try—in more ways than one." She slanted Will and Candy a knowing look.

Briggs raised his hand. "See you later, guys."

"Have fun," Jessica encouraged.

"It'll all go as planned," Will said positively.

"I wish I had your confidence." Tamara didn't sound convinced.

Will bent his arm and put his hand to his chest. "Sometimes you just have to have faith that it'll all work out—more than you can imagine."

"I'M PROUD OF YOU," Drew said. "You only panicked for a few minutes when Candy and Will disappeared on their way into town."

Tamara exhaled a sigh of relief. "Will made sure to give me the heads-up earlier. Now that we actually talk to each other, it makes everything so much easier—including this little playdate. And speaking of making the playdate easier, the way you exhausted Sheba and Buddy with your dog version of 'Here We Go Round the Mulberry Bush' was pure genius—even if it did go on and on and on…" She fell back on the grass.

"It really helped that everyone kept singing and that both dogs got into the all-fall-down part."

Tamara rubbed her stomach. "I don't know who landed harder on me, Sheba or Will. Or maybe the combination of Will and Sheba. I don't think my ribs will ever be the same."

Drew dropped his pencil on his sketch pad. During the outing, he'd stolen a few moments here and there to draw Will and Candy playing hide-and-seek with the pets, and Tamara diligently taking guidance from Will on how to gain Buddy's confidence. She'd thanked them both with spontaneous hugs. Now, he was attempting to capture her peacefully reclining on the lawn. It had been the most relaxed fun he'd had in…in… Well, he couldn't remember when.

He glanced at the pile of sleeping dogs. Sheba was lying on her back, her legs splayed immodestly wide. Her lips were curled inside out, and her tongue was lolling to one side. A collection of wet tennis balls dotted the lawn nearby. They had quickly learned that Sheba's favorite activity besides listening to music was to collect tennis balls. Buddy, on the other hand, had his own way of sleeping. He was coiled in a tight doughnut shape, his nose buried in the long fur of his tail. After every few breaths, he exhaled contentedly.

There was something remarkably satisfying about staring at sleeping dogs, Drew thought, and he could have gladly let himself be mesmerized longer. But then he sensed Tamara shifting her position, and he moved his gaze in her direction.

She was looking at Drew. "I was so busy at the market and then nervous about the playdate, I forgot to ask you earlier."

"Ask me what? If I'd been thinking about you? If I was wondering if you'd been thinking about me? And so on…" He made a rolling motion with his hand and gave her a teasing smile.

"Are you inferring that you warrant a kiss for all your help and so on…"

He grinned. "I wouldn't say no."

She anchored herself up on one elbow and seemed to consider her options. Then she rubbed her chin and offered a half grin. "You know what they say. All good things come to those who wait."

"I could grow old waiting."

"Somehow, I don't think so." For a moment she looked like she was going to lean closer, but then she stopped. "Besides, the kids should be back soon.

I'm not sure I'm prepared to have my son see me kissing a stranger."

"I'm hardly a stranger."

She waved her hand. "You know what I mean."

"Do I?" Did he?

"Enough! Actually, what I wanted to know was where you were this morning. I'd expected you at the market sooner."

Drew was disappointed at the failure of his flirting, but he did his best not to show it. "Yeah, sorry about that. Pops asked me to take him to Laura's gallery. He wanted to see the setup and talk to her about the show."

"That's amazing! Does that mean he's going to donate paintings?"

"No guarantees, but I think he's moving in the right direction."

She nodded. "I'm so glad. I think it'd be good for Norman, even if he just loans a few. But I hope he realizes he'll have to decide soon. I mean, when's the opening?"

"A little under three weeks. Laura was pretty clear that she was flexible but basically, he's got one to two weeks max."

"Hmm. I'm not sure whether talking to him more will help, but I'll see what I can do."

"It couldn't hurt."

The dogs snored: Buddy a snuffle, Sheba more a long whistle with a whine at the end.

Tamara chuckled and fell back on the grass.

"It's good here, isn't it?" She closed her eyes and breathed in.

"You meant about being with the dogs?" he probed.

She paused. "That, too."

He looked at her lying kitty-corner to him, her fingertips almost touching his knee. He watched her plain T-shirt (not some designer number) rise and fall with each easy breath. Her wisps of dark hair fluttered in the mild breeze, and her long eyelashes cast spiky shadows on her freckled cheeks. He wanted to point out her freckles, but she'd probably deny she had any. She looked young and innocent, not the hard-bitten professional woman making it in a tough world.

He dropped his gaze. Tamara and Will had obviously started to form a closer relationship, but that still left things between him and Tamara up in the air. The two of them seemed to be performing a continual do-si-do around each other. But given their uncertain futures, didn't it make sense to remain simply breakfast buddies? That's what they had vowed to be in the beginning, not all that long ago. Yet, could he leave it at that, especially when breakfast seemed far from the only thing they shared?

Drew ditched his pad and pencil and lay on his back next to her. Now was the time to say something. Be forthcoming.

He opened his mouth. "I can truthfully say that I'm exhausted." So much for being forthcoming.

Tamara swiveled her head in his direction and placed a hand over her eyes to shade them from the sun. "Actually, about my not freaking out when Will and Candy left to buy Myrna a birthday present? I wasn't totally shocked 'cause I'd already talked to him about arrangements I'd made for her birthday, which, to be fair, stem from a suggestion Signora Reggio made. As you probably already know, when Signora Reggio makes a suggestion—"

"There's no saying no," Drew finished her sentence.

"Just keep that in mind when I explain to you your part in the plan."

Drew moaned.

"Oh, stop it. I'm not dragging you into something just for my own benefit."

"So you claim. And I'm supposed to believe that because…"

"I'm grass stained and smelling of disgusting liver treats. Is that the image of a totally selfish person?"

Drew smiled and inched over, still lying on his side. "Before you launch into the details of my contribution to this newest adventure, let me just say what I was thinking."

"Always dangerous."

Dare he? "You know how we say we should be absolutely truthful with each other?"

Both dogs snored extra loudly at that moment.

Tamara laughed. Drew shook his head.

"You were saying?" she prompted.

He cleared his throat. "This is going to sound strange coming from me."

She wiggled closer. "Is this where you tell me that you think you might've met the woman of your dreams?"

Had she guessed, or was she joking? He was pretty sure she was joking. But if she wasn't…

Which of course was when Will and Candy chose to make their grand entrance.

"Hey, everybody, we're back!" Will shouted. He and Candy came running across the lawn.

Drew turned and really groaned. Tamara sat up and patted her hair, pulling out blades of newly mowed grass. At the sound of Will's voice, Buddy instantly awoke. Sheba flipped to her stomach and barked in a low rumble. Both dogs went running toward the teens and almost bowled them over.

Drew sighed. "How quickly our babies abandon us." And how quickly the moment had passed for true confessions.

"It lets you know where you stand in the pecking order, that's for sure," Tamara admitted. She waved hello, seemingly having forgotten their truncated conversation. Her eyes were focused solely on Will, the affection apparent. "So, were you successful? Did you find the best present ever for your aunt?"

"We didn't do too bad," Candy said after they'd finished saying hello to the dogs.

"We got two, actually." Will reached into a shopping bag. "First, we got Aunt Myrna a gift certificate to Denise's salon. She's the owner of Earl the boxer. Anyway, it's for a pedicure."

"My mom says a girl can always use a pedicure," Candy explained.

"Wise words. And I can vouch for Denise's expertise myself," Tamara said.

"Then we stopped in at the library to ask Amy Pulaski about a book. She took us to the cart with the Members' Sale books and showed us some mysteries by this Australian writer—"

"The Jack Irish series by Peter Temple." Candy supplied the details.

Will agreed. "That's right. Anyway, she recommended we get the first book, *Bad Debts*. See?"

He waved the book around a little too quickly for Drew to read the title.

"Amy said if she likes it, she can always read the rest of the series," Will finished.

"Sounds like solid advice. I'd expect nothing less from Amy," Tamara agreed.

"Oh, and she said to say hello to you, Tamara. She didn't say that about you, Drew," Candy said.

"That's because she knows he's still mad that she beat him out to be high school valedictorian," Tamara informed them.

"No, I'm not," he argued. Well, maybe a little.

Will dropped down on one knee and cuddled both dogs again. "Were you guys good? I bet you were the best for Momara and Drew, weren't you?" He buried his head between the two dogs' muzzles.

"Momara?" Drew asked.

"That's my new name for Tamara—Mom and Tamara combined. Kinda silly." Will lifted his fist in Tamara's direction, halfway to their signal.

She beamed. "We landed on it together last night. It's only to be used sparingly—like with Buddy. But enough about that. Mayor Park should be finished with his meeting pretty soon, and we should return Sheba. Maybe you guys could round up the dogs while Drew and I gather the rest of the stuff up. Then I'll take you to Teddy Sweet for ice cream like I promised."

As Will and Candy marched to the nearby picnic table to retrieve the leashes, Drew noticed how Candy poked Will in the ribs with her elbow. He glanced at Tamara and whispered, "Tell me I'm just seeing things. But I could swear there's something more than two birthday presents going on."

"Maybe true love?" she joked. "Though, somehow I doubt it."

If she only knew.

CHAPTER TWENTY-TWO

THE FOLLOWING FRIDAY MORNING, Tamara dropped off Will at tennis before swinging by Chubbie's to pick up Drew. She opened the front passenger door when she spotted him waiting outside. He didn't look all that enthusiastic. "No need to be so sullen," she admonished him. "This is for a good cause. Making Myrna happy will make everyone happier."

Speaking of Myrna… Tamara let Drew know that Gloria Pulaski had volunteered to help out by inviting Myrna to a birthday lunch today as well. (Amazing how these Hopewell women seemed to stick together!)

"Apparently, Gloria's chicken salad is legendary, and she reserves it for only a chosen few," Tamara explained. "Needless to say, Myrna was tickled pink when she informed us at dinner last night."

"Little did she know," Drew supplied the obvious.

"Exactly. I even reminded her about Norman's invitation to take her to Daniel's Restaurant in Lambertville this evening, saying she clearly was a lucky birthday girl. At which point, Will piped up and mentioned how he'd offered to spend Saturday together."

"So, I'm not the only one you've corralled into your plans, am I?"

"If I said you were the most important person, would that make you feel better?" She didn't give him a chance to say *yes*. "Just remember. All these carefully orchestrated plans mean Signora Reggio can give us our cooking lesson today, and tomorrow I'll be free to ready the house for the celebration later in the evening. So hop in and we can get going."

Drew slipped into the passenger seat, balancing a cardboard take-out holder on his lap. "I'll have you know I gave up eggs over easy for this," he complained. "But at least, all is not lost." He nodded at a white bakery bag.

Tamara poked open the top. "Freshly baked scones. You are the most important person in this endeavor after all."

He smiled, placated.

Then she looked up, concerned. "You got one for Signora Reggio, I hope?"

"Oh, ye of little faith. Of course I got one for Signora Reggio! The only person who scares me more than Mrs. Horowitz is Laura's *nonna*."

La Signora lived on the first floor of a two-family house close to the farmers' market. (Where else!) The exterior of the 1940s dwelling was stucco. A screened-in porch greeted visitors, and the roof of the porch served as the base of the top floor's open balcony. The south side along the driveway provided a sunny spot for growing tomatoes, basil, oregano and pepper plants.

Tamara parked the car in front. Drew was contentedly drinking coffee and leaning against the passenger door. "So, you remember the drill, right?" she asked. "This morning we make of the meat sauce, and this evening we finish everything up."

Drew placed the to-go cup in the holder. "You can make all the plans and drills you want—whatever makes you happy. But just so you know, my response is…" He sang slightly off-key in Italian. "Loosely translated, it means, I talk of love in my dreams."

Tamara's eyes grew wide. "What?"

"What do you mean *what*? I'm not allowed to listen to opera on my phone? It's *The Marriage of Figaro*, by the way—my form of preparation for today's Italian-oriented activities."

Tamara tried to be cool, but why did he choose to recite that particular line? "I gotta say—just being candid—"

"Absolutely, it's part of our breakfast buddy pact."

Hmm. The old breakfast buddy thing. Well, there was being candid and then there was being candid. "I'm just surprised you felt the need to prepare," was the best Tamara could manage.

If she were being truly honest, she'd admit she'd watched numerous YouTube videos on making lasagna.

But she wasn't being totally honest, was she? About a whole bunch of things.

SIGNORA REGGIO PUT Tamara to work dipping fresh tomatoes into a pot of boiling water to loosen the skins. ("No more than two minutes! Two minutes!") Next, Drew ran them under cool water before peeling them. The skins came off easily. At which point, La Signora cored and seeded the tomatoes.

"The key to a good ragù is fresh ingredients," she informed her apprentices. "Now, who wants to break up the tomatoes with their hands while the other chops the onion?"

Both sets of hands went up.

"You, Tamara, you will do the tomatoes. I show you how." La Signora dunked her hands into the large stainless-steel bowl holding the tomatoes and squeezed the pulp until it broke into bits. Then she wiped her hands on the towel wrapped around her waist. "Tamara, I will let you finish this step. While you, Drew, will do the chopping of the onions. From what I have been told, you are handy at fixing things around the house. Therefore, I believe I can trust you with sharp implements." She held up a large chef's knife with terrifying gusto. "You know the proper technique?"

"Why don't you show me," Drew wisely deferred.

Tamara looked up from smashing the peeled tomatoes—a surprisingly rewarding exercise—and bit back a smile. Drew—big, outdoorsy Drew

Trombo—was wearing a floral apron. The ruffled edges and cabbage-rose print covering his faded black T-shirt was wildly feminine. She had expected him to make some silly joke when he was handed the overtly frilly garment. Instead, he'd good-naturedly tied the strings into a bow and stood ready for action.

That Drew was able to dice the yellow onion into precise pieces after getting his brief instructions was less surprising. The man clearly handled tools with finesse.

Luckily the next step required Tamara's full attention. La Signora pointed to a large cast-iron casserole dish on the stove, where she was heating olive oil and butter. She ordered Drew to dump in the chopped onions. Tamara's job was to sauté the mixture over medium heat. When the onions had properly wilted ("No browning! Never!"), Tamara, under close supervision, added ground meat to brown, followed by the tomatoes, wine, milk and nutmeg. From then on, it was a question of simmering the ingredients on a low heat.

"So, when do we get to layer the whole thing? Tamara mentioned something about this evening, but really?" Drew asked.

Signora Reggio looked at him in horror. "The ragù, it takes five hours to cook. That is why we started in the morning and why you will return later. At which time, we will also make the fresh pasta. Though I think I will prepare ahead of time the béchamel sauce—the traditional element in Emilia-Romagna, where I come from."

"What's béchamel?" Drew whispered to Tamara.

She covered her mouth. "I believe it's a white sauce made with milk and flour."

"Drew, I need you here in the kitchen at six. You, Mr. Muscle Big Man, you will have the job of rolling out the pasta dough. Tamara, you do not need to come until six thirty, at which point the dough will be ready. You will be in charge of layering all the ingredients. And do not be late—either of you—if you want to stay on my good side."

"We'll be on time," they said simultaneously.

"Good. Now go practice your piano before you see Mrs. Horowitz. I wouldn't want you to disappoint her."

LA SIGNORA SHOOED them out the door before going to the wall phone in the kitchen. (Hers was olive green. Everyone above a certain age in Hopewell still had a landline.)

Mrs. Horowitz picked up immediately. "A success?"

"It went better than I expected."

"You are being kind. I can tell."

"It is true. But my kitchen will survive. I sent them away so that they would practice before coming to see you."

"Good. They will be too busy to think about what's really going on. And they're supposed to come back to your place tonight?"

"Exactly." Signora Reggio smiled and rubbed her neck. "After tonight's cooking session, there is nothing more I can do. The outcome will be in the hands of the gods and my lasagna."

CHAPTER TWENTY-THREE

TAMARA DIDN'T SLEEP well that night. She kept thinking about the lasagna. More like obsessing about the lasagna.

She kept referring to the index card with Signora Reggio's reheating directions. There was also a second card with the directions for making a vinaigrette for the salad. Tamara was worried that even with these detailed instructions, there was a chance she'd mess up.

On a positive note, at the end of the day's work, La Signora had welcomed Tamara into the family, so to speak. "Sharing the kitchen like this is the greatest pleasure," she had said after pouring Tamara and Drew generous portions of the sweet Italian dessert wine vin santo. "It is like we are related now. I insist you call me Nonna, which means Grandma."

It was a loving gesture that had warmed Tamara's stomach as much as the alcohol. And she kept thinking about it as she lay in bed that night. She also kept picturing Drew in that flowery apron kneading the flour and egg to make the fresh pasta.

Even though Signora Reggio's instructions had been to come at six thirty, Tamara had figured there was no harm in showing up early. No harm indeed! She got to admire Drew's powerful forearms as he mixed and rolled out the combination of flour and egg. Of course, it also meant that she got to fish out the large rectangles of pasta dough after they'd cooked in boiling water and lay them on towels. Granted, Drew did most of the work since his command of the large tongs far exceeded hers, but it was fun to share.

And simply watching him in action was entertaining enough. Perhaps *entertaining* was too mild a word, she admitted. He took it in stride when Nonna corrected his use of the long rolling pin. And he laughed at his initial attempts at rolling the dough into thin, neat rectangles. ("It looks more like the map of South America than a lasagna noodle," he'd announced in mock horror. "I'd say roadkill is more like it," Tamara had commented after close inspection.)

He was a good guy, she thought. More than a good guy. Decent, helpful, self-effacing, smart and really, really attractive.

No wonder her brain wouldn't shut off.

DREW ALSO TOSSED and turned. He'd been given two tasks: storing the cooked lasagna in Pops's fridge and picking up the cake and salad greens at the farmers' market the next morning. Theoretically, everything was under control.

The hard part would be letting his dad in on the surprise. The harder part would be getting him to keep it a secret from Myrna. Fortuitously, Norman's leg was getting better and better, and the doctor had said he needed the boot only on occasion. As long as he sat whenever possible, he was even cleared to work. Which meant that with Jessica away for the long weekend, Norman was at the veterinary clinic—and out of direct communication with Myrna. To be on the safe side though, Drew "misplaced" Norman's cell phone, checking it occasionally to make sure nothing crucial was left unanswered.

But all these machinations weren't what kept him awake. For whatever reason, Signora Reggio had had to take a phone call from Gloria Pulaski during the evening lasagna-making session. "The bedroom phone will be more private. You can hang up this kitchen phone when I tell you to," she'd announced.

"Should we wait until you come back to continue?" Tamara had asked.

"No, no," La Signora had insisted as she headed out of the kitchen. "You have it all under control."

Famous last words, Drew couldn't help thinking. Tamara, ever the good student, had mastered the proper layering technique. But it was the way she did the layering! Drew kept picturing her nose inches from the pan. She'd extended and bowed her lithe upper arms with the grace of a prima ballerina, letting her wrists undulate as she'd carefully spread the ingredients with a spatula. And she breathed through her slightly open mouth, a picture of utter concentration, as she carefully added the meat sauce, fresh pasta, grated Parmesan and rich béchamel.

Drew had been struck—heck, he was still struck now as he lay in bed—by the picture of her deep brown eyes and quick smile. If he hadn't been convinced that Signora Reggio was secretly eyeing them from the other room, he would have chanced a kiss—something highly uncharacteristic for mere breakfast buddies.

TAMARA AND DREW may have had restless nights. Not so Will. Theoretically, Myrna had left him home with Tamara while she went on her dinner date with Dr. Trombo. But of course Tamara and Drew were up to their elbows in lasagna making at Signora Reggio's. Will chuckled at the thought. The more Will saw of Drew, the more he realized that Drew was a good guy—a good guy who was helping Tamara loosen up. Will was all in favor of that. Just look how successful the doggy playdate had been.

And he was especially in favor of the fact that Tamara had said that at fourteen, he was old enough to remain by himself for a few hours that Friday evening—provided he stayed off the internet and texted her regularly. ("You're starting to sound like Aunt Myrna," he'd kidded her. She'd nodded. "I'm taking that as a compliment.")

She'd even ordered him his favorite take-out

dinner—pepperoni pizza. Will had found his new independence exhilarating—and tiring, and he'd slept as only an exhausted teenager can.

On Saturday he had the added responsibility of keeping Aunt Myrna out of the house, and the sense of growing up gave him more confidence. He felt like he was doing something nice for his aunt, not just fulfilling an obligation. And she seemed to get a kick out of spending some quality time with him. They went to the latest Superheroes movie. ("Long," was Will's opinion. "Loud," was Aunt Myrna's.) Afterward, feeling the need to stretch their legs, they took a leisurely walk along the canal, counting the number of baby ducks floating on the water. And because they'd had some exercise, a snack was absolutely essential. Teddy Sweet beckoned, and, for once, Aunt Myrna let Will have three scoops. She was feeling mellow.

"This is the best birthday present a gal could ask for," Aunt Myrna said as she squeezed his shoulders. (That part wasn't so great because they were out in public. But, oh well. It was for a good cause.)

Just you wait, Will thought. *Just wait for your present to come.*

As soon as Myrna parked by the barn, Will jumped out of the car. "It's been a long afternoon, Aunt Myrna, and…and I… I…have to use the bathroom—if you know what I mean." He raced toward the kitchen door.

"Do you need me to unlock it?" she called out as she gathered her purse from the back seat.

"No, I've got my key," he shouted, already tripping over the threshold.

Myrna shook her head and laughed. Some things never changed.

The small red stones of the drive crunched under her footsteps as she headed to the kitchen door. Some other things never changed either—like Will forgetting to close the door. "Will, you might have been in a hurry, but—"

"Surprise!"

Myrna came to an abrupt halt. Mostly because a large bunch of helium balloons blocked her view. "What the—"

"Happy birthday!" Will shouted.

Buddy barked.

Will pushed the balloons into Myrna's free hand. "These are for you. I was so afraid you'd find out. We all were."

Myrna tried to get a grip on the balloons, which was not easy when Buddy was dancing around her feet. "Oh, my goodness. Let me just put my bag down on the chair and get my breath."

"I'll take your purse," came another voice.

"And I'll relieve you of those balloons, if that makes life easier," came another.

Myrna let her burdens be lifted and sat. Will and Buddy, but also Tamara, Drew, Norman and Candy crowded around her. She gazed at the unexpected throng. "I never guessed…" She was at a loss for words.

Buddy was so excited he jumped up and put his front paws on Myrna's lap. "Oh, Buddy, Buddy, thank you for the surprise, but you shouldn't jump on people. Still…" She sniffed and wiped the corner of her eye. "Could somebody pass me a treat? He clearly needs one." She held out her hand.

"Here you are, Ms. Longfellow," Candy said with authority. "He's been excited all afternoon. He could sense something was in the works."

"Have you been excited, Buddy?" Myrna fed him one of his favorite liver treats. She wiped her nose. And that's when it hit her—not the smell of liver on her fingers, but something far more appealing. "Is that…is that…?"

"Lasagna," Will announced. "Tamara made you lasagna for a surprise birthday dinner. Can you believe it?"

Myrna blinked. "Frankly, no." Everyone laughed. She looked around the tight huddle and located Tamara, who was hanging back. "Did you really make dinner?"

Will grabbed Tamara's hand and pushed her forward. "Tell her."

Tamara waved her hands nervously. "Yes, but with a lot of help. From Nonna mostly, Signora Reggio, that is. She was the one who first suggested the idea and who guided me through everything. It was just amazing. But I also couldn't have done it without Drew's help, and of course Nada Bellona. She's the dessert maven."

"But still." Myrna was in shock. "You cooked. I always assumed you didn't know how."

"You're right. I'm normally a mess in the kitchen, but it's your birthday. What better occasion to learn how?" Tamara replied.

Will reached down and encouraged his aunt to get up. "Come to the living room now, please. Candy and I have some things for you to open."

"And we all get to toast the birthday girl. Lemonade for the underage crowd and, courtesy of Mr. Portobello, prosecco for the adults," Drew announced with a flourish.

"Then by all means." Myrna rose to her feet and let herself be escorted to the living room. "This was really your idea, wasn't it?" she whispered when Norman got nearby.

"On the contrary, it was all Tamara's. She even organized Drew to pick up Candy and me. Letting himself be ordered around is not his usual style, I'll have you know," Norman remarked.

"Maybe it's a question of who's doing the ordering?" she suggested.

He nodded. "You could be right."

What was definitely right was the triumph of Will and Candy's presents. "I can't wait to get the pedicure," Myrna said as soon as she saw the gift certificate. "Will insisted I buy a new pair of sandals today when we were out together, and now I know why."

Will beamed. He was sitting on the footstool by the rocking chair where his aunt was seated. Buddy was curled up at his feet and looked very pleased since Myrna had passed him the wrapping paper.

"Amy Pulaski recommended it," Candy piped up as Myrna started to open the second gift.

"My word, a mystery book! If Amy recommended it, it must be good." Myrna scanned the blurb on the back cover. "I've never read anything from Australia. I'm sure I'll love it. Thank you both very much. It was so thoughtful." She had to stop because the tears were starting to come again, and Myrna never cried in front of people. Ever.

"And now that the gift giving is over, and we all have a drink in hand, I think it's time for an early dinner. I've followed Nonna's cooking directions to a T, and I wouldn't want to ruin things at this point," Tamara declared.

A cream-colored damask tablecloth covered the dining room table. "Why, we haven't had the occasion to use this in a long while," Myrna exclaimed as she thumbed a corner. It was one of the few things she had left from her failed early marriage.

"I hope you don't mind. I found it in the bottom drawer of the kitchen hutch. I decided it needed a bit of a touch-up, but I've never ironed something so big in my whole life. What a chore!" Tamara admitted.

"You iron?"

"I don't usually advertise that skill set, but yes."

Myrna surveyed how Tamara had set the table

with the everyday crockery and flatware and wine-glasses that weren't theirs. ("From my house," Norman would later tell her.) A large glass bowl—one of Myrna's finds from the Lambertville flea market—contained three tea lights floating in water. The girl was trying, the girl was really trying, Myrna told herself.

"Well, I'm ready for this lasagna if nobody else is," she pronounced. "I presume this is my seat?" she thought to ask before taking the chair at the head of the table.

"Of course. Your place is always at the head," Tamara replied, the tone of her voice sincere. Clearly, she and Myrna had evolved to a truce of sorts, not necessarily an easy one, but a truce, nonetheless. "Now if everyone will be seated, we'll serve the lasagna family style. After that there's salad and dessert—so don't forget to leave room." She quickly headed for the kitchen.

"I'll come get the wine." Drew followed her.

Myrna beamed. She directed Will to sit on her left, with Candy next to him. Norman sat to her right.

"Who do you think is more nervous? Tamara or Drew?" Norman asked.

Myrna smiled wisely. "They're both adorable." Her tone was sincere as well. "Let's leave it at that."

All during the meal, the conversation flowed freely. Myrna hadn't heard so much laughter in the house in…well…forever. She eyed Tamara at the other end of the table, smiling as Will told her the plot of the movie that he and Myrna had seen that afternoon.

And even though Norman was fading after a long day, she could see the warmth that he had for his son, and the way Drew listened for probably the umpteenth time while his father told some story about how he and Mr. Mason once drove all the way to Watkins Glen, New York, back when there was a Formula 1 race there. And how it rained the whole time, and their tent leaked.

And goodness, there was Candy laughing and answering questions about her job at Chubbie's.

And Buddy? Sweet, sweet Buddy. Every member of the table was sneaking him tidbits. He particularly liked the crusty corners of the lasagna.

In the end, after they'd sung "Happy Birthday" over Nada's incredible plum cake, Myrna tapped her wineglass with her dessert spoon and rose to have the last word. "Quiet everyone," she ordered. And they were.

"I want to thank you all for such a wonderful birthday celebration. I had no idea."

"For true, Aunt Myrna?" Will asked.

Myrna beamed at the boy. "For true, Will." Then she raised her glass. "I realize it was a group effort, and I want to acknowledge all your contributions, including Drew, who seemed to have had a hand in all aspects."

"Hear, hear," went around the table.

"But above all, for making this joyous celebration happen, which I know was not an easy feat, I want to thank Tamara. I never thought I'd be eating a lasagna made by you—" Candy snickered until she caught Myrna's stern gaze "—but I can honestly say it's the best lasagna I've ever eaten, and not just because it was delicious—which it was. No, it's the best because it was made with caring and…and, while you may not realize it, with love. I know we've had our moments, but I'd like to think that we're moving on—to better things." She had to pause so she could regroup. "And for that, I want to thank you from the bottom of my heart." She raised her glass higher. "To Tamara—and all her helpers around the table," she said, and everyone joined in and drank.

From the other end of the table Myrna could see Tamara blush. And she watched her nod her head in thanks before she made some excuse and rushed to the kitchen.

"Is everything all right?" Will asked Candy.

"Some people don't like to cry in public. Just ask your aunt," Candy informed him.

No fool, that girl.

SOON, TAMARA WAS BACK. "I just realized I never offered any coffee. I just put a pot up. Any takers?" She carried in the sugar bowl from the kitchen table and a small creamer (another flea market find).

"Why don't you sit down for a change and allow me to take the orders," Drew suggested. "And Candy, you're the experienced waitress here. I know I can trust you to help me out."

Tamara let the others do the work while she

sniffed quietly and rubbed her nose with a tissue she'd snagged in the kitchen. "I am a little tired, I must admit," she said. "But it's been so much fun. Really. I don't know if it's Hopewell or what, but this place must be special..."

"Looks like the big-city gal has become converted to the small-town way of life," Myrna said.

"Thanks to everyone in town and especially you guys—even if it's been a learning experience on my part." She gave Myrna a knowing glance before addressing the whole table. "And it's been a real eye-opener to discover all the great things here in Hopewell."

"Like Teddy Sweet," Will volunteered.

"For sure," Tamara laughed. "And of course, Chubbie's."

"Ballroom dance classes," Drew said when he reentered. He didn't sound completely sardonic.

"Amy Pulaski and the wonderful way she runs the library," Candy suggested as she passed around the coffee cups.

"The farmers' market and Nada's baking," Norman said. He stole a corner off the remaining cake on the table.

"Coach Keith and the tennis program," Will said, not to be outdone.

"You know what?" Tamara made a circle motion with her hand. "All this talk right now, all your suggestions, have me thinking. What about a short TV feature story on all Hopewell has to offer? Say, for someone looking for a day trip. It could run on the local Philadelphia news. What do you think? Let more people in on a good thing. In fact, you probably don't remember, Candy, but you actually planted the seed for this idea a while back—when you told me about all the things to do in Hopewell."

"I don't really remember. I say a lot of stuff. But you think you could make it happen? Get something like that on the air?" Candy asked.

"I may be persona non grata at my station in Phoenix, but I bet a short feature for the Philadelphia affiliate wouldn't go unwanted—not with my credentials and not if I offered to supply it for free. I think there's a good chance we can convince them."

"But how are you going to do it? I mean how can you produce the story? We don't have a local TV crew, let alone sound people, an editor and I don't know who else would be involved," Norman pointed out.

Tamara banged the table with the heels of her palms. Buddy stirred from his slumbering position and poked his head out from under the table. "Oh, Buddy, I'm so sorry. I didn't mean to scare you. I just got excited. Here." She broke off a mouthful of cake.

"I think we could make it work, Norman," she explained. "This is off the top of my head, but bear with me. Since it'd be for the Philly station, the pitch would be that now that it's summer, it's the perfect time for day trips to the surrounding countryside. Most people already know the more famous sites in Bucks County—the theater in New Hope and the fancy boutiques in Doylestown. But what about the charming, less-well-known towns in this picturesque part of Pennsylvania—sorry for the alliteration—for instance, Hopewell."

"I like the idea." Myrna nodded. "And what would it focus on? Restaurants? Shops?"

"Food, for starters. Chubbie's and Teddy Sweet. But we'd highlight Laura's art gallery and the antique shops. The farmers' market."

"You could suggest a stop at the library for more ideas. See my archnemesis Amy," Drew said.

Tamara grinned and nodded. "Especially if the visitor plans to stay some extra days. And if so, the possibilities are endless—free classes like ballroom dancing, tennis programs—or you could test your mettle and go skydiving. But even just one day provides ample opportunity to enjoy the beautiful scenery. Bike or walk along the canal's towpath. Stop to sketch some of the charming scenes. We could include brief testimonials from some of the local residents and showcase others in the scenes."

"But what about the technical side? You need to consider that," Norman mentioned.

"You're right. I'd do the narration. As to videography, Amy Pulaski is a pro already. I've seen her stuff on the library's website, and it's terrific."

"A veritable superwoman," Drew conceded.

Tamara squeezed his hand. "I'm proud of you, Drew. There wasn't a touch of irony to your words—well, maybe a touch." Her hand rested in his for several seconds longer than necessary. She hastily removed it and went on. "And, Will, with your superior computer knowledge, you can help with the editing. Wouldn't it be great for the two of us to work together?" He nodded enthusiastically.

She stopped, abruptly losing her chain of thought. *Focus on the piece*, she told herself, *not how Drew's hand had felt*. She cleared her throat. "But I think we should first make a short version of what the story would entail, a teaser, so to speak. That way the station manager will have something concrete to evaluate."

"Don't forget to check with the mayor and, of course, Gloria Pulaski," Myrna reminded her.

Tamara nodded. "Absolutely. The heartbeat of Hopewell."

"And with that, I think we've found the title of the feature. 'The Heartbeat of Hopewell,'" Drew declared. "I don't know about anyone else, but I think this calls for another round of prosecco."

CHAPTER TWENTY-FOUR

AFTER THEY ALL adjourned from the dining room, Tamara volunteered herself for cleanup duty, shooing the rest of the party to the living room. Most of the dishes and cutlery went into the dishwasher, but she stood at the sink washing the pots and pans. Norman had disobeyed her orders and was firmly in control of the drying. "That was a wonderful idea on your part, the surprise dinner and all," he said. "I can't believe Drew helped out, too. Normally, he runs away from this type of family get-together."

"I don't think he had much choice. Nonna and I—mostly me—didn't give him any alternative. And, really, don't sell him short, Norman. You should have seen him kneading the dough for the fresh pasta."

If Norman noticed Tamara's glassy stare out the kitchen window as she spoke, he didn't comment on it. Instead, he bit back a smile.

She finished rinsing the cake platter and put it in the drainer. Norman lifted it out and began drying. "You know, events like these remind me again of the importance of family and of sharing. I've given more thought to Vivian's paintings, by the way." He wiped both sides of the platter dry and rested it on the countertop. "I've come around and decided to donate some of her work to the show. Not all, mind you, but some."

Tamara stopped washing. "That's wonderful."

"You were right. I want other people to see the pieces that are really dear to me. I'd be able to show off her vision to the world and get to hear their reactions. And I think that's the lesson Vivian wanted me to learn. Not to be afraid to open myself up, to share what's most important to me and, in the process, maybe find out more about myself and the world around me."

"I think you're being incredibly generous, Norman. And brave. It's not easy to let go even if you know it's the right thing to do." She paused, lost for a moment in her own thoughts. "If you want, I can call Laura for you. I'll even come to the house when you show her Vivian's works. She can help you decide what things to contribute. She's the expert after all."

"It's not necessary, but thank you." Norman leaned over and gave Tamara a peck on her cheek. "I believe it's important that I be the one to contact her, and if you're free, wonderful. If not, I'm strong enough to face her myself."

She grinned and rubbed the spot on her cheek with the soapy back of her hand.

"So, now that I've made the big leap about my family, I'm going to keep being bold," he went on.

"At the risk of upsetting you, I want to bring up the subject of your family. Hear me out. That's all I ask."

Norman waited until she nodded.

"Have you given any more thought to seeing them?" he asked. "I believe you said you're originally from Philadelphia. It'd be an easy trip into the city."

Tamara dried her hands on the striped apron she was wearing. (No florals in Myrna's kitchen.) She wet her lips. "I gotta admit that tonight made me jealous of everything that you all have—that sense of love and security—not to mention the bouts of silliness. Even the little tensions. And I know you mean well, Norman, but you've got to understand. I never had any of that—ever. My mother and my father—they had nothing like the kind of relationship you had with Vivian. And my father made it abundantly clear to me that I wasn't fit to be a mother because I'd made all the wrong choices, made too many mistakes. No surprise that I felt like I was unlovable."

Norman looked shocked. "I'm so sorry."

"I somehow managed to graduate from high school, but after I had Will… I had real difficulty coping. Being a mother was overwhelming, and I had nothing in my family life to draw on. Like I mentioned the other day, Briggs and Myrna were there to help, but still… Well, you know the rest. Myrna and Briggs took full custody, and I went off to college. End of story." She shook her head before eking out a brave smile. "Besides, when I checked online recently, I saw that my father had died. So, there's no hope of reconciliation there." She didn't mention that she'd only decided to check on her parents after their earlier talk.

Norman sighed. "I can't imagine going through all that. And I don't mean to pry or stick my nose in where it's not wanted—so stop me at any time if you want. It's just that I finally realized that unless I found peace with the past, I would never be able to move on. I learned I had to face my fears. Now that I've done that—or tried to do that—I am finally able to really appreciate the happiness that surrounds me."

He gently placed a hand atop hers. "I want you to have all the happiness you deserve. Especially after seeing the events this evening, I can tell you've found contentment in your growing relationship with Will, the Longfellows in general—dare I say, Myrna, too—besides the rest of Hopewell. But I think there's more out there for you—including Drew." He let the last name hang in the air. Then he added, "So don't sell yourself short. Never think you are unlovable. And I believe to achieve that peace of mind, you must reconcile with your past— either truly put it to bed or bring it into your future. Your mother was and still is your mother. And don't forget, she's Will's only grandmother."

Before tonight, Tamara would have brushed off Norman's advice without giving it a thought. But the closeness of the evening had her second-guessing such an impulse, and his words about Will especially hit home. She nodded. "I'll take into consideration what you've said, Norman. And if I decide to do anything, it'll only be after I consult Will."

"As it should be."

No sooner had Norman departed for the living room than Myrna came in. She was carrying the tablecloth and napkins, which she deposited in the laundry room off the side of the kitchen.

"We could've done that," Tamara said. "The whole idea was for you to sit and enjoy yourself. You're the birthday girl after all."

"Unfortunately, or fortunately, depending on your point of view, I wasn't born to sit around—which is no comment on everything you've done. I thoroughly enjoyed myself, and I can't thank you enough. It was totally unnecessary."

"Of course it was necessary. It's your birthday. And besides, it was a group effort."

"Don't be so modest. You didn't get to be the confident career girl by being self-effacing."

"News alert. I'm confident, but only when it comes to my career." Tamara squeezed the sponge. She watched the water dribble between her fingers and onto the apron.

Myrna pulled out a chair. "Why don't you sit with me at the kitchen table. I have something to say." She patted the chair next to hers.

Tamara liberated herself of the sponge and apron. Then she sat. "Is this okay?"

"It's more than okay," Myrna assured her. "Tamara, you and I haven't always seen eye to eye. I think that's fair to say."

Tamara clenched her hands.

"Things are better, but they're still not ideal. Seeing as you're Will's mother, and Will is my nephew's son, we can't go on like this."

"Well, we could. But it would be awkward."

Myrna set her mouth. "Awkward is all right from time to time but not for a long-term relationship. And since we're part of the same family, we're in a long-term relationship."

"I'm sorry if I haven't been more open, more accepting of your suggestions," Tamara offered.

Myrna shook her head. "Don't go assuming it's all your fault. I'm sorry, too—that I haven't been more accommodating. We're talking a two-way street. As I see it, there're a couple of fundamental issues we need to talk about. One—" she held up an index finger "—I'll always feel that I don't deserve the family that miraculously came my way. That somehow, I was a part of something special that was rightly yours." She saw Tamara try to speak and she put up her other hand. "Wait. I haven't finished. And two—" she held up a second finger "—you may have worked on patching things up with Will, but you're still not willing to forgive yourself for abandoning your baby, even if you believed back then that it was the right decision to make. Don't deny it either—I know you admitted as much to Briggs in the first days after you arrived. Am I being open enough?"

Tamara studied her knuckles. She remembered Briggs pointing it out to her after she'd forgotten to pick up Will after tennis. So much had happened since then. She cocked her head before lifting her chin. "I'd say you're being pretty darn open. So, where do we go from here?"

Myrna reached out and took Tamara's tense fist in her larger hand. "We tell ourselves that those feelings of doubt are utter hogwash," Myrna continued. "That we made choices that at the time we were convinced were the best for everybody, including Will. But we also recognize that in times of weakness, these doubts and anxieties are going to rear their ugly heads."

Tamara's fingers gradually relaxed under Myrna's grip, which softened in turn. "And then what do we do? When the anxieties seem too big to cope with?" She dropped her face again as if not wanting to risk rejection.

"We turn to each other for guidance and reassurance. Because that's what families do. They may kick and scream on occasion, but when the going gets tough, they're there for each other. So, tell me. What do you think?" She lifted Tamara's chin with her other hand and looked at her directly. "Would you like that?"

Tamara sniffed and nodded. "I'm going to cry, and I never cry."

"Neither do I, but there's a first time for everything." Myrna reached across the table for the box of tissues. "Here. Take one. Take two, even. And now, let's agree going forward that we'll each try to forgive ourselves and accept each other, even though we will possibly not agree at all times—"

"Possibly?" Tamara blew her nose loudly.

"Okay, probably. But now that we've gotten this far, how about you call me Aunt Myrna and not just Myrna?"

"I've never had an aunt before."

"Well, now you do. If Signora Reggio can be your *nonna*, I have just as much right to be your aunt— more, in fact. Now, when you feel ready, come join the party." Myrna smiled and pushed her chair back on the hardwood floor. The scraping noise woke up Buddy. Myrna hadn't realized the dog was sleeping under the table. "And you, Buddy, come with me. Will must be wondering where you are." She rose and was just about to pass through the doorway when Drew came wandering in with a glass of wine.

He stepped aside for Myrna. "I realized that the chef was without any libation. I came to remedy that fact." He offered an absolutely magical grin. Then he frowned when he saw Tamara wiping away tears. He turned to Myrna for insight. "Is everything all right?"

She patted him on the shoulder. "Not to worry. We've just come to realize that I've acquired a third member of the family who's pretty great." She looked down at Buddy, who was waiting patiently by the jar of dog treats. She lifted the lid and rewarded his polite begging. "Make that four." Buddy trailed obediently after Myrna as she left the kitchen.

DREW RESTED THE glass on the kitchen table and knelt next to Tamara. "Are you all right? I was worried." He put his hands on her shoulders. "Pops told me the good news about the paintings, but then he said that he'd talked to you about reconnecting with your mother. I mean, maybe it's a good idea, but I hope he didn't upset you."

Tamara didn't pull away. "First your dad. Now Myrna."

"She didn't say something she shouldn't have, did she?" His protective instincts had kicked in but good.

"No, just the opposite. Still, I didn't expect it." She slumped against him.

Her shoulders, which he normally thought of as so firm, so determined, felt fragile. He worried that touching her was too much. "Well, I'm glad that Myrna behaved herself. And I promise you that I won't bring up the issue of your mom again. I'll even tell Pops to lay off. If you're ever ready, you'll know."

"Do you think there'll ever come the perfect time?"

"Maybe not perfect. But you'll know when to decide."

"I'll need to discuss it with Will first, and if

the time comes—that's a big if—I'll need moral backup, you know." She raised her head and looked into his eyes.

"You've got it." He smiled. The corners of his eyes crinkled. "I'll be with you all the way. Don't forget—I'm your wingman. I'll drive us, and I'm sure that Pops will insist on coming along."

"It's a tempting offer. I don't know how to thank you enough."

"I can think of a way." There, he'd said it. Drew lowered his head slowly. "I don't want to overstep my bounds, or exploit you in a moment of weakness, but I absolutely have to say this. I really, really want to kiss you. What do you think?"

Tamara wet her lips. "I promise, you wouldn't be exploiting the situation. I... I think I'd like that."

In the background, there was a muffled sound of a phone ringing.

"Ignore that," Drew said as he slowly, gently brought his face close to hers.

"I will," she answered softly. Her lips were close enough for him to feel the warmth of her breath. She smelled of plums and sugar and coffee and something utterly Tamara.

"Drew! Drew!" Norman's voice penetrated the kitchen walls as he came huffing and puffing into the room. He held up. "Oh, sorry."

Drew and Tamara pulled apart. Tamara coughed. Drew shook his head. "Not good timing, Pops."

"I'm sorry. If I had known... But you see, while we were in the living room I thought I heard my cell phone ring, I mean, bark. That's the ringtone for your sister, you see. But for the life of me, I don't know where my phone is. It's been missing all day."

Drew sighed. "My fault, Pops. I had it—a long story, too much to explain for now. But the good news is it's in the pocket of my jacket hanging by the door." He motioned behind him.

Norman looked relieved.

"Why don't you head back to the others, and I'll bring it to you?"

Norman agreed and headed to the living room.

Drew turned back to Tamara. "Rain check?"

She nodded. "Definitely. Rain check."

They rejoined the others, and Drew handed Norman his phone. "Here, Pops. You know how to call her back?"

"I may be a Luddite, but I can redial. You just go to make a call and…ah…let me see."

"Why don't you let one of the teenagers show you, Norman? That's what we have them around for," Myrna recommended. She was sitting at the end of the couch, curled up with her stockinged feet tucked under her.

Will got the hint and jumped up from the floor where he was rubbing Buddy's belly. "I'll show you, Dr. Trombo. I'm sure you'll get the hang of it after that."

"Why, thank you, Will. I'm kind of anxious to find out why Jessica would have called. I thought they were going out to some fancy restaurant tonight. I hope nothing's wrong." Norman seemed to half listen while the boy demonstrated what to do.

When Will finished, he quickly took the phone back. The call must have gone through because he soon spoke up: "Sorry I missed your call, Sweet Pea. Is everything all right?" There was a pause while he listened. "You and Briggs have good news, you say?" He nodded. "What's that? Yes, Drew is here, as is everyone else for that matter—Tamara, Myrna, Will, Candy and Buddy, of course." He frowned while he listened further. "Just a minute. I need to figure out how to do that." He held the phone at arm's length and studied the keypad. "She wants me to put it on speakerphone so everyone can hear."

"Let me, Pops." Drew didn't have Will's patience and immediately punched the correct icons. "Hey, Jess, what's up?"

"It's just I wanted you all to know as soon as possible. We were having chocolate mousse at the restaurant—"

"Skip the menu and get to the good part." It was Briggs's voice from the other end of the line. He sounded very happy.

"But the dessert was *so* good. Okay, if you insist." There was a momentary pause for what sounded like a quick smooch. "The good part is that Briggs proposed, and I accepted."

Norman looked at his phone and blinked. "Are you saying…?"

"We're getting married, Pops!" Jessica announced.

"That's so wonderful! I can't think of better news." Norman was shaking.

"About time, too," Drew responded. "Congratulations, Briggs, and welcome to the family!"

Myrna gave Norman a hug and spoke into the phone. "Wonderful news, you two. I'll want to hear all the details when you get home. And thank you so much for calling us right away. We couldn't be happier."

"Same here," Jessica replied. "In fact, we're so over the moon that we decided to cut the trip short. It'll only take a day or two more to sort out stuff here anyway, and then we'll be back to share the announcement in person with everyone." There was a bit more chatter before the call ended soon afterward.

Needless to say, everyone was giddy.

"THAT...THAT NEWS means you'll officially be my uncle, Drew," Will announced.

"And it will be an honor." Drew was doing his duty and opening another celebratory bottle of prosecco.

"And just think, Buddy—" Will turned to his best four-legged friend "—more people to love you and for you to love." He and Candy started dancing around the pup, who pranced on his back legs while Candy held the front ones.

Norman beamed at Myrna. "Our families keep getting bigger and better all the time."

"They sure do," she said. Myrna grinned in Tamara's direction.

"What a night!" exclaimed Norman.

"To Briggs and Jessica!" Myrna raised her glass.

"To Hopewell!" Tamara clinked her glass in a toast.

DREW PULLED TAMARA to the side. "I can think of another way we could celebrate." He gave her a quick peck on the cheek.

She slyly took his free hand behind his back. "I like your style."

He moved in closer. "Not to get off the subject—which frankly is not my intention—but speaking of phone calls, you really should call whoever's in charge at the Philadelphia TV station about that story and get Amy Pulaski in on it, ASAP."

"That can wait, Drew." Tamara squeezed his hand. "Tonight's special."

"It'll be even more special if you can get Amy involved. Her participation's crucial."

"You're right. I want to make it to happen. I owe it to all the people in Hopewell."

"You really owe it to yourself. You're too good a reporter to sit around and just eat English muffins and take ballroom dancing lessons."

"Maybe I had other things in mind. Like sky-diving lessons?"

"Really?"

"No, not really."

"Enough joking around then. You need to do this. It's in your blood."

"As much as your sketchbook is a part of you?" She pointed to his back pocket.

He shrugged. "We're even. Look at it this way—if you're happy, I'm happy."

She smirked. "So, in the end, it's all about you, huh?"

"I'm merely suggesting—"

Tamara touched his cheek. "It's okay. I'm just giving you a hard time because…because…well, because what I really want to say is thank you for having such faith in my abilities and encouraging me not to give up on my career."

"We promised each other the truth." He just needed to work up the courage to always voice it. Meanwhile, he walked over to Myrna. "Myrna, important question. Do you know Amy's phone number?"

"Not by heart, but she's in my contact list."

"If you'd give it to me, I'd be grateful," Tamara said.

Drew watched the two of them scurry for their phones. Then he turned at the sound of Candy, Buddy and Will falling down in a heap on the floor in front of the fireplace. It was hard to say who was panting more.

Will looked around. "Where's everyone going?"

"They're just doing stuff," said Candy. "Hopewell stuff."

Drew smiled at them. "You can say that again."

CHAPTER TWENTY-FIVE

"YOU SHOULD…should have heard Tamara. The way she talked about the TV segment—what it'd show, who could help with it. She…she was great! So… so…" Will was practically jumping up and down in the Hopewell Public Library. His words came in starts and stops, evidence of his excitement conquering his innate shyness. The evening before, when they were all sitting in the living room recovering from the birthday meal, Tamara had managed to connect with Amy Pulaski about the story. Amy had agreed to meet the next morning.

And here they were on Sunday in the library— Amy, Tamara and Will, who Tamara explained was her indispensable assistant. They huddled in a converted closet that was laughingly called the librarian's office. With the door removed, there was barely enough room for a child-size desk and a folding chair. Which meant that Will was standing.

"You don't mean Tamara acted bossy, do you?" Amy Pulaski asked in response to his description.

"More like she was fierce," Will answered.

Amy took in Will's words before she addressed Tamara. "This boy will go far. Now—" Amy twitched her fountain pen back and forth in her hand "—when do we get to work on this segment about the joys of Hopewell?" The question was asked without a hint of mockery, which Tamara found amazing given Amy's futuristic appearance. A black bodysuit and white go-go boots were not the norm in Hopewell.

"As soon as possible," Tamara replied. "It's still the very beginning of summer, so it's prime time to air something about day tripping. But you must understand. This is strictly on spec. I'm not on assignment for this. But the good news is I managed to get the home phone of the Philly station manager." She'd decided not to wait until Monday after all. "And I floated the idea by him pretty hard earlier this morning. He sounded genuinely interested. They always need this kind of story, especially in slow news times. But I need to be up front. There might be a complication."

"You're talking about your suspension."

Tamara nodded.

Amy shrugged knowingly. "It's unfortunate. I could tell you stories…" She stopped herself. "But that's for another time." She knocked her knuckles on her desk blotter. "Now, let's work on the assumption that the station manager sees that your supposed problem is all nonsense. I could use stronger words, but there's a minor present, and I already get enough flak for my black lipstick."

"But it's fabulous! And in case you're interested,

I saw that Denise carries black nail polish at the salon."

"Good to know. But to get to the proposed feature. What exactly did you have in mind, who's doing what and what's the time frame?" Amy fired up a tablet and began a new document.

Tamara gave a rundown as Amy typed away. "I'll write the script after we're done today, and I'll be the on-air narrator. There'll be a couple of interviews—very short stuff—like the ballroom dancing class, Chubbie's and, if we have enough time, the farmers' market. This is just a teaser for the real thing."

"Shots of Briggs's flower stall would be amazing," Amy added.

"Exactly. Then we could have some beauty shots of town and the canal path—"

"With me and Candy walking Buddy," Will proposed.

"Absolutely," Tamara agreed. "Nothing raises the Q-score like having a cute dog in the shot. That's the industry's measure of appeal. And I was hoping, Amy, that you'd be the videographer. I've seen the library's website, and your work's excellent."

"Thanks. The stuff I do helps attract people who wouldn't otherwise get out. For that alone, I'm happy. But it's nice to get praise from a professional."

"Will here is fantastic with software programs, and I was hoping you could teach him enough for him to take over the editing."

"No problem," Amy agreed. "It's always good to have another set of eyes on a project. And I'm happy to show you how to use the camera at the same time, Will. In fact, I don't see why we can't film some beauty shots today, say, after lunch. We could meet at the canal. The weather's supposed to be sunny, and we can start there and move on. What do you say, Will? You ready to roll?"

Will nodded eagerly. "Let me just call Candy and see what time she's free. And I'll get in touch with Aunt Myrna about getting Buddy there." He pulled out his phone and wandered into the magazine section.

Amy looked at Tamara. "He's come a long way. Your good work has paid off."

Tamara waved off the compliment. "It's all Will, really. He's taught me a lot."

"You want to get this done as quickly as possible, correct?" She didn't waste any time or words.

"Like yesterday." Tamara rose. "And I can't thank you enough. I think the project has real potential and, as a side benefit, it will help give Will even more confidence, never mind some new skills. And it wouldn't do me any harm either. I just hope people don't look at this as a vanity project."

"Don't worry. Everyone will be clamoring to be part of the action." Amy stood in her latex techno-garb. She was so tall that the top of her head nearly scraped the bank of fluorescent lights that hung from the ceiling. "If you don't mind, it's time for my thirty minutes of meditation, followed by a dose of the Shopping Network. I can't resist when they have kitchenware on sale."

TAMARA AND WILL were already at the canal's towpath when Myrna swung by with Buddy. Myrna begged off sticking around. "You know me. I can't stand not keeping to my schedule," she admitted without remorse. Candy arrived by bike a few minutes later. As they waited for Amy, Will and Candy walked Buddy.

Since she had a moment to spare, Tamara decided to call Drew. "How'd it go? I'm just sorry the timing didn't work out for me to be there." Drew had told her at breakfast first thing in the morning that his father had contacted Laura, and she was coming by the house to see Norman and Drew about the paintings.

"You were missed, but the meeting worked out better than I could've imagined. Laura was great the way she dealt with Pops. You could tell she's handled all sorts of clients, including reluctant ones. Turns out that my mom's later works are some of her best. They show real maturity."

"Oh, I'm so pleased. Can I get a peek ahead of time?"

"No way. I want you to enjoy the full experience on opening night, which I'm trying not to panic about since it's coming up pretty soon. I can't believe how much work is left to do."

"I guess that means that I won't see you tonight?"

"I don't think so. I've got tons more framing jobs to do. It's going to be tight, but it'll be worth it."

"I understand—but tell me our breakfast time together is still sacred."

"Nothing could ever touch it."

At his casual mention of touching, Tamara remembered his see-ya kiss when they parted ways earlier at Chubbie's. There was nothing casual about that.

So, as much as she wanted to expand their time together, Tamara was aware of the pressure he was under. Lessening his stress was just as important as actual face-to-face time. "We can put our mind-expanding outings on hold, and if you want, I can send your regrets to Mrs. Horowitz for our lessons. I'm sure she'll understand."

"I'm not sure at all. With the piano recital in three weeks, she'll insist on the lessons. My practices may take a hit, but she's used to that from me."

"The old you, not the new, totally adult you," Tamara said with a laugh. "Listen, I won't hold you up. Amy's just arrived now anyway, and we'll start filming."

"Good luck with that. But one thing before you go."

"Yes?" She waved to Amy but pointed to her phone. Amy nodded and approached Will and Candy to discuss filming.

"I have something I want to get off my chest," Drew confessed. "Like I told you last night, I was so proud of the way you handled the whole situation yesterday. It only made you more special."

Tamara blushed—and felt a tingling that was

caused by more than embarrassment. "Thanks. That means a lot to hear you say that." Did he understand what she was implying? She turned away for some added privacy. "But you're giving me too much credit."

"Not true. For all her positive attributes, Myrna didn't exactly welcome you with open arms when you first arrived in Hopewell."

"I've learned we all have issues. And to give her credit, Myrna apologized."

"Which proves how crucial it was for you to take the first step, opening up like that. And that kind of courage has inspired me to act the same way. You deserve it. I didn't have the guts to tell you this before, but I want to now."

Tamara heard him inhale.

"You remember after we went skydiving? When we were back on the ground?" Drew asked.

"How could I forget? Talk about a rush! But, you know, I couldn't help noticing how strange you were acting. I hope the skydiving didn't trigger a bad memory from work. You looked almost fearful."

"That wasn't it. I wasn't afraid. Honestly, it almost would have been better because at least I would have felt something. No, it was much worse. You see, I'd always been an adrenaline junkie, and, truthfully, that was part of the attraction of my job. I could get this high and help people at the same time. But the job finally got to me."

He took a deep breath. "You might recall how I said that I was taking a forced break. It wasn't simply burnout. You see, I wasn't so much depressed at all the suffering I'd seen—which was humongous. It's that I'd become numb. And after skydiving with you, the same feeling reoccurred—no high, no fear. No anything. And that kind of dead feeling is what can really lead to trouble. Long term."

"Oh, Drew. That's terrible. And so sad."

"Not to worry. The way you faced your demon head-on—"

"But it wasn't dangerous like yours. And I did it with the help of you and Nonna," she added.

"Exactly. The way you were willing to open yourself up and accept help—you made me realize that it's time to alter what I'm doing in life."

"You're saying what exactly?"

"I'm saying that I don't know what's in store, but whatever it is, it requires me to change. And it's because of you that I understand that."

She found herself sniffling.

And he clearly heard. "Aw, c'mon. This conversation is supposed to fill you full of joy, not tears."

"I am happy," she protested, her voice cracking.

"Just hold that thought. Because I am, too."

WHEN TAMARA'S PHONE rang later that evening, she was sure it would be Drew. It wasn't. It was her agent.

Sidney listened patiently—well, patiently for Sidney—as Tamara told him about preparations so far on the Hopewell feature story.

"That's nice, Tam. A real boost to the community, and I hope you pull it off, even if you've offered it completely gratis, which, as your agent, I would have advised against. Now, however, it's time to talk turkey. I'm referring to forcing the powers-that-be in Phoenix to get off their behinds and come to a decision—in your favor!"

"I agree, but I'm not sure how we can speed up the clock," Tamara replied.

"It's time we got tougher. Pushed them harder. They're dragging their feet."

Normally, Tamara would have been the first one to urge this tactic. This time she wasn't convinced. "I don't know. I know you said management agreed that me giving up my baby was off the table. But what if the people who are behind the lies feel the added pressure and claim my past prejudiced my reporting? They might be desperate enough to leak Will's identity. I've told everybody here that there's no need to worry, and I'd die if I had to go back on my word. And just think of the damage it could do to Will."

"As a fellow parent, I agree with you. We never want our kids to be pawns in a negotiation. But this is your career, Tam. You've been working for this your whole life."

"It's out of the question. And that's final."

Drew had his earbuds in and was blasting AC/DC when he began framing this incredible work of his mother's, one of the paintings his dad had donated to the show. She'd used mad dashes of brushstrokes to depict a corner of her attic studio. Her easel and paints, a ratty upholstered armchair with an eclectic collection of pillows, stacks of paintings leaning against the rough wood walls and a window. Yes, a window, with a view of her cherished zen garden. In contrast to the riot of color of her studio, the raked pebbles conveyed an ethereal calm. But back in the studio, if one looked closely, they'd discover small photos of the family tacked to the top of her easel. Her personality was all there to see: her daring, free spirit coupled with her sense of tranquility and above all, her love of family.

Drew tried out a number of framing options, but none of them did the painting justice. And then it came to him—a simple, blond wood edging, turned so the narrow side barely outlined the work. That way the painting wouldn't stop. It would appear to continue out into the world.

The process of complementing each of Vivian's pieces as best as possible was exhausting, and when he felt his phone vibrate in his pocket, he breathed a sigh of relief. Drew turned off the music and checked the screen, hoping it was Tamara. So much for hope—it was the logistics supervisor from the international relief agency. He let the call go through to voice mail. When he was ready, he hit Play. "I haven't heard from you lately, so I thought I would check in," the message went. "Just wanted to see how you're doing. No pressure from our end, but we should talk."

Drew rested the phone on his thigh. It was one thing to come to grips with his emotional state.

It was another to plan for the future. He had a lot going on. He just wanted to enjoy the moment. And he had a lot of work to do before he and Laura could finish mounting the show.

And then there was Tamara. Boy, was there Tamara.

CHAPTER TWENTY-SIX

THE NEXT TWO weeks passed quickly. All of Hopewell seemed abuzz with news of Jessica and Briggs's engagement, and when the pair weren't greeting well-wishers, they were trying to work. Meanwhile, Tamara was busy writing and filming. Not to mention cajoling the Philadelphia station manager. He'd been happy with the teaser, and she was waiting on a final decision.

And Drew was up to his eyeballs in framing and mounting his mother's show at the gallery. Responses to opening night were still trickling in, and Laura was struggling to get a grasp on the numbers in order to arrange for refreshments and entertainment. Drew was helping out as much as he could on that end as well.

In the few moments in between, Tamara and Drew squeezed in lessons with Mrs. Horowitz. Tamara would practice at the house during the day, and Drew would suffer the wrath of Jessica and Pops with some late-night piano practicing himself.

When they did grab a few moments together, it consisted of a rushed breakfast, either at Chubbie's or gobbled down as takeout on the stools at the gallery. They would hold hands between bites and sips of coffee and talk about what Tamara was filming that day or which artworks Drew still had to frame.

It was all close, wonderful and fraught with tension. And somehow, every time one of them would mention how they had to talk or how there were questions they needed to answer, a meeting or a deadline inevitably cropped up to delay the crucial conversation.

A stolen kiss or a smile would have to be enough—for now.

Then there was the matter of Tamara talking to Will about her mother. After dinner one evening, she, Will and Buddy nestled together on Will's bed. Buddy was in the middle, taking up more space than a medium-sized dog should physically be capable of doing. Still, his presence provided a soothing relief, especially for Tamara, who stroked the silky fur on Buddy's ears.

"I can't believe he lets me do this," she whispered to Will.

"Of course he does," Will encouraged her. "You're part of his family, Momara." It was one of those times when their special term for her was totally appropriate.

She smiled and leaned back against the headboard of the twin bed. They were surrounded by posters of animals, mostly dogs. Will's backpack lay on the floor next to the desk, which was cluttered with notebooks, a laptop and worksheets. Tamara had had to step gingerly around the piles of clothes and sneakers when she'd entered, but she didn't criticize. She had more important things to discuss.

"You already know how your dad and Aunt Myrna raised you from a baby. That I wasn't on the scene," she began.

"It's all right, I understand now how it was just too much for you, that your parents weren't there for you. And I'm proud how you were able to go to college even though you were all on your own. Now look at all the great things you've done on your job."

Tamara looked at her son with love. "That means so much to me. Thank you, Will. But what I want to talk to you about has to do with something that might potentially happen now. You see, I've found out my mom is still alive and still in the same house in Philadelphia. For all these years, I didn't want to have anything to do with her or my late dad. But now I'm starting to wonder if I should find out what went wrong between them and me. It's like I've come to realize that if I don't put these past problems to rest—if I don't face my fears—I may never be the best mom I can be for you. And I don't want a sense that there's something lacking in me getting in the way of our relationship." She searched Will's face.

It was Will's turn to look to Buddy for security. He ran his fingers through the dog's downy belly fur, and Buddy sighed a doggy sigh of contentment.

"I'd never think there was something wrong with you, Momara. I might get frustrated or not understand you sometimes, but I think you're a good person. You always try—even if you don't know what you're doing." He raised his head and smiled at Tamara.

She returned the smile. "You think I don't know what I'm doing?"

"Well..." he begged off.

Tamara laughed. "Okay, I'll give you that. Sometimes I haven't a clue. But listen, there's another reason I think I should go see my mom. Because maybe, just maybe, if things work out, you'll be able to meet your only remaining grandmother. Would you like that?"

"Sure, why not? Once I just had Dad and Aunt Myrna. Then came Buddy. Now there's you and Jessica and Dr. Trombo, and who knows, maybe Drew." He mischievously dropped the last name.

Tamara rolled her eyes, but secretly she was pleased that Will was happy to have Drew around. But for how long? Another matter to be resolved. Meanwhile, fingers crossed...

"So, I guess that means you're okay with me getting in touch with her," she concluded.

"Sure. If you want my help, too, I'm here for you. We're family after all."

AT LAST, the Friday evening of the art opening arrived. Drew was already at the gallery, having dashed home hours earlier to change before running back to check on the final preparations. Jessica and Briggs decided to make their own arrangements, while Myrna insisted on driving Tamara and Will as well as picking up Candy and Norman.

And Myrna being Myrna, they arrived at the opening time on the dot.

Tamara slipped her arm through the crook of Norman's elbow and guided him up the steps to the gallery. A drawing on the partition just inside the entrance greeted all the visitors. Tamara stopped and turned to Norman. "I can't believe you agreed to take it out from behind the door. What a perfect way to meet Vivian!"

"It is, isn't it?" Norman's voice was unsteady. On the wall was a short biography, ending with Vivian's philosophy of life: "Never wait for inspiration to come to you. You go to it." And next to her words was Drew's portrait of his mother. It was charming, accomplished and full of love.

"It almost breaks my heart," Tamara confided.

Norman nodded. "It breaks mine. That's why it had to be here."

Tamara patted his arm. "I'm proud of you. And look." She swept her arm around the room. "All the people who knew and loved her are here as well as those who want to find out more."

She was right. The gallery was already hopping. Members of the community had turned out in force, from Mr. Portobello, Mayor Park (for once, minus Sheba) and Signora Reggio to Mr. Mason, Gloria Pulaski and various of her children and grandchildren. Even Robby Bellona was there with Nada. "I can't believe we've never met in person," Tamara exclaimed when she shook hands with Robby's wife. "I feel I know you so well through your jams and baking."

And still, there were more. Laura had enlisted students from Vivian's school, and they mingled among the guests, serving trays of hors d'oeuvres. And for a soothing cultural ambience, Mrs. Horowitz had the town hall's piano moved over. ("The upright fits better than my baby grand, and it'll loosen the purse strings," Mrs. Horowitz had informed Drew. Maybe, but he'd sweated bullets while two of Robby's plumbers, moonlighting as movers, carried the heavy instrument up the steps to the gallery. Talk about requiring a big tip.)

As additional people made their way inside, Myrna turned to her little group. "I think it's time we moved farther forward, don't you?" Then she made a point of addressing Will and Candy. Will was wearing the blue blazer and chinos from his recent middle school graduation. (The sleeves were already getting too short.) For her part, Candy had traded in her usual overalls and hoodies for a demure, tiny-flowered midi dress and Doc Martens. Myrna smiled. "Will, why don't you and Candy check out who else is here? There may be some other kids from your school." They didn't need further encouragement and cheerfully took off.

Then Myrna ushered Norman and Tamara along. She did a quick survey of the art and acknowledged the throng of viewers with a nodding respect. "Quite a turnout and a lovely way to celebrate Vivian and her art. Tell you what. Let's go seek out that son of yours, Norman. Tell him what a great job he's done. It goes to show he's not just all smiles and easy charm." And with that, she liberated Norman from Tamara and marched him toward the back of the gallery. Her white trousers and flaming-red tunic with brass buttons made her look in charge—which was true no matter what clothes she was wearing.

Left to herself, Tamara took her time to admire the exhibit—the dazzling landscapes, the family portraits and the still lifes. Vivian had exquisitely captured the innate beauty and vigor of her surroundings and everyday life, making them all seem far from mundane. Like her son, Tamara realized.

Drew had so much to offer the world. His big heart, expressed here in honoring the mother he loved and cherished, and whose memory he wanted to share in a way that would help others. That giving spirit, that sense of generosity, that was such an integral part of both of them.

She needed to find him. And not surrounded by so many people.

Tamara pushed toward the back. The sound of laughter and conversation almost drowned out Mrs. Horowitz's rendition of a Chopin Nocturne. Almost but not quite. Mrs. Horowitz was nothing if not determined.

"Yoo-hoo! Tamara, Tamara, it's been too long."

Gloria Pulaski waved mightily. She zoomed in with Amy trailing behind. "You must be so excited." Amy had chosen to wear a vintage double-breasted black pantsuit with enormous shoulder pads—very sixties. She'd also omitted a blouse—very risqué.

"Yes, the opening is going really well," Tamara responded.

"I agree, but I was talking about the feature story. I'm convinced they'll green-light it. I told Amy she should have brought the camera to the opening, but she said it would work better when the gallery's less crowded." She looked Tamara up and down. "You look wonderful, by the way, but that's not one of your usual outfits, is it?" She pointed to Tamara's dress.

"No, it isn't, but isn't it fantastic?" She did a little curtsy and held out the pleated skirt of the flapper-style frock. The silk moiré fabric was a dusty rose. Keeping with the Roaring Twenties theme, Tamara had used gel to curl her bangs. "I was telling Amy how much I admired her look, and she told me all about the Salvation Army used clothing store. I stopped in after my piano lesson with Mrs. Horowitz and saw this. I couldn't resist. Very retro, don't you think?"

Gloria agreed.

Amy tapped her mother's arm. "Mom, look. There's the mayor. You wanted to ask him about the brew pub building proposal." The thought of Hopewell politics was strong enough to carry Gloria away. For that alone, Tamara thought she'd take Amy up on her offer of a meditation session.

But most of all, she wanted to locate Drew. She attempted a step in that direction, only to be stopped by Mr. Mason, looking very jaunty in a yellow V-neck sweater and plaid pants.

"Like the kicks," he said, pointing to Tamara's white tennis shoes.

She smiled. "I figured I'd be standing, so it was better to be practical and throw fashion to the wind."

"White sneakers are always classic. Terrific show, isn't it?" He raised his wineglass and tottered away without waiting to hear her answer.

Mrs. Horowitz had moved on to *Rhapsody in Blue*. Tamara put her head down, determined not to be thwarted despite the snippets of conversations that reached her ears.

"That's not a designer dress, you know…"

"You heard what she's trying to do for Hopewell, didn't you…?"

"Will appears to have grown in one week…"

"And so much more confident. I'm sure having Tamara here has helped…"

The last comment elicited a smile, which widened when she saw Laura.

Even though well-wishers mobbed around her, Laura managed to grab Tamara's hand. "Come talk to me. We couldn't have done the show without you persuading Norman. It made a huge difference. Did you see all the red stickers indicating sales? The proceeds will go a long way toward the scholarship fund." She pivoted and put her other hand on the man standing next to her. "And let me introduce my husband, Phil LaValle. Phil, Tamara Giovanessi."

Tamara nodded at the handsome man with close-cropped hair and a faded scar on his cheek. "You must be very proud of Laura. She's done a magnificent job."

"I am. But she benefited from this fellow's help, too. I think you may know him?" Phil pointed to the tall blond gentleman on the other side of Laura.

The gray suit and white dress shirt were unfamiliar. The short wavy hair and minimal beard were also a new look. But there was no doubt. It was Drew.

"Maybe we should give Tamara and Drew a little time together? Catch up on things. Word has it that they've both been too busy to see much of each other." Those words of wisdom came from Jessica, who was standing between her brother and Briggs. The circle of garnets on her ring finger signified her newly engaged status.

"Yeah, get lost, you two," ordered Briggs good-naturedly. "You deserve a few private minutes before someone insists you do something else for the denizens of Hopewell."

Drew didn't need any encouragement. "It's so busy already, I wasn't sure I'd be able to find you," he confided to Tamara. He steered her to a quiet corner in the back near the framing table. Strains of "It Had to Be You" floated above the din. "You look amazing," he said. He ran the back of his fingers up and down her bare upper arm.

She grinned. "Not too bad yourself. I almost didn't recognize this cleaned-up version of you. And if anyone had told me you owned a pair of long pants I would have laughed in their face."

"I like that I can still surprise you."

"I've never been a fan of surprises until now."

He wet his lips and smiled.

Tamara cleared her throat. "Drew, I have to tell you. The whole thing's magnificent. I know that Laura worked hard, too, but it's clear you put your heart and soul into the show. I can't imagine what the whole process must have been like for you. Difficult? A relief? A sense of pride?"

"All of the above, if I'm being honest."

"Which we must be with each other."

He nodded. "Mounting the art, in terms of the chronology and putting different subject matter together, was a collaboration with Laura, for sure. But I wanted the show to tell a particular story. We both knew her but obviously in different ways. I wanted to make certain that my point of view as a family member and wannabe artist prevailed, and finally Laura agreed. As to the framing? That was another challenge. I really worked on doing justice to the art—in essence, partnering it. And you know what? Doing that taught me a lot about myself, how I can be a better partner."

His words held such promise. "You mean like

dancing together?" She asked the obvious—but hoped for more.

He laughed at her choice of words before taking on a more thoughtful tone. "Something like that, but not in an ordinary sense, more like dancing in its most idealized form. A complete sharing of trust and respect, so that in the end, it looks polished but effortless." Drew turned away from the crowd and bent down. "I need to tell you something, too, but it's not for public consumption yet. This morning, in the middle of one last-minute crisis after another, Laura offered me part-ownership of the gallery." He waited for her reaction.

Her eyes widened. "That's amazing. What did you say?"

"I said it was very tempting, but I'd need time to think about it. I said that if I took her up on the offer, I'd want to try and integrate the gallery into the local schools. Introduce art and a love of art into kids' lives. Maybe give them a venue to showcase their works, too."

"I love that idea. You should be proud. I know your mother would have been." Was this a sign that Drew was considering giving up his wandering ways and settling down? She reached for his hand. "I have some news, too. I didn't want to steal your thunder, but I heard from the Philly station manager this morning. He spoke to a bunch of people at the network, and I quote, 'You'll be glad to hear the climate is finally right.'"

"That sounds positive."

She nodded. "It is." The phone in her tiny purse started vibrating, but Tamara ignored it. "The upshot is they want us to go ahead with the feature on Hopewell. They said they'll even pay—not great, mind you, but enough to cover expenses."

"That's fantastic! I knew you'd do it. And you'll do a wonderful job. You have to let people know. They'll be so excited."

"I will. But not right now. The opening is the news tonight."

The music switched to Richard Strauss's *Der Rosenkavalier*, and Tamara, who was still holding Drew's hand, found herself beginning to sway.

He swept her into his arms. "I think this is our cue, and luckily the waltz is the one dance I know—thanks to you."

By some miracle of acoustics and Mrs. Horowitz's piano playing, the music rose above the noise of the crowd. Tamara moved closer and leaned her cheek against his chest. Drew rested his chin on the top of her hair.

They let the music do the rest as they moved in their own little world. (Mr. Portobello would have been proud.) And when the piano stopped, Tamara reluctantly awakened from her trance. "Thank you," she said.

"For what?"

"For being you. For being here. For telling me the truth. For kicking my derriere when I needed it." She gave him a lazy smile. He gave her one back.

"Before we get too involved—" she continued before being cut off.

"Involved? I like the sound of that."

"Just calm yourself," she teased him. "Before we get carried away with…with whatever, I want to let you know that I've decided to try to reconnect with my mom."

"Tamara, that's amazing! Are you sure? But, please, I don't want you to do anything that will cause you distress. And I certainly don't want you to do it on my account."

"No, it's on my account. I need some kind of closure about when I was young and my relationship with my parents if I'm ever going to be truly secure as a parent." *And a better partner*, she thought but didn't voice aloud. "There'll never be a better time than now."

"So, you're going to call her? Soon?"

She shook her head. "No, I think it'd be better just to show up, talk in person—that way there's no backing out. I was hoping to go tomorrow, if possible—while I still have my courage up. Will's given me his blessing, and I don't want to let him down." Her phone vibrated in her purse again. She had the urge just to shut it off. Instead, she ignored it.

"Tomorrow's perfect," said Drew. "I'm free whenever to drive you. And your mom still lives in the same house in Philadelphia?"

She nodded, not sure what she'd set herself up for. "And Norman?"

"Wild horses couldn't keep Pops from coming." He held her close. The music started up again: "Strangers in the Night."

"More than anything right now though, I'd really like to—" He lowered his head, his lips parted, as did hers...

"Tamara, there you are." Gloria barged into their intimate little corner. "I've been searching all over for you. I just got off the phone with Sidney. He's been trying to reach you." She glanced at Drew, but he was frowning at his own phone.

Tamara stepped back and stared at Gloria. "Sidney has your number?" She shook her head. "Never mind. Of course he has your number." She glanced over at Drew. "Is everything all right?"

He looked up, distracted. "Sorry, I have to take this," he said and slipped into the office.

"Yes, it seems the people from the Phoenix station called," Gloria continued undeterred. "You've been completely exonerated. They want you back."

Tamara stared dumbfounded. "That's...that's great." She was in shock. "I'll call Sidney now." She pulled out her phone, saw that he was the one who'd been trying to reach her. She pressed Redial.

He responded immediately and repeated what Gloria had just told her.

"Did they say what changed their mind?" Tamara asked.

"Just that the evidence indicated the accusation was based on lies, and apparently the other reporter from the station finally confessed she'd taken the money in exchange for spreading the false statements about you. Probably she was also hoping to take over the anchor position, but she wasn't willing to admit it. Needless to say, she got the boot. I don't think she'll show her face in town anytime soon."

"I don't know which motive would have been worse—that she did it for money or out of jealousy. Either way, I'm just glad the truth has come out. But please tell me none of the teenage moms got caught up in the investigation. That the crooks didn't somehow try to intimidate them in order to get away with their crimes."

"Rest assured, they didn't. In fact, one girl came forward and let us know the adoption agency had tried to pressure her into lying. But evidently, you'd made such a good impression that she swore she'd stick by your reporting no matter what. Said she'd never had an advocate like you before. High praise. Even the police took notice, and they've opened an investigation into the agency's illegal practices."

"At least that gives me some faith in humanity." Tamara pursed her lips. "When is this all supposed to happen? My return, I mean?" she asked.

"As soon as possible."

Tamara blanched. "Sidney, to tell you the truth, I don't know… There are some things I need to do here first…" Her voice trailed off.

"What's to know? I tell you what—call me when this little shindig is over. Gloria said you're at some sort of art opening. Anyway, when you can, let's talk. We'll discuss details, especially about you getting a raise."

Tamara ended the call and looked around. She felt utterly confused. When Drew came out of the office, she rushed over. "You'll never guess what I just heard." She gave him the news.

"I guess congrats are in order," he said. He didn't sound as enthusiastic as she hoped.

"I suppose so. It's just…just I hadn't counted on it. I was too busy with everything here. Imagine, going back to my old station. I know it's petty, but I gotta confess, I'm looking forward to certain people eating humble pie. It's…it's almost too much to fathom. What do you think?"

"What do I think? About you wanting to go back and prove that you were right all along? I thought you were tired of that jealous backbiting. That you'd moved beyond seeking revenge."

"What if I haven't—completely?" And if she hadn't, did that mean she wasn't ready to take the next steps—in her career? In finding love? She had no doubt that Drew was someone special to her. But where their relationship was headed in the long term was still so much up in the air.

"Well, I just got word, too, by the way—from headquarters." He held up his phone. "The coordinator in Geneva has had a stroke. He's alive, but the extent of his recovery is up in the air. They need someone to step in right away and quite possibly permanently. To make a long story short, they offered me the job. It's mostly an administrative position at the headquarters in Switzerland. But, of course, there'd be times that would require me to go in the field. Anyway, they were wondering if I could manage…"

Tamara shook her head. All this news from out of the blue was overloading her brain. "And what did you say?"

"I said I'd think about it. I need to let them know soon though. They're in a bind."

"I thought you'd realized that this wasn't the healthiest work for you to do anymore. That you needed to change course."

"But this could be an opportunity to make a difference, and who knows, maybe now that I've recognized the problem, I'll be able to deal better with the stress."

It was all too much. "So, I guess congrats are in order for you, too," she said, her voice listless.

"I guess, but it's not like I've made any final decisions."

She dropped her head. "But you will. I know you. You won't be able to resist." After a thoughtful moment, she raised her chin. "I know we said we'd talk when all the hullabaloo here in Hopewell died down, but it seems that the outside world has other plans for us. Maybe our breakfast buddy arrangement is coming to an end sooner than we thought."

"Don't say that. I'm sure we still have time. To discuss the options," he insisted.

"What kind of options? Can you promise a life that won't consist of a few precious weekends here and there, with long-distance phone calls in be-tween until it all becomes too hard to even think of us *as* us—as a couple?"

Because, as unlikely as it might have seemed from the get-go, that's what they'd become—a cou-ple. A couple in love. The issue wasn't whether she was capable of finding love, Tamara realized. It was that she'd already found it.

She loved him—deeply. The feeling had been lurking all along, but she'd never had the courage to admit it, let alone accept it. And the sudden real-ization was overwhelming, causing her to overreact to his news. It was simply too much to take in all at once. She peered at Drew, but he seemed equally at a loss.

"Tamara, right now, I don't... I don't know what to say," he managed to sputter. "I'm sure... I'm sure..." But he seemed sure of nothing.

She rubbed her forehead. "You know, Myrna's migraines must be catching. I've suddenly got this bad headache. I need some fresh air. If you'll excuse me." She held her purse tight and ran toward the door. "Sorry," she said repeatedly as she bumped into people along the way.

"Tamara," Will called out when she went rushing by. He turned to Briggs. "Dad, what's wrong with Tamara? She just ran out the door."

Briggs looked at Drew, who had suddenly ma-terialized next to him. "Did something happen?"

"I don't know. It all came so fast." Drew looked uncertain.

Jessica looked at her brother. "Did you guys have a fight?"

"No. Yes. I'm not sure."

"You're not going to let it hang there, are you?" Briggs asked Drew. He looked down at Will. "I'm sure Tamara will be all right, son. She just needed a little air, I guess."

Will moved to the window and saw Tamara run down the sidewalk. He turned back, distressed. "It's starting to rain. She'll get wet." He pushed his way to the front door and opened it. "Hold up, I'm coming," he shouted. "Tamara! Momara! Mom!"

The door shut behind him. The drops fell more heavily as he reached her. He hugged her fiercely. "What's wrong? Don't cry." Tears stained his cheeks.

She shook her head. "I'm sorry. I got upset. But there's nothing to worry about." She tried to push him away. "You should go back, enjoy yourself."

He kept his arms tight around her. "No, I'm here for you. Just like you're here for me."

CHAPTER TWENTY-SEVEN

DREW WAS SO desperate and confused about what was going on with Tamara and her job, his job, their future, her outburst and his own heart, that he did the one thing he shouldn't have. Nothing. Or almost nothing.

His usual response to a crisis was to muscle his way through it, all the while putting on a happy-go-lucky front. But this time he knew that what he had with Tamara—or at this point, maybe no longer had—was too important to act like nothing serious had occurred. Because even a numbskull like him finally got the message—he was in love. For the first time.

And what was his reaction to that realization? Later that evening, he showed up unannounced at the Longfellow farmhouse, but when Myrna greeted him at the door, she informed him that the others had gone out for a drive to points unknown. He figured he was lucky she hadn't slammed the door in his face.

He followed up this futile gesture with a phone call and then several more phone calls. But Tamara didn't pick up. Not that he could blame her. Finally, he managed to apologize in a text. (*A text, for goodness' sake!* Even he recognized how cowardly that was.) Hoping against hope, he kept waiting for Tamara to take the first step—to be braver than he was. But he didn't hear from her.

Finally, he decided to offer an olive branch. He left a voicemail message, renewing his offer to take her to Philadelphia to confront her mother. She had said it was important for her well-being and her future with Will, and however much he'd messed up things between the two of them, at least he could do the right thing about this.

Which meant that at ten o'clock the next day, he and Norman rolled up in Pops's Subaru wagon outside Briggs's farmhouse. Tamara was already waiting outside the kitchen door. With Will.

Norman put down a back window. "We thought my car might be more comfortable than the truck. Why don't you hop into the front?"

Tamara turned to Will and gave a quick squeeze to his shoulder. "I'll let you know how it goes," she said.

Will nodded. "You sure you don't want me to come with you?" He compressed his lips.

She shook her head. "Thanks, but it's something I have to do myself."

"I know it's going to be tough, but if it helps at all, just look how great things have turned out for me. I've got a mom! I want the same for you."

"I hope so, too." She reached up and kissed the top

of his head. "I'll keep in touch." Then she opened the passenger door and slid into the seat.

Norman leaned forward and gave Tamara a pat on the shoulder. She nodded and glanced at Drew.

He handed her a to-go cup. "Soy milk latte." But when he saw her stern countenance, he wondered the wisdom of their journey. "Are you sure you're up for this? We can do it anytime. If I'm making things worse, I don't have to be the one to drive you."

"No, let's do it now. I'm ready." She held up her phone. The screen displayed her mother's address.

Drew studied the directions, put the car in gear and drove silently. Everyone appeared to be deep in their own thoughts with nothing to say. Once he got off the highway, he maneuvered through the city streets to the address in South Philadelphia. He leaned forward to search the house numbers and finally pulled over. He cut the engine. "This is it."

Her childhood home was typical for the neighborhood—an attached, two-story building dating from the 1920s. A green-and-white metal awning hung over the front porch. Concrete steps rose from the sidewalk, and a black metal railing connected twin concrete columns positioned at the corners. A heavy curtain shrouded any view into the front window.

"Do you want to call first? Let her know you're outside?" Drew asked.

Tamara shook her head. "No, it's Saturday, and she should be home. Mom never liked to go out on Saturdays because she avoided crowds."

"But maybe just to warn her?" Norman asked gently from the back seat. "It could be quite a shock after all this time."

Tamara worked her bottom lip. "I suppose you're right." She pressed the number on the screen and brought her phone to her ear. "Hello, this is Tamara. I'm outside the house, and—" She blinked and let the phone drop to her lap. "Whoever answered hung up."

"Maybe she's changed their number. It could have been anyone picking up," Norman reassured her.

Drew spoke up. "Tamara, why don't you and I ring the doorbell and find out what's going on." Then, without waiting for a reply, he opened his door and circled around to the sidewalk. He stood there, waiting for Tamara to join him.

Tamara looked over her shoulder at Norman. She put her phone in her tote bag and left it on the seat. "Well, here goes nothing."

Norman winked. "You're being very brave. I'm proud of you. Just remember that."

Tamara and Drew mounted the three steps. He hung back and let her approach the entrance. A metal security gate covered the solid front door. Tamara rang the doorbell and waited.

The curtain covering the picture window fluttered momentarily.

"Try the doorbell again," Drew said softly.

She did.

After more than a few minutes, the wooden door

slowly opened inward. A small woman, an older, more tired version of Tamara, stepped forward. Her hair was salt-and-pepper, and her clothes consisted of pull-on charcoal pants and a gray fleece jacket. Everything about her was gray. She didn't bother to unlatch the security gate.

But through the bars and black grating, Tamara recognized her. "Mom, it's me, Tamara," she said tentatively.

Her mother shook her head. "After all these years."

Tamara drew a long breath. "I'm sorry to hear that Dad died. I didn't know until recently." She paused. "Anyway, I just wanted to tell you that I'm living in Bucks County, not too far away. And that my life has worked out well. I've got a great job. Wonderful friends. I've even reconnected with my son, who I gave up. You'd be so proud of him, Mom. He's a terrific kid—bright and polite. Knows everything there's to know about dogs. I've got pictures of him. They're on my phone. I left it in the car, but I can go get it." She started to turn to retrieve her cell.

Her mother grabbed the inside handle of the security gate but hesitated before lowering her eyes. "No, wait. I want to see them, I really do, but I'm just not sure. So much time has passed and…and besides, what if we went from there? What if I did actually meet him? I can't imagine what he would think of me." She winced. "I never learned to be brave the way you always were."

"I wasn't brave, Mom. I was a kid—a kid who was convinced that you and Dad didn't love her because there was something wrong with her."

Her mother looked up. "No, I always loved you, and you were never the problem. Your father was, but I didn't question his ways. I should have, many times. And despite what you claim, Tamara, you always had the courage to follow your own path. You still do. And I'm so proud of all you've done. And now, your son... I don't know what to say."

"You could still meet him if you want," Tamara offered. "It's not too late."

Her mother seemed tempted, but she still held back. "Easy for you to say." She shook her head. "No, he wouldn't want to see me, not after how we treated you...how I treated you. I'd be too embarrassed."

"Don't be. Don't you want to be a grandmother?"

"More than you could imagine, because it's something I never thought was possible." She held her breath before letting it out slowly. "But I need time, time to stop regretting the past. Like I said, I'm not brave. Can you give me that time? I can't guarantee anything, but can you let me try?"

"If that's what you're prepared to give, I'll take it. But know this, believe this, you'll always be in my heart."

"HOW DID IT GO?" Norman asked when Tamara and Drew returned to the car.

"Not as well as I could have hoped," Tamara responded quietly. She folded and unfolded her hands on her lap.

"Not the worst either." Drew tried to put a more positive spin on it. "Probably best to let Tamara just mull it over, Pops. It was a lot to digest for one day."

Norman got the message, and for the rest of the trip he remained silent except to offer a few remarks about the traffic or something he saw along the way. Soon he stopped when even those comments didn't generate any response.

And as he drove, Drew kept thinking that if only Tamara would let him, he'd take her in his arms and reassure her that she was loved by everyone. Him especially. Yes, him, no matter what she decided to do in the future. But for now, he just drove.

Tamara didn't cry. She didn't speak. She just sat there, mute.

When they were on the outskirts of Hopewell, Drew looked in the rearview mirror and spoke to his father. "Pops, maybe you could send a text and let people know we'll be arriving soon."

Tamara nodded. "That would be helpful, actually. I'm okay, you know—really, I am…"

No, you're not, Drew thought.

"I told Will I would call, but I don't think I'm up for it quite yet. He was so positive about the whole thing."

Finally, they pulled into the driveway. Drew parked the car. His heart was breaking as he watched Tamara unhook her seat belt and gather up her bag. She put her hand on the door.

Myrna and Will were standing outside. Buddy was bounding around their feet.

Tamara stepped out of the car and slowly marched toward the huddled group.

No words passed, but somehow Myrna and Will knew instinctively what to do. They opened their arms and embraced her. Buddy, too, seemed to sense what was needed because he stopped his wild greeting and instead curled his body protectively around Tamara's legs.

"I'm home," Drew heard her say. "How good it is to say that. I'm so lucky, and you all give me hope."

CHAPTER TWENTY-EIGHT

"I KNOW YOU had your difficulties last week, but I expect the best from both of you." Mrs. Horowitz placed her arms in front of her ample bosom and clasped her fingers. The semiprecious stones in her broach of musical notes sparkled on her maroon twinset. She eyed Tamara and Drew, who were seated together on the piano bench but as far away from each other as was logistically possible. They had sat that way for much of the entire lesson.

Tamara looked up at Mrs. Horowitz. "Do you know? About our jobs and…and what that might mean?" She didn't mention Drew's name. "And even how we visited my mom? That, too?"

"Everyone who was at the art opening heard about the phone calls, and they told the few people who weren't there. We're a tight-knit community. And word went around about your trip to Philly. People here are interested in what happens to their neighbors because we like to think we look out for each other. But despite all your personal dramas and decisions to make, the reality is the recital is tomorrow. And, as the saying goes, the show must go on." She gave them a stern stare. "Do you hear me, Drew?"

"Yes, Mrs. Horowitz," he said as meekly as he could.

She nodded briskly, her double chin providing a coda. (Fitting when you thought about it.) "It's good to hear that you recognize your responsibility—to me, your fellow students and, most of all, to yourselves. And remember, your loved ones will all be in attendance."

"I didn't invite anyone," Tamara admitted from her side of the piano bench.

"I didn't either. I didn't think anyone would be interested," Drew confessed.

"Knowing that would probably be the case, I went ahead and sent out invitations."

They both looked up, stunned.

"Throughout today's lesson, and especially during your performance of the duet, I've sensed a palpable awkwardness."

"The understatement of the year," Drew murmured as he gazed at the Persian rug under the piano.

"No smart talk," Mrs. Horowitz reprimanded him. "Despite your collective discomfort, I'm counting on you both to overcome life's travails and perform at the highest level. Tamara and Drew, you should know that you have shown real progress. Tamara, your rendition of Bach's 'Prelude to a Well-Tempered Clavier' showcases your rigorous attention to keeping time. I'm very impressed. Drew, you still need to watch your fingering, but the liveliness you bring to Offenbach's 'Can Can' is admirable."

Drew stole a glance at Tamara. "You're impressive. I'm merely admirable."

Tamara looked away.

Mrs. Horowitz breathed in deeply. "As I said from the beginning, this is not a competition, rather a collaboration. That's why I assigned you a duet, in this case, Gershwin's 'I Got Rhythm.' Not only did I think the audience would enjoy it after sitting through more than one dreary Chopin Etude—"

Tamara interrupted. "You don't like Chopin?"

"I didn't say that, merely that I assign pieces to my students for pedagogical reasons, not necessarily because they're my favorites. But to get back to your duet. I also chose it because by working together, you've learned to bring out the best in each other. Tamara, Drew's natural liveliness and, I might even say sense of pizzazz—"

"Pizzazz. I like that," Drew quipped.

Mrs. Horowitz narrowed her eyes. "As I was saying, Drew's sense of fun has leavened your emphasis on technique and precision. But your strengths have also forced Drew to concentrate on the fundamental mechanics of the music. Jazz may seem free-flowing, but it's actually a complex interplay of different musical keys and rhythmic changes. It requires you to listen to each other and be generous with each other. One performer has to mesh chord progressions with the other player's rapid repetition of notes. It's like…like a dance—a collection of movements that, taken together, captivates the audience and the musicians playing the piece. Think of it as being hypnotized by each other." She looked at them both. "Do you see what I mean?"

Drew and Tamara stared at each other silently. He breathed in slowly and didn't shift his gaze. She licked her lips and moved imperceptibly toward him.

They got it, Mrs. Horowitz decided.

"That's enough for today's lesson," she said. "We will end a bit early because I believe in tapering before a performance. Get a good night's sleep tonight, and I will see you both here tomorrow at quarter to four in the afternoon—sharp." (The musical pun escaped them.)

"Of course," said Tamara.

"I'll be sure to set the alarm on my phone," Drew complied.

"And you're sure I can't bring anything? Snacks? Drinks?" Tamara gathered up her sheet music in her Moana folder.

"That won't be necessary. I've got it all covered. Chubbie's has always been my go-to caterer for these events."

"You can't go wrong with Chubbie's," Drew agreed. He backed out of the piano bench. "I don't suppose you ordered any eggs over easy?"

"Drew," Mrs. Horowitz said sternly. But because she couldn't help herself, she laughed. "Go home. The two of you. And think about the lesson of the music."

WITH SCHUBERT CURLED at her feet, Mrs. Horowitz dialed a familiar number from the kitchen phone. She munched on a saltine cracker while she waited for Gloria Pulaski to pick up. The lesson had taken a lot out of her. In retrospect, she rated it an A minus. She questioned whether she should have had Tamara and Drew sit together longer on the piano bench. It was impossible not to feel the tension—a positive kind of tension. If they'd just wake up and let it happen.

"So, tell me," Gloria answered the phone.

Mrs. Horowitz swallowed the remainder of the cracker. "I did my best. The rest is up to them."

"I understand. But I just hate to sit back and watch them mess it up. You know and I know—the whole town knows—that the two of them were meant to be together."

"That may be so, but unfortunately, they're adults. They're free to make their own mistakes."

"So true, but we all need happy endings."

"I agree. But I've decided not to worry anymore. I have faith that Tamara and Drew will figure it out. When? I don't know. But eventually, I'm sure they will recognize the inevitable. After all, love is the strongest source of inspiration. As mere mortals, we can only do so much."

"Oh, my gosh. Now I'm starting to worry that with all of us trying so hard, it might have backfired. You know how strong-willed they both are."

"Strong-willed—yes. Appreciating what's right in front of them—not so much." Mrs. Horowitz sighed. At the moment, all she wanted to do was cuddle Schubert, let the softness of the dog's fur calm her nerves and allow the slow, methodical rhythm of his breathing to lower her blood pressure. (Luckily, she'd followed Jessica's advice and had gotten Schubert's teeth cleaned.)

And she would do so as soon as she got off the phone. "Gloria, you must calm down," she ordered. Mrs. Horowitz was good at ordering without somehow offending people, maybe because her ordering served to snap people out of their anxious states. "Go hug one of your grandchildren and forget about all of this. As for Tamara and Drew, my prediction is that all will go well. And I know exactly the piece I'll be playing on a certain date in the months to come."

CHAPTER TWENTY-NINE

THE NEXT DAY in the early afternoon, Tamara held up two different dresses. "Do you think this black one—" she waggled the hanger in her left hand "—or this white one?" She thrust the hanger in her right hand in Myrna's direction. The white A-line dress had lace around the neck and sleeves. "Or maybe I should go with slacks? That would be practical. I have my good black crepe ones here. They'd look very smart with a blazer."

"The black one on the left looks like you're going to a funeral. And the other one would be good for a Communion." Myrna took the two dresses from Tamara and hung them up in the closet. "And definitely not the slacks. You'll look like you're preparing to interview the governor."

Tamara squinted at her with exasperation. "Did anyone ever tell you that honesty sometimes isn't the best policy?"

Myrna sat down on Tamara's bed and glanced around. The younger woman had lived in the guest room for more than a month now, and except for her tote bag hanging off the arm of the desk chair and her phone stationed at a perfect right angle on the side table, the place looked as unoccupied as when she'd first stepped foot in it.

Myrna studied Tamara nervously biting on a fingernail. "Why don't you wear that lovely dress you wore to the art opening? It's bright, and it's fun. This is supposed to be a celebration of all the piano students' accomplishments, a showcase for all they've learned."

"I suppose you're right." Tamara brightened. "I'll just touch it up with an iron. It's a little wrinkly from the last time." She went to the closet and pulled out the silk dress.

"I tell you what. You do your makeup, and I'll iron the dress. That way you won't feel rushed. And, really, I'm sure there's nothing to worry about. Look how hard you've practiced."

Tamara didn't look convinced. "Easy for you to say."

Myrna patted her shoulder. "I'm sure you'll be very happy in the end." She didn't elaborate but left Tamara standing in the middle of her room. She headed downstairs, and while she waited for the iron to heat up, she called Norman. "Is Drew as much of a wreck as Tamara is?"

"It's horrible to watch," he said. "This is the same man who's rushed into disaster sites—countless times. He was so nervous he couldn't tie his tie. He asked me to do it for him. Do you know the last time I tied someone else's tie? The two ends don't come close to meeting."

"Not to worry. When we get to the recital, I'll re-tie it. I brought up two boys. I've had lots of prac-tice."

"I knew you were good to have around."

Myrna mulled that one over but decided Nor-man probably didn't mean anything by it. Some-how, he could be astute in evaluating the feelings of others, but absolutely hopeless when it came to reading his own.

"I can't believe all this anxiety just over a piano recital," Norman added.

"It's stress, all right," Myrna agreed.

"Our families are going to be okay, aren't they?" Norman asked.

"Trust me. We're all working on it—in more ways than one."

TAMARA STOOD AT the kitchen door, her music folder in her hand, her tote bag over her shoulder. "I'd drive you all, but Mrs. Horowitz told us to get there early, and there's no sense you guys hanging around any longer than necessary." Myrna, Briggs, Will and Buddy were all gathered in the kitchen to wish her good luck.

"It's not a problem," Briggs assured her. "The extra car will come in handy. I'm sure Will and Candy have plans for afterward, and that way I can drop them off." He made a show of nodding his chin up and down at his son. "Will?"

"What, Dad?" Will looked at him blankly. Then, it was as if enlightenment had descended from the heavens. The boy walked over to the hutch and picked up a small package wrapped in brown paper. "This is for you." He held it out for Tamara.

"That's so nice." Tamara reached out to take it as she juggled her music folder and tote bag.

"Here, let me hold all your stuff while you open the present," Myrna offered.

"Thanks." Tamara did an awkward handoff and unwrapped the package.

"Careful. It's delicate," Will warned.

Tamara glanced up as she worked the tape loose. "Good to know." She opened the paper and discovered a single pale pink rosebud with a sprig of green fern. She recognized the delicate blossoms as coming from Briggs's garden.

"There's a pin there, too, so don't stick yourself," said Will, coming closer. Buddy followed and gave an approving sniff.

"I've never gotten a corsage before. Thank you, Will. It's beautiful. Would you pin it on me?" She pointed to a spot on her dress. "I think here on my shoulder would be perfect."

Will sighed. "I'll try. I've never done this before either." He did his best and stepped back. Buddy barked in approval.

Tamara gently touched the flower. "Thank you all. It's very thoughtful. And almost as beautiful as Buddy's bow."

"Candy and I found the tie at the card shop, and we thought it'd be good to get," Will informed everyone.

"Definitely," Tamara agreed. Buddy wore a ribbon around his neck with a black-and-white piano keyboard pattern. Tamara smiled at the dog, who immediately sat and wagged his tail. "You look very spiffy, Buddy."

"Enough dawdling now." Myrna handed Tamara back the folder and her bag and shooed her out the door.

Tamara slid behind the wheel of her car and rested her various items on the passenger seat. "Please tell me this day will end," she pleaded to any higher power that might be out there. "And, while you're at it, let it end on a good note." She groaned at her choice of words. "And I promise, I will never, ever use that pun again. Even if it is appropriate."

TAMARA WAS SWEATING BULLETS. And the program hadn't even begun.

The six pupils participating in the recital sat in the front row in the order of their participation. Tamara was second, since she played her solo piece after the young boy with the polka-dot tie. Drew was two chairs to her right. For their duet, scheduled to close out the concert, they would each rise and meet at the piano.

Additional rows of chairs lined the large oriental carpet, and the floral curtains at the picture window were pulled back to let the sun stream in. The mahogany furniture had been polished until it gleamed. For once, Schubert appeared to have been banished to a bedroom.

Practically all of Hopewell had squeezed into the living room. Tamara looked around and spotted Myrna, Will, Candy, Norman, Briggs and Jessica. Will waved enthusiastically. Candy discreetly wiggled the fingers on one hand. Gloria Pulaski and a thirtyish redheaded woman, whom Tamara guessed was another daughter, sat smack in the middle. Nonna Reggio, Laura and Phil were seated to one side. Near them, Mr. Portobello sat with Mr. Mason, who'd removed his favorite touring cap. Even the tennis coach, Keith, was in attendance, and Candy's mother, Alice, was sitting happily next to him.

The crowd was so thick that Tamara could barely make out who was who, but amid the waving and nodding she spied two people giving her the thumbs-up from the back row. None other than Robby and Nada Bellona. And hovering by a side window was Amy Pulaski, video camera in hand. Tamara moaned. Her potential failure was to be preserved for all humanity! It was best to stop looking around, and she zeroed in on the piano score on her lap instead.

At four o'clock on the dot, Mrs. Horowitz rose and introduced the performers. She explained that she would be stationed at the piano, not as a participant, but as a page turner. "So, ignore me, please," she instructed, a declaration easier said than done since she was wearing a floaty dress featuring blue-and-green Impressionist splotches—Monet's "Water Lilies" in chiffon, size 14 Petite.

And then it all happened. Tamara's fellow pupils earnestly performed their pieces to much warm approval. She played the Bach with her laudatory efficiency. Drew delivered a lively "Can Can" that got the right amount of buoyant response. And then there was no further opportunity for denial—it was time for the final piece. Mrs. Horowitz announced their duet.

Tamara and Drew reluctantly rose and positioned themselves on the piano bench. They looked to Mrs. Horowitz. She gave them an encouraging nod. *Breathe*, she mouthed silently.

And they did. Tamara nodded her head, and, on cue, they launched into the Gershwin. Tamara wasn't sure where the inspiration came from—whether it was Mrs. Horowitz's pep talk the other day or some positive form of stress that sprang from the act of performing, much like the exhilaration that accompanied her skydiving adventure. Whatever it was, she and Drew played like they'd never played before. She bounced off him in a give-and-take of notes and joy. The punchiness of their rhythm was hypnotic, and the audience spontaneously swayed and bobbed. The room seemed to be dancing, yes, dancing, to the magic that she and Drew created as one. The audience began clapping before they'd played the final note, and there was even a wolf whistle—Robby, no doubt.

When they finally finished, their hands remained on the keyboard as if the music was still flowing through their fingers. They were both breathing heavily.

Drew reached out with his pinkie finger and touched hers. "I really need to talk to you," he said, his voice low.

"And I want to speak with you, too. There's something—some things—I need to say." She didn't pull away.

Mrs. Horowitz shifted from her page-turning position and spoke to the gathering. "Thank you all for coming. I think we can completely agree that every pupil did themselves proud. It was worth all those hours of practicing."

"Or not," someone called from the back of the audience. A scattering of knowing laughter followed.

Mrs. Horowitz clapped. Obedient silence followed. "And now, as part of the festivities," she continued, "there are drinks and munchies for all our wonderful performers and their families and friends. Please, come enjoy and mingle. And as I always say, nothing brings people together better than music." She turned to her pupils and blew them a big kiss.

Drew looked around the living room. "There's no way we can talk in the middle of everyone."

"Maybe in the dining room?" Tamara proposed.

Drew nodded and grabbed her hand. The dining room table had been pushed against one wall to serve as a buffet. A curio cabinet was jammed in an opposite corner between a window and the door to the kitchen. Drew steered them to that small niche.

Tamara glanced inside the cabinet's glass doors and discovered a collection of music boxes. (What else!) *Forget the music boxes*, she told herself. *Concentrate on what's important.* She bit the inside of her cheek and stared with all her might at the man she loved, a love she had finally admitted to herself that evening at the gallery opening. An admission that had set off a tailspin of emotions when he'd announced the possibility of taking the job in Switzerland.

"First off, I wanted to thank you for taking me to Philadelphia," she said. "That meant a lot to me, and you and Norman were right to encourage me to go. It didn't end exactly as I wanted it to, but just confronting my mom, showing that I still wanted her in my life, has given me more confidence with my son."

Drew suddenly stood up taller. And his tie looked miraculously straighter. "Thank goodness. I thought you'd never forgive me after what happened at your mom's house."

She took his hand in hers. "No, it helped me realize that families can be messy, but that I'm capable of dealing with that situation, that I have the capacity to love and be loved. More than anything, it made me appreciate my true family—the one here in Hopewell."

He squeezed her hand. "Does that mean…?"

She nodded. "Yes, I've decided to stay in Hopewell. I already contacted Sidney to tell him to turn down the Phoenix offer. For my own sense of integrity, not to prove other people wrong—I'm glad that I've been exonerated. That vindication was important, and, I'm sure, a big reason I got the green light on the feature story on Hopewell. In any case, the station in Philly wants more local features from me. Naturally, I've asked Sidney to negotiate better terms than the ones they offered. I may have turned all sweet and cooperative, but I'm not completely squishy. And the really good part is that I'll see Will regularly."

He laughed. She did, too. "And what about you?" she ventured.

Now he took her other hand. "I'm staying. In Hopewell."

A man in a black suit maneuvered by, carrying a serving dish of deviled eggs. "Excuse me. I'll just leave this tray on the table."

"No problem," Drew said. Then he did a double take. "Chubbie! I didn't recognize you without your apron."

Chubbie winked at them. "I wouldn't have missed the festivities for anything." He vanished back in the kitchen.

Drew turned back to Tamara. "Where was I?"

"You were saying that you're staying in Hopewell," she said with a smile of pure happiness. "And do I need to remind you that this is not the moment to be tempted by those eggs?"

He grinned. "You know me too well. Now, as to remaining in Hopewell…that's the plan."

"What about the job in Switzerland?"

"I've already declined the offer, explaining it was time for me to put down roots."

"And your roots run deep in Hopewell."

"And hopefully they spread wide." He raised her hands to his chest. "I wish I had talked to you right after the art opening and saved us all this misery. In my own feeble defense, I did try, although, we never seemed to connect. But, you know, maybe it was just as well we didn't. Too much was going on, and I just couldn't think straight."

"That makes two of us. I really regret how I handled that evening. It was all too much, too fast, one thing on top of another."

"Good to know I wasn't the only one feeling that way. But now I've had time to think, quietly and calmly. I want you in my life, Tamara. You started out as my breakfast buddy, but you're so much more, and I want to give you so much more. I love you."

She leaned back. "I suppose you want me to be honest?"

He looked fearful and eager at the same time. "Please. Always."

She cocked her head as if thinking it over, which she really didn't need to do at all. "You say you love me. I get that. But I love you more."

He beamed. "Impossible."

Tamara stretched up as far as she could on tiptoes—for once, wearing heels came in handy—and brought her lips to his.

He abandoned her hands and took her in his

arms. He lowered his head and pressed his lips to hers, his kiss filled with longing and promise.

When they finally broke apart, Drew and Tamara looked around to see Gloria Pulaski and Mrs. Horowitz standing nearby.

"Deviled egg?" Mrs. Horowitz asked, lifting the tray.

"I've been told by someone wiser than me that now is not the time for refreshments," Drew demurred.

Gloria gave Tamara and Drew both the once-over before addressing Drew. "I presume the corsage is from you?"

"Actually, no." Drew cocked his head. "Does this mean you have another admirer, Tamara? Should I be jealous?" He looked at Tamara with laughter in his eyes.

"I don't think so," she assured him, not that he seemed to need any assurance. "It's from my family." She raised her head to find Will and Candy, Myrna and Norman, and Briggs and Jessica standing to the side. She blew them a kiss.

Gloria waved a finger at Drew and Tamara. "So, are you two getting together—and not just temporarily?"

Tamara nodded. "You're the first to know. To think that two such opposites could somehow be attracted to each other is amazing. When I least expected it, love came calling. It took me a while to recognize it—and accept it—but even a newbie to love like me was finally able to catch on."

Mrs. Horowitz put her arm through Gloria's and pulled her away. Yet even from a distance, her commanding voice penetrated above the buzz of the crowd. "Tamara can think what she wants," they heard the piano teacher proclaim, "but you and I know how much work it took to get them both to this point."

Signora Reggio approached the couple. She was carrying an aluminum container with foil wrapped over the top. "You played beautifully, Tamara. And you, too, Drew," she thought to add. She thrust the container in Tamara's hands. "I made a little eggplant *rollatini* last night and had a few leftovers. I thought you might be hungry afterward. And it was also to thank you for the flowers you sent me."

"Nonna, that's so unnecessary. The flowers were meant to thank you for teaching me how to make the lasagna."

Signora Reggio eyed Drew before she addressed Tamara. "If you like, I will teach you more recipes. I think the two of you will be spending a lot more meals together, besides breakfast, right?"

"Right," Tamara said. She kissed Nonna on the cheek before the woman scampered off.

When the coast was clear, Tamara's family closed in. Alice, Candy's mom, trailed shyly behind.

"You guys did great!" Will exclaimed.

"Not bad for amateurs," Myrna declared with a glint in her eye. She reached out and touched Tamara's forearm. "The dress looks beautiful," she added, before moving closer and whispering, "I presume it did the trick?" She waited.

Tamara nodded. "You were right—as always."

Myrna smiled. "Not always. But I'm pleased about this time. And I also have a surprise for you." She motioned toward the living room, and a small woman in a gray knit dress walked reluctantly closer.

Tamara peered around the milling people, then caught her breath. "Mom?"

Tamara's mother let Myrna pull her into the little group. "Will's aunt called me and told me about the recital. She can be very persuasive."

"Don't I know it," Tamara kidded.

Myrna let her mouth turn up. "As is only fitting."

"I hope you don't mind my coming?" Mrs. Giovanessi asked her daughter.

"Mind? Of course I don't mind." Tamara reached forward and hugged her mother before standing back. "But how did you get the phone number, Aunt Myrna?" She shook her head. "Never mind. If anyone could make this happen, it's Aunt Myrna. We'll have to have a long talk and make sure you get to know Will."

"There's plenty of time for that. I'm not going anywhere for a while—at Myrna's suggestion," her mother explained. "Meanwhile, why don't you enjoy the moment and see all your friends." Tamara's mother may have been estranged from her daughter in the past, but she clearly was trying to make up for lost time.

Tamara turned to her unlikely guardian angel. "I can't thank you enough, Aunt Myrna." She reached over and gave her a big hug, too.

Myrna didn't say no to the embrace, but when they broke apart, she returned to her no-nonsense self. "Enough of that now." She looked at Norman, who was standing there smiling. "What do you have to say to your son?"

"About his playing? It never was this good when he took lessons as a kid, that's for sure," Norman joked.

"The playing's one thing. I'm talking about the fact that he and Tamara are staying in Hopewell— together." Myrna gave him a c'mon-already stare.

Norman opened his mouth in surprise. "They told you that?" He looked at his son and Tamara.

Myrna shook her head. "They didn't need to. You can see it plain as day. But never mind. Why don't I usher you over to the table to get something to eat? I think I spotted rugelach. Will? Candy? You coming, too?"

CANDY HELD BACK and drew her mother to the side. She pulled an envelope out of her pocket. "Mom, this is for you. To help you buy a car. You really need one."

Alice opened the envelope and viewed the thick wad of cash. "Where did you get this?"

"I haven't robbed a bank if that's what you're thinking. I've been saving up from my jobs. I figured you could use it more than me right now."

Alice fingered the bills, and with tears in her eyes, she gazed at her daughter. "Thank you, thank you so much. I promise I'll pay you back."

Candy wasn't counting on it, but she'd already accepted that fact. "Whenever, Mom."

"You're such a good daughter," Alice went on. "But you know, maybe you should keep it. You worked hard for the money, and I suppose I could always ask your father." She held out the envelope.

Candy pushed it back at her mother. "No, Mom, this is for you. I want you to have it. It's my way of helping out—it's what families do."

Alice shook her head. "That's so generous. What did I ever do to deserve you?"

Candy shrugged. "You got lucky, I guess." Her mother probably deserved more, but just then, it felt good knowing they were there for each other. Candy stepped back, wary that her mom was going to hug her in public. "So, you want some ginger ale and sherbet punch?" Candy asked. "I heard from one of Mrs. Horowitz's students that it's her specialty."

"Why not." Alice slipped her arm through her daughter's. Candy flinched but didn't pull away, and they angled to the table.

TAMARA LEANED AGAINST DREW. "I'm exhausted. Is there anyone else we need to be happy with?"

Drew scanned the crowd. "Not right now. Besides, I want you all to myself." He put a hand under her chin. "You do look a little pale. Can I get you something to eat, drink?"

"No, just hold me. That's all I need." She rested her head on his chest. The silk of his tie was cool. It felt reassuring against her hot cheek. "You know, before I came to Hopewell, I was convinced that I could do it all on my own. You changed that, Drew Trombo."

"Same here. And I can't believe how good it feels to reach out, and—"

"And have someone incredible catch you," she finished his thought.

"Exactly."

In the living room, someone started playing the piano, and the sound of music floated over the chatter.

Tamara perked up. "'Moon River.'"

Drew listened. "You're right."

"I never realized before, but it's a waltz."

"In which case, should we put our lessons into practice?" He stepped back and held out his arms. "Tamara Giovanessi, may I have this dance?"

"I'd be delighted, and I'll even let you lead," she offered.

"Just this once. After that, I'll think we'll trade off. It seems only fair."

"That's allowed?"

"Only in Hopewell."

"Then we'll dance together always."

* * * * *

HARLEQUIN
Reader Service

Enjoyed your book?

Try the perfect subscription for Romance readers and get more great books like this delivered right to your door.

See why over 10+ million readers have tried Harlequin Reader Service.

Start with a Free Welcome Collection with free books and a gift—valued over $20.

Choose any series in print or ebook.
See website for details and order today:

TryReaderService.com/subscriptions